Ps...I Love You

By

Erin Mack

Dedication
I want to dedicate this book to my mom. Thank you for always loving and supporting me through any path I have chosen in this life. I am grateful for all I have learned from you and continue to learn. I am who I am today because you have loved me through it all.

Table of Contents

Prologue
Ginger

I recheck my hair and reapply my lip gloss again, even though I don't need to. I had nothing to do today, and after everyone agreed over our group chat this morning that we should meet up tonight for drinks, I spent an embarrassing amount of time getting ready. I have this nervous energy I can't seem to shake off or put my finger on the source.

I was so relieved when everyone wanted to go out tonight and get a drink. After the week I had to endure, I needed some fun. I am catching a ride to the Thirsty Moose with Stella and Bubba. I am normally the designated driver due to the fact I have never been a bigger drinker. Plus, it doesn't help that I just turned legal a hot five minutes ago, but when Stella suggested that she and Bubba could swing by and pick me up, I jumped at the offer.

The doorbell startled me, even though I was expecting them. Stella pops her head in. "Hey, girl! Wow, you look amazing. You realize we are only going to the Thirsty Moose, right?"

"I know. I was bored today, and apparently, by the look on your face, I went overboard. Should I go change?" Now feeling self-conscious as I look down at my dress.

"Abso-freaking-lutley not are you changing. Every guy in the bar will be checking you out in that dress all night. It is time Larry has some competition," Stella says with her hands on her hips with all the confidence in the world.

I love Stella, even though she is a little over nine years older than me; she is like the sister I never got. Stella and Bubba have been inseparable since they met in the 2nd grade. Bubba was already buddies with my older brothers, Max and Noah. To round out the group of misfits, there was also Ralph, Henry and Harrison. When Bubba started bringing Stella around on the playground and invited her to eat with them, it was a no-brainer that Stella was adopted into the group by all the guys.

When I entered the picture, they were all nine years old. I always wanted to tag along with them but was always told I was too little, but really, I think the boys were afraid I would snitch on them for the less-than-stellar mischief that they got into. Stella was always kind to me and always took time to do my hair or nails.

This is how the group stayed until Noah found Emma, the best sister-in-law ever while attending college. Emma also always tried to include me in activities, but it wasn't until I graduated high school that I really started hanging out with everyone more often. Then, three years ago, Jane moved to town and became an instant friend.

"Stella, you have to stop calling him Larry. You know he hates it." I say as I grab my purse and head for the door.

"I am sorry, is Sir Lawrence the third here to rebuke me for such a slanderous name-calling opps?" Stella asks in dramatic fashion, which only she can.

I try not to smirk but fail miserably and bow my head as I shake it. "No, he is not here. He chose to stay in the cities and not come back with me for the rest of the weekend."

"Girl, when are you going to cut that guy loose and start living your life? He is smothering you to death with his hoity toy stuffiness."

"What are you talking about, Lawrence is the perfect guy. He has an amazing job lined up at a top law firm this fall. He checks all the boxes," I say as we climb into Bubba's SUV.

"Hey, kid! How's the weekend treating you?" Bubba asks as he starts the car and starts to reverse out of the driveway.

"Great. I am excited everyone wanted to meet up. I am in serious need of some fun tonight." I answer while putting up my seat belt.

"Because Larry is no fun," Stella mumbled under her breath, but we both heard her.

"So Bubba, what do you think about my older brother making out with Jane last night on the Ferris wheel?" I ask nonchalantly, trying to get the goods. It was revealed this morning in the group text thread that my brother, who recently moved home from California, was caught making out with our other friend Jane last night. Now, I am dying to get details without the gross details.

"Come on kid, you know the bro code is too strong to break." Bubba starts to chuckle. "But honestly, you probably know more than I do if you girls interrogated Jane this morning. Max is being very tight-lipped about the said make-out session."

"What good are you, Bubba, if you don't share the goods with me?" Stella asks.

Bubba stares at her for a brief moment, then shakes his head and mumbles under his breath while looking out the window, "I will show you the goods."

Stella doesn't notice, or if she does, she is playing stupid as she reaches for the radio to play DJ. We all fall into a comfortable silence as the music fills the car. I let my thoughts drift to the others in the group that we will be hanging out with tonight. In the last three years, I have built a better relationship with my older brother Noah. Doesn't hurt that his wife is one of my best friends or that they made me an auntie to a perfect little girl. I hope now that Max as returned home, we can work on our relationship as well. Ralph and Henry are easily like sudo-big brothers to me. They all annoyingly call me "kid," like Bubba does. That just leaves Harrison. That man does not exude big-brother vibes for me at all.

I have never uttered the words out loud before, but I have a serious crush on Harrison Stone. From Junior year in high school till the present if I was being truthful. He came over to hang out with Noah and Max on a break from college and found me home alone. I was super upset that I didn't get a dance part that I auditioned for. Harrison made us ice cream sundaes, and we watched cheesy rom-coms all afternoon. I am sure he didn't give that afternoon a second thought, but for me, it meant everything.

Clearly, nothing could ever become of my crush for so many reasons, but a girl can still dream. I shelved my crush on him, put myself out there, and dated more when I started college. There were a few boys here and there, but no one serious until Lawrence. He graduated a few weeks ago and is starting with an impressive law firm in the fall. On paper, he is great, but in real life, I am so bored. This past week, I went up to be with him as his firm put on a week of team-building activities. Those invited were asked to bring wives or significant others. I thought this would be a great time for us to grow closer together as well. That didn't happen, and I was ignored all week. I even ducked out early on the weekend with a lame excuse that I had come down with a cold I didn't want to share with anyone else there. Lawrence didn't even bat an eye at me leaving.

So, even though it is highly inappropriate, I have found my thoughts wandering back to Harrison. During summer break, I usually come home and spend time with family and friends and work. So naturally, I see Harrison more. I thought that hiding my crush was a flawless performance on my part, but the girls have been making comments lately, making me think I am not as covert about my crush as I thought. I need to stop being a silly girl and get over this unrealistic crush. I need to get over Harrison Stone for good. Harrison is known around town as Little Falls OG playboy. Everyone knows his reputation. He would never go for a girl like me or for someone who has annoying older brothers like I have. Doomed, simply doomed.

"Earth to Ginger, girl, are you listening to me?" Stella asks.

I pull myself from my thoughts and shake my head for good measure. "Sorry, lost in thought. What did you say?"

"I was asking if you had a good week, but now, I really want to know what has you so distracted?" Stella turns in the front seat to look at me.

"Umm, yeah sure, it was a fun week. Lawrence's firm spoiled everyone. Not sure I really fit into that world. Everyone is so fancy." I say, moving my attention out the window again. I could still feel her gaze on me, so I continued on. "Not distracted, just excited to see everyone. You know me I love a good night out with you all."

That seemed to do the trick. Stella turns back around, facing forward. Stella and Bubba start discussing the merits of the current song that is playing. Allowing me time to drift in my thoughts again.

As we pull up to the Thirsty Moose, I find myself on edge again, like before when I was getting ready. We walk in and head to our regular tables in the back. The owner doesn't care that we push some tables together to accommodate our group size. Ralph, Henry and Harrison beat us to the punch and already have the tables pushed together and are waiting on us. Noah and Emma walk up right behind us. We all find spots and start to sit down.

Sadie comes by and takes our order. We always order way too many appetizers and a few pitchers of beer. Every once in a while, the girls grab specialty drinks that the guys would not be caught drinking. Finally, Max and Jane show up.

After an awkward moment of staring at them like they grew two heads, Jane speaks up.

"This is happening. You get two minutes to ask your questions, and then the night moves on," Jane says iindignantly.

We all laugh and start talking at once. Noah excuses himself and heads for the bar. Emma looks worried about his sudden departure. Max stands and goes after him. I have always wished we were closer in age. Maybe if we were, I would feel comfortable standing and

joining my siblings over at the bar for what looks like a private
moment. There is a small part of me that still feels like an outsider
looking in on my brothers and their group of friends.

Bubba takes control and starts telling stories and distracting
everyone. Soon enough my brothers return looking like all has been
made right in the world again between the two of them. Max leans
over and kisses Jane. There is a tenderness that they seem to share
after only knowing each of a few days. I have known Lawrence
almost a year and never has he ever looked at me that way. Get a grip
girl, pull yourself together. You came here to have fun tonight, no
more moping. I try giving myself a pep talk and ignore my thoughts.

"I need to work off some of these nachos, Stella, want to take a
turn around the dance floor?" Ralph asks.

"Sure, old man, try and keep up," Stella says while rising from her
chair. Ralph grabs her hand and leads her out onto the dance floor.

"I miss dancing" I hurump out with my shoulders drooping down
as I look out at the couples on the dance floor.

"What are you talking about Gin? You dance all the time? That is
literally what you are majoring in at school." Emma states matter a
fact.

"It's not the same. What I do for school is different than cutting
loose on a dance floor with a partner," I say as I look back toward the
table.

"With all the fancy parties you attend with Larry you don't dance
at them?" Bubba asks.

"First of all, his name is Lawrence, Stella is rubbing off on you.
And secondly, no, he doesn't like dancing. He finds it frivolous and a
waste of networking time."

"I will take you out on the dance floor, Ginger," Harrison says
quietly. I look at him wide eyed "Really? You wouldn't mind?"

Harrison stands, and his chair slides back. He walks around the
table to me and extends his hand out. For being in a noisy bar, it
seems to go quiet suddenly, at least at our table, where everyone is
watching the interaction. I slowly place my hand in his hand and
stand. Harrison leads me out on the dance floor. The current song is
more upbeat, so you would think that would limit our touching, but
Harrison finds ways to touch me and look at me which has me feeling
totally lost in the moment.

The song is coming to an end. Crushing disappointment hits me.
I do not want this moment to end. I want to be greedy and have a few
more seconds together. The song ends. We are left standing, staring at
each other. A slow song starts up next. Resigned to the fact he would
never want to slow dance with me, especially in front of my brothers
and everyone else. As I was turning to go, Harrison grabbed me by the
waist and pulled me into him. I am holding my breath. I should not
love the feeling of being in his arms as much as I do. His mouth is
right by my ear as he whispers, "Please, Ginger, don't go yet. Dance
one more with me?" There is a pleading in his tone.

I turn in his arms and look up into his eyes. "Ok" is all I can
manage to get out with his arms around me already. I put my arms
around his neck, and we started to move. I want to scream with sheer
joy and excitement; why does this feel so good?

"Hi," so apparently, I have no chill. Who says hi randomly after
already dancing one dance?

"Hi," he chuckles and shakes his head at me. "You look beautiful
tonight."

I feel the blush creeping up my cheeks. I look away from him. I
hate that my skin betrays me every time I am feeling any emotion.
Stupid blushing! I can't believe he just said I was beautiful.

"Why are you blushing, Sunshine? It is just me and you?" He
asks with not one under tone of mocking in his voice.

I whip my eyes back up to his. What is happening? And did he
just call me sunshine? It is not the two of us, we are in a bar
surrounded by people, people we know. Feeling like I am on the verge
of a panic attack, he pulls me closer.

"What are you thinking, Sunshine?"

"Umm, Sunshine? That is new. You are not going to go with
what everyone else calls me?" That felt like a safe response.

"When was the last time I called you kid? Plus, I much prefer
Sunshine."

I take a minute to think. I cannot remember the last time he called
me "kid." Everyone else does it so often that I never really paid
attention. Confusion must be all over my face because he answers
before I can ask my own questions.

"It was your junior year in high school. That day, I came over,
and we ended up hanging out all afternoon. After that day, I guess I

stopped seeing you as a kid. The nickname didn't fit you anymore."
He seems nervous sharing this with me.

I decide to go easy on him and not ask more about his sudden confession and instead ask "Why Sunshine, then? And why all a sudden? I have never heard you call me that before."

"Sunshine is not obvious to you? You are pure light and joy and happiness and everything good in this world, Ginger." He almost whispers his response with a reverence that has me off balance.

"W-why now?"

"The table full of guys over there, two of which are your brothers, that would pummel me for calling you my Sunshine. Plus, there is that annoying detail: you have a boyfriend." Like he can read my mind, he continues, knowing I still have questions.

"You came in tonight a little off, maybe on edge about something. I hate seeing you upset. I just wanted you to know that I see you and am always here for you."

I can't respond. My mind is a jumbled mess. I lean in, rest my head on his shoulder, and hold on tight. He, in return, holds me tighter. I don't' care who sees us. All I can focus on is he called me his Sunshine and he pointed out that I have a boyfriend. But for the moment, I am in his arms, and nothing else matters.

Chapter 1
Ginger

I lean back and let the sun fall over my already over heated skin. This is one of the perfect summer days that I wish would never end, but they all do. This will probably be the last day on the river for the season. Summer will be ending soon. The weather in Minnesota is unpredictable at best. So, when you have one of these perfect days, you grab hold of it and enjoy it while it lasts.

I was trying to catch up on some reading, but eventually, the sun wins and gets all my attention and I lean my head back and cast my face upward toward the sky. I lean back on my hands and stretch my long legs out. I used to hate being the tall girl in class. Being 5'9" can be intimidating to some guys, but I have learned that those are just not the guys for me. As I have gotten older, I have learned to appreciate my body and all that it can do. The warmth feels amazing on my skin. I feel at peace and relaxed for the first time all summer. This summer has been one for the books. I started the summer with a boyfriend, close to graduation, with the promise of an audition at a premier dance school in New York City. And now that summer is ending, I find myself single thanks to my cheating, good-for-nothing ex. I spoke with a graduation counselor and realized that I miscalculated my credits and can graduate right now and not in December as I previously thought. Let's not forget the prestigious, once in a life time audition with Julliard, yeah, let's not forget about that. I called them last week and canceled it. They warned me the invitation would not be offered again, and I was fine with that. I still haven't been able to bring myself to tell family or friends any of my secrets. I just bury them with more secrets. Something has got to give soon. I am going to have to let people in soon before everything implodes on me.

In the depths of my multitasking about how to salvage my seriously messed up life at age 21 years old and soaking up the sun, a large shadow falls over me, blocking my rays. I can't bring myself to open my eyes to see which well-intentioned friend is coming to check on me.

"Hey, Sunshine!"

I try my hardest not to groan with annoyance. Of course, it was this friend that would be coming over to me now. Ever since we shared that dance six weeks ago at the Thirsty Moose, things between us have been off. Whenever we have been alone, he will call me

Sunshine, but in front of others he ignores me, or it is back to Ginger. He also started a text thread for just the two of us. I might be a little sensitive on the topic after catching my boyfriend in bed with another woman, but this secret makes me feel like a dirty little secret. It does not feel great, and I am growing tired of it.

"Hi, Harry." I can't even be bothered to open my eyes. Maybe he will take the hint and leave my sourpuss self alone.

"Harry, really? Where did that come from?" Harrison asks with an amused tone as he takes a seat next to me giving me back my sun.

"Only fair, you have a secret nickname for me. I thought I would start one for you. And seeing your single girl fan club in town calls you Capt. Hottie, I thought I would come up with one of my own for you. Don't want to step on their toes and steal their nickname for you." I snip back.

"It's not a secret, I don't care if anyone knows that I call you Sunshine," Harrison says, going from amused to hurt. "And I don't have a fan club of single girls in town."

I am a jerk. It is not his fault I am drowning in secrets. I turn my head and look at him. "I am sorry. I am in a bad mood, I guess. It is not fair to take it out on you. And for the record, I love that you call me Sunshine, and I kind of like calling you something that no one else gets to. I think Harry is very fitting for you."

"I know it hasn't been the best summer for you. I am sorry." He glances over at me and then back out to the water, where everyone is still playing and relaxing.

I only shared with the girls that Lawrence cheated on me. I asked them to keep it to themselves. I really didn't want the guys to know. For some reason, I really didn't want the man sitting next to me to know most of all. Can someone explain to me why I am the one who feels shame and embarrassment when my loser ex was the one who was caught cheating? The girls promised to keep my secret, but we were having a game night, and some drama with my brother and his ex-girlfriend came up, and because of my reaction the guys pieced it together why I was currently single. Harrison looked like he could kill someone that night. Even though I am sure they all know, no one will bring it up with me.

"It has definitely been hard, but there have also been some highlights as well," I say as I lean over and bump my shoulder against his shoulder. "And for what it is worth, I think you look like a Harry. Is it okay that I call you Harry?"

"You can call me anything you want, Sunshine. I kind of like that you are the only one that calls me that." He is full-on smiling at me now as he leans into me.

"You know you can talk to me about anything, right? I will always be here for you." He says it is so earnestly that I want to crack and give him all my failings and secrets and plead for him to fix the mess I have weaved myself into.

Instead of leaning on him and letting him support me, I deflect with the best of them. "Why are you not out on the water enjoying one of the last good days we have?"

He looked disappointed. I was unwilling to open up to him, but he still answered me "I was designated to come start the fire to get dinner started. Apparently because I am a firefighter, I am the only one that is capable of starting the fire." He rolls his eyes at what I can only imagine was a ridiculous conversation he had out in the water about his fire skills. "They really didn't have to twist my arm that hard. I have been looking for an excuse to be alone with you all day."

"Harry you don't need an excuse to come hang out with me or talk. I am always available to you." I cringe at the words that even sound pathetic and needy to my ears.

He takes pity on me and lets my neediness roll without further thought. "Want to help me get the fire going and keep me company while I prep dinner?"

"Sure, I would love too."

Chapter 2
Harrison

I knew I was in trouble today when I showed up and saw Ginger walking down the dock. All she is wearing is very short cut-off shorts with a freakin tiny yellow bikini top. The nerve of this woman. She is going to be the death of me. Resisting her all summer has taken all my self-control, and that pathetic excuse for a bathing suit will be my undoing.

I know I shouldn't want more with her. I know all the reasons that it would never work. I am too old for her. Her brothers have been some of my best friends since before I can remember. I never thought anything about Ginger growing up other than she was the little sister of my buddies. I came home one weekend from college, and it all started to change. That one freakin weekend was what started the change in how I saw Ginger. I went to her house to hang out with Max and Noah but found Ginger home alone crying. I hated that she was alone and had tear streaks running down her cheeks. I couldn't leave her alone while she was so miserable, so I stayed and tried to cheer her up. We had the best day of movies and junk food. By the end of it, she was smiling and laughing. It wasn't until she graduated high school and started hanging out with the group more that I started to not think of her as the little sister of my best friends but the woman that I couldn't stop thinking about.

I also really hate summers now, which sucks because it used to be my favorite. She comes home and spends all her free time with us. It has been harder and harder to resist her each summer. This summer, she came home with a boyfriend, a real tool. I can't believe any of the guys, let alone her brothers, were okay with her dating that loser. I didn't think I would survive having to hear about their dates and weekends away. The few times he graced us with his presence were the worst. I could never understand what my Sunshine saw in him.

Luck was on my side, and they broke up mid-summer. Which makes me a complete jerk; seeing it clearly broke Ginger's heart, she must have really been in love with him. She has not been herself since the breakup. I felt awful for being happy about the breakup when she was so miserable. My time with her is coming to an end again with summer ending, she will be headed back to school for her last semester. After that, she will be off to New York for Julliard's. I am not sure it will ever be the same around here. She won't have summers off anymore. I am losing her and any chance of spending time with her.

"All right, Mr. Fire expert, where do you want me?" Ginger asks with a mocking salute.

What I would like to say and what I answer are two very different things: "I already have the fire pit set and ready to go. Do you mind helping with food prep?"

"Sure. What is on the menu tonight?"

"Ralph was in charge of the food tonight. Guarantee it is some meat and potato concoction." I say while lifting the cooler and bringing it closer to the fire.

Ginger opens the cooler and looks at the already prepped food in the foil packets. "Umm, Harry, when you said you wanted my help, you meant…" She trails off, looking up at me with confusion lacing over her face.

"Is that what I said?" I look away as I pretend to concentrate on the fire. Out of the corner of my eye I can see Ginger smiling, shaking her head. I turn and look at her and we lock eyes. What would I give to be able to claim this girl as my girl? Not sure how long we stay in this moment before my so-called friends ruin it.

"Harrison, how have you not got the fire started yet? Your expert level will be taken away and given to a more worthy recipient if you can't get that fire started." Henry says with the straightest of faces. I hear Ginger let out a giggle and move away from the fire pit and head toward the other girls. *Thank you, Henry, for driving my girl away.*

"Instead of critiquing my work, you could help, ya know."

"Oh, I am helping you, man. If Noah catches you devouring his sister with your eyes like I just did, he will kill you dead. So, your welcome."

I look over, and Ginger is now helping the girls set up the drinks and deserts. I want to tell him that he has lost his mind, but it would be a lie. Before I can come up with a comeback that doesn't make me sound like an idiot, Ralph and Bubba walk up to join us.

"Dude, I am starving; how much longer?" Bubba whines.

"The fire looks good and the packets won't take long. Just need to throw them on," Ralph adds as he moves toward the cooler. After arranging the packets on the fire, Ralph turns to me.

"What is up with the weirdness going on with you two?" Ralph asks as he is looking between Henry and me.

"I would have to agree with the Chief of Police on this one, even though I am starving, I can even see we walked in on some weirdness." Bubba adds.

"You guys are insane. We are just standing here waiting for dinner like you." It sounds lame even to my ears as soon as I say it.

Ralph looks around. Being the natural-born investigator of the group, he can't just let it go. "Ah, I see. Did something happen that involved someone wearing a tiny yellow bikini? Ginger is looking very fine in that contraption today."

I lunge forward and shove Ralph as hard as I can. I can hear Bubba let out an obnoxiously loud laugh. Henry pulls me back. "Bingo, nailed it on the head with your assessment, their Chief," Henry says, holding back a smirk. Even Ralph is smiling.

"Finally, it is about time you got our boy to admit to his feelings. We have been trying all summer to get you to admit you have feelings for Ginger," Bubba says, wiping his eyes from his obnoxious laughing fit.

I am fuming mad. I hate that Ralph noticed her in her bikini. I am mad that my friends seem to be getting joy out of this situation. I am mad that I have no chill and that they even notice that Ginger means more to me than she should. But what really has me pissed is that no matter how much I want things to be different, that will not change a thing. I can't have her, and I need to find a way to be okay with that.

Feeling the steam leave my fight. "Sorry, Ralph, for shoving you, but don't talk about Ginger like that."

"Harrison, listen, dude. I meant no disrespect. Ginger is like a little sister to me. I was just trying to get you to admit that she means something to you."

"Well, it doesn't matter what I feel. It can never go anywhere. So can we drop it before her very protective brothers come over here and join the conversation." I whisper, desperate not to let this conversation include all my friends to join in on.

"You are being ridiculous. Max is so happy, stupidly in love with Jane that he would probably welcome you into the lovey-dovey group of suckers who fall in love group. I think he is the president of the group. Noah you might need to worry about, but I can protect you until he calms down." Bubba says as he crosses his arms over his chest. He has a few inches on me and about 50 pounds of muscle, the man is a beast.

Before I can reply the others start toward the fire. Noah walks up, holding Emma's hand. Max has his arm around Jane's shoulder. Annoyed that there happily ever after came somewhat easy for them. Then Stella and Ginger follow behind, whispering and giggling about something.

"Is the food ready? I am starving," Noah says.

Thankfully the guys take pity on me and drop the subject of Ginger. The food will be ready soon, so I welcome any distractions. Everyone digs into their food when it is ready. The conversation flows naturally with everyone. Thinking to myself that the disaster confession before is the worst the day has to offer, I am proven wrong.

Chapter 3
Ginger

"So, Ginger how many more days do you get to stay before you head back to school? I was thinking that maybe the girls and I could come with you and make a girl's trip out of it to set up your new apartment." Emma asks me with genuine concern.

Everyone has been so worried about me since my breakup. I hate that I can't snap out of my funk. I have so many secrets. I feel like if I tell them one it will unravel the whole mess.

"Yes, girls trip! I am totally down." Stella adds.

"Yep, count me in too -eekkk!" Jane squeals before she can get it all out.

"Um, excuse me. I don't like girls night and you are only gone for a few hours. Now you want to leave me for a whole weekend. Nope not going to work for me." My annoying brother, Max, says between his tickling attack on Jane.

"Hey lover-boy, calm down, she is going." Stella stares Max down. Even though Stella is the tiniest of the group, coming in at 5 foot nothing, she can be terrifying.

"Yeah, babe, love you more and all but I am going. Ho's before bro's, right?" Jane offers, then leans in to kiss his cheek. I'm not sure which emotion is stronger, the urge to throw up from sweetness overload or laugh because my brother is sitting there pouting that his girl will be gone for two days. Oh wait, crap, I am not leaving. I should say something.

"Now that Max has been set straight, and I will set Jane straight later that she might have delivered the last saying wrong, when are we doing this weekend, Ginger." Emma beams, so excited for a girl's trip.

Crap!! I have to say something. I look around the fire pit and all the eyes are on me. "Umm, well, funny thing about that. I decided to do an internship in my last semester. It will not mess with my graduation date, but I will not be returning to campus this fall." I decide to stop talking before I give more away than I want to. That, however, does not stop the questions coming in from the girls.

"What?"

"Why?"

"Where?"

All questions are spewed out all at once. I grab my water bottle and take a huge chug, hoping for a miracle or divine intervention to get me out of this. Nothing comes, shocker. I let out a breath and dive in. "It's really not that big of a deal. I decided to take this internship opportunity. Like I said, it doesn't affect my graduation." They don't need to know that I already graduated and my degree is already in the mail. That is a problem for the future Ginger; tonight, I need to deal with one secret at a time.

"Ginger, do Mom and Dad know? How does this affect your Julliard's audition?" Noah pipes in; the look on his face is killing me. He looks hurt that he didn't know.

"Noah, not sure if you know this, but I am an adult. I do not need Mom and Dad's permission to make changes to my education or my life, for that matter." I know Noah loves me, and he is just concerned about me, but it feels so condescending to bring mom and dad into this like I am still a child in his eyes. Everyone is being weirdly quiet. I can't even bring myself to look at Harrison.

"Hey, kid, I think it is great that you are taking an internship. Where is it at? What will you be doing?" Max steps in as the family peacemaker.

"I will be running a dance studio and teaching classes."

"How does that help you? You are going to get into Julliard's, and this feels like a waste of your time and talents." Noah gets his second wind into the conversation. Emma looks around nervously. Jane reads the situation and stands and grabs the plate of cupcakes she brought and shoves them in Noah's direction. He reluctantly takes one, but he is still focused on me answering his questions. It was a nice try on Jane's part to distract my brother. Normally, cupcakes are his downfall but apparently, my future is trumping cupcakes right in this moment.

"Well, guess what, big brother? I am sick and tired of other people telling me what is right for me and when it is right. This is what I want to do, and I am going to do it whether you agree or not." I huff it all out. Not sure where it came from or how long that has been festering waiting to get out.

An awkward silence falls over everyone. I never have outbursts or speak up for myself. I apparently have no filter tonight.

"Girl, where is this dance school? Please tell me it is close, but if it is far away, I am down for a road trip to see you, too." Stella asks, trying to rescue me.

I avoid looking at Noah now because even though I know he loves me, I need a break from the judgment in his eyes. "I will be running Mrs. Hannigan's School for Dance." The silence is deafening. I can't take much more.

"Yes, girl!! I am so excited. I always hated the end of summer when you left us to go back to school. This calls for more girls' nights!!" Stella beams, genuinely happy for me.

I hear Max mumble under his breath, "Great, more girl nights." It brings a smile to my face. He is so in love with my friend Jane. As if Stella broke the ice or the tension with her excitement, everyone joins in congratulating me except for Noah and Harrison, who both look hurt and or pissed at the revelation that I will be staying in town. I understand what Noah's problem is. He takes his overprotective brother to a whole new level, but what is Harrison's problem?

We wrap up the night on a better note than the dinner conversation. We all pitch in to help clean up and pack everything up. By the time we get the boat back to the dock, and we all make it to the parking lot, I am exhausted. I don't linger chatting with everyone. I duck into my car and make my exit. Even though I love all those people, I need a little space. I head toward my parents' place. Now that my brothers know about the so-called internship, I need to loop my parents in.

I stay with them during the summers, but I will be moving out this week. It is hard to claim you are an independent adult when you are still sleeping in your childhood bedroom. There is a studio apartment above the dance school that I will be moving into this week. The lights are still on when I drive up to my childhood home. Better rip another band-aid off tonight.

I throw my purse and keys on the table by the front door. I start walking toward the family room. I hear the TV and my mom and dad laughing at whatever they are watching. "Hey, mom, dad. I am home. How was your night? Did you two stay out of trouble?" I say with a giggle as I enter the room. The idea of my parents getting into trouble is an amusing thought.

"Oh sweetie, your home! How was your day? Did you kids stay out of trouble?" My mom will forever refer to all of us as kids, even though the majority of people she is referring to are approaching 30. I stifle a giggle that my brothers and the other boys traumatized my mother so badly that she is genuinely asking if we stayed out of trouble.

"Mom, when was the last time the boys got into trouble?"

"Just because we don't hear about it anymore does not mean that they are not up to something."

"Ha, very true Dad. It was a perfect day out on the river. No complaints from me." Just as I was about to lead into my big news, my mom's phone starts ringing. I don't even need her to tell me who is calling, I know. One of the world's most annoying Buttinski brothers.

"Oh, look, Noah is calling…". Before I let my mom finish her thought, I blurt out, "Don't answer that!" a little too loud.

My outburst was not a smooth transition. Both my mom and dad are staring at me now. The phone stops ringing. "Sorry Mom, I just need to talk to you and Dad, and I would like you to hear the news from me and not Noah."

"Oh, cheese and crackers, you're pregnant? You were arrested and need money for a lawyer? A mafia boss wants you to marry him. You decided to become a vegan?" My Mom is a trip. I think the only reason the insane suggestions stopped coming out of her mouth was because she needed to take a breath.

"Okay, first of all, Mom, no more dateline for you. Maybe raising the boys did more of a number on you than we originally thought."

"What is it sweetie? We are always here for you." My Dad offers.

"Well, I am not headed back to school next weekend because I am going to take an internship this upcoming semester. I will be running Mrs. Hannigan's School of Dance in town. And before you say you are disappointed in me or worried about my future. I have given this a lot of thought, and I really think this is what I need to be doing right now."

"That is it? That is your big secret news that your brother is calling to tattle on you about?" My mom asks.

Unsure if it is a trap, I nod my head.

"You are staying in town, running the dance school that you grew up learning how to dance in, and you were worried we would be mad at you?" My dad jumps in, a little confused.

"Well, it just deviates from my original plan, and I was worried you would be disappointed in me."

"Honey, we could never be disappointed in you. I am so very proud of the woman you have grown into. I am just relieved you didn't say you were getting back with that bonehead Larry. I think I would have preferred you marrying a mafia boss between rehab stays while becoming a vegan."

I shake my head at my mom's ridiculous antics. "You guys are crazy, but I love you so very much. Thank you for being the best parents ever."

"It is easy when you are the best daughter ever. And don't worry about your brother. He will come around. I think he still thinks of you as a little girl running around with pigtails and a tutu in the backyard. He will come around." My dad says as I get up to head to my room. Suddenly feeling relieved but still very much exhausted.

"By the way, I am moving out this week. I am moving into the studio apartment above the dance school. You old people need your space, and I have cramped your style long enough." I start heading to my room when I hear my dad yell, "What old people? I am just as hip as you young people."

There was a huge smile on my face by the time I hit my room. My parents are ridiculous but amazing and great. Starting to feel a little more optimistic about the next few months. I throw myself face-first on my bed. I am considering if not doing my nightly bedtime routine would rank on my mom's ridiculous list of things that would upset her.

Before I can give it too much brain power to consider it, my butt starts to vibrate. Great. It could be one of the girls checking in, wanting more details about me staying. More likely, it is one of my annoying brothers, well, being annoying. I reluctantly take my phone out of my back pocket and enter the code seeing face ID won't work with my face smooshed into the bed.

CRAP, anyone but him. I would rather have a lecture from Noah right now than a text from Harrison.

Harrison: I have questions.

Chapter 4
Harrison

Me: I have questions.

I text Ginger the minute I get home. I am impressed I used such restraint to wait that long. I wanted to pick her up and drag her away when she made her announcement tonight. What am I going to do? I needed her to go back to school for a little space. I am never going to make it another four months of constantly hanging out without crossing the line and claiming her as my girl.

Ginger: I have answers but whether or not I will give them to you is a different story.

Me: Funny. When did you decide to stay?

Ginger: Why do you care, Harrison?

Me: What do you mean, why do I care? You know I care about you. You should have told me.

Ginger: Actually, what I know is that you ignore me 95% of the time. And only halfway through this summer did you want to be secret friends where you only text me. So no, Harrison, I don't know why you care.

I can't believe she thinks I ignored her. I messed this whole thing up. I was trying to protect her and not blow up my friendship with her brothers.

Harrison: Sunshine, I am sorry. I never meant to make you feel that way.

Ginger: Doesn't matter. If you were looking forward to me going back to school because having your best friend's little sister always tagging along cramps your style, you don't need to worry. I will be busy and won't crash your activities anymore.

Me: Stop!! That is not what I want or what I am saying.

Ginger: It is fine, Harrison.

Me: I hate when women say that "F" word.

Ginger: I am sure the girls you date are always better than fine.

Me: Whoa, where did that come from? What has gotten into you?

Ginger: Maybe this is the new me. Sorry if it isn't all sunshine and rainbows for you.

Me: Sunshine…

That is all I can text because what I really want to text her is I don't care about sunshine and rainbows, all I really want is her.

Ginger: Doesn't matter. Sorry, I am cranky tonight. Noah is annoying me with his older brother's protectiveness. Nothing will really change with me staying in town. I will be so busy with work that you won't even know I am here.

Me: That is not what I want.

Ginger: Sometimes we don't get what we want, Harry.

Harrison: Did you mean what you said tonight…about how you don't feel in control of your life? People making decisions for you?

Ginger: Yes, kind of…I don't know; it's complicated.

Me: Uncomplicate it for me.

The blasted three dots appear like she is texting then they disappear. Then they are back.   It is killing me to wait for her response. I am so tempted to abandon this and just call her when her text comes through.

Ginger: My mom said something tonight that sums up how I feel. We were talking about how Noah would always see me as a little girl in pigtails in a tutu running around the house.

Ginger: Answer something for me first…please. Is that how you see me, too?

Me: No…that is not how I see you.

Ginger: Harry, how do you see me?

Me: Sorry, not how this works Sunshine. I answered your question, now answer mine.

Ginger: Yes, I meant what I said tonight. For as long as I can remember, my life has always been dance. I was always the good girl who had a plan and never deviated from it. What if I want different things now?

Me: Ginger, you deserve all the good things this life has to offer. You pick what path you want and do that. I will support you no matter what.

Ginger: It has been a long day. I am going to crash. Good night.

Me: Sweet dreams, Sunshine.

I feel like garbage. I know that Ginger can never be my girl, but I don't want to make her feel bad, either. I have feelings for the one girl that is off-limits to me. Without thinking, I start a group thread for the guys minus Max and Noah. I know this makes me a crappy friend, but I am sure the guys will know what to do.

Me: Boys I need help

Bubba: Admitting it is the first step

Ralph: Why did you start a new guy thread without Max and Noah?

Henry: My money is on this has something to do with a tall blonde ballerina.

Me: Don't start Henry.

Bubba: You are doing a piss poor job hiding that you are into her. Every time someone mentions her in any way, you wig out or become violent.

Me: I pushed Ralph once, and I apologized.

Ralph: So I am assuming because Max and Noah are excluded from this thread you need advice in reference to everyone's favorite ballerina.

Me: Any way you can just give advice and make it painless.

Bubba: Do you know us?

Henry: Good point Bubba.

Me: Fine, get your jabs in as long as you give me something useful to use.

Ralph: What exactly do you want advice with?

Me: Well you might have guessed but I might have feelings for Ginger that are less brotherly and more…just more than you all have for her.

Bubba: Color me shocked.

Henry: This is a bigger revelation than I expected.

Ralph: Man, I really want to give you crap, but that admission was pathetic…and I do not kick puppies.

Me: You all suck, you know that right.

They all shoot off laughing emojis like we are in middle school. I desperately want to send the middle finger emoji, but I can't risk them abandoning the text thread without me getting some help.

Me: Focus please. Apparently, I did not hide my feelings for Ginger as well as I originally thought. But I have been barely hanging on with Ginger this summer. Larry made it worse. I thought I was going to get a break when she went back to school. Finding out tonight that she is not going anywhere is killing me. What do I do?

Henry: You are making this sound like the end of the world. Maybe she is busy and we rarely see her?

Ralph: Is she the reason you are on the longest dry spell we have ever seen you on?

Me: Maybe…

Bubba: We need all the details if you want our help.

Me: Ugh, fine, yes! I have tried going out with other girls but I spend all evening thinking about Ginger. So, I gave up and quit dating. If I can't be with Ginger, I don't really want to be with anyone else.

Bubba: Umm, this is worse than we originally thought, boys.

Henry: Agreed.

Ralph: I thought you were just wanting to make out with her and move on to the next girl

Me: Ginger is the forever type of girl.

Bubba: Why don't you ask her out on a date then?

Ralph: Interesting that Bubba has a useful suggestion, seeing his love life is a mess.

Henry: True, but when Bubba finally figures out his life and claims Stella as his girl, he will not have to deal with two angry brothers.

Ralph: Is that what is holding you back, Harrison, the brothers?

Bubba: You guys have no idea what you are talking about with me and Stella. But Harrison answer the question. You afraid of the brothers?

Me: Not afraid of them but I have known them almost my entire life.

Henry: Give them more credit. They know you and you are a good man. What else could they ask for in a guy for their sister?

Ralph: Either step up and make a move or move aside and watch as someone takes the girl of your dreams away.

Me: Can't decide if you all suck or if this was helpful.

Bubba: All helpful except Ralph's misguided views of Stella and me. Am I right boys?

Bubba: Am I right?

No one responds to Bubba. As messed up as I am with my feelings for Ginger, it is safe to say the Bubba-Stella love affair is a mess and has been going on way longer. So, he takes the cake for being more screwed up in the love department than me. Not that it is a comforting reward.

Maybe the guys are right. Maybe it is time to pull myself together and let Ginger know what she means to me. I have nothing to lose at this point.

Chapter 5
Ginger

The past few weeks have flown by. I moved into my new apartment above the dance school. It is tiny and nothing special to write home about, but the best part is that it is all mine. I have never really lived on my own before. I went from living with my parents to the dorms and eventually sharing an apartment with five other girls. During the summer breaks, I would move back in with my parents to save money.

This apartment, even though it is very small and bland in style, is still very much mine, which makes it kind of perfect. The girls came over when I first moved in and helped me paint and decorate. They were impressed that Mrs. Hannigan would allow me to change so much about the space if I was only here for a semester. I came close to giving away another secret when the girls would not let it go, but I could not bring myself to share my secrets with them just yet.

That is the problem with secrets and half-truths is that they seem to take a life of their own, and before I knew it, I was unable to find the words to explain to the people I love the most in this world about the biggest moments in my life. Although I am failing to share my secrets, I have been successful in avoiding the guys or the group activities. I have successfully avoided game nights, nights out at the Thirty Moose, and dinners at each other's homes.

I fear my luck is running out in dodging everyone. The girls started this morning on the girl's text thread.

Emma: Has anyone seen a slightly tall ballerina? I am related to her. Rumors have it that she is currently living in town but there have been no sightings of her in the wild.

Stella: Is there some type of reward for locating such a rare find?

Jane: I am slammed at the bakery this morning and have nothing witty to contribute but let me know if you locate said missing person.

Me: All right you weirdos, I am picking up on some underlining issues you would like resolved.

Emma: EEKK, she is alive and makes contact. Make sure not to spook her back into hiding.

Me: You are ridiculous Emma.

Stella: I would have to agree but she has a point Ginger. Where have you been? We never see you. I thought it was a bonus that you were staying in town this semester, but I am rethinking that.

Emma: I agree. Admit it, you are avoiding us.

Me: Dramatic much ladies? I have been slammed at the dance school.

That was not completely a lie but also not the whole truth. I could make time if I really want to, but there is a glaring reason stopping me and his name is Harrison. I can't bring myself to face him especially how we left it a few weeks ago.

Stella: Come on, kid!! Come clean what is up with you.

Jane: We can have a girls night at my place tonight so we can grill you in person.

Me: That sounds tempting and all but…

Emma: No buts or I will sic your brothers on you about this.

Me: You drive a hard bargain. Fine. I will be there. But only girls tonight. I am not in the mood for everyone.

Stella: Victory!! See ya tonight, girls.

Jane: Max is going to whine about girl's night…

Emma: That is your problem, girl. HE will get over it. I will see if Noah can take Max out to distract him.

Jane: Thank you….I will make tacos.

Stella: I will bring the Margaritas.

Me: Thanks ladies that sounds perfect.

If I would have come up with another excuse, they would have shown up at my door. In truth, I have missed hanging out with everyone. I was super excited at the thought of not leaving at the end of the summer. But the news I was staying didn't go like I thought it would. Noah was overprotective and annoying. Harrison is the one who took me by surprise, though. His response was weird and conflicting. He ignores me more often than not, but that night, he seemed upset I was staying. It puts a damper on my crush that I have been harboring for that man since before it was appropriate for me to have a crush on him. Avoiding everyone was my only course of action if I wanted to stop being a silly girl and get over this stupid crush. Except now I am being summoned before the firing squad, so to speak, and they are not going to go easy on me about my lack of being present at get-togethers.

When I pull up to Jane's bakery, I stall and don't immediately get out of my car. She is also living above her business and her studio apartment is so cute. The exposed brick, beams on the ceiling, and lots of windows make the space perfect. I am gathering my stuff up to head upstairs to hang with the girls when my phone starts to vibrate, alerting me to an incoming text message. I pull it out, kind of wishing the girls are canceling so I can have a quiet night at home with a frozen pizza and a movie. I regret pulling my phone out to check the message.

Harrison: So you are not dead.

Not sure how he would like me to respond or why he is randomly texting me. Maybe if I ignore it, he will go away. It's not in the cards for me tonight when my phone alerts me to another text message.

Harrison: Glad to see you are not ignoring the girls anymore. They have been worried about you.

Me: I am not ignoring anyone.

Harrison: Then why have I not seen you since the last time we went out on the boat this summer?

Me: You are being dramatic….You have seen me. Plus I told you I would be busy with my internship and nothing would be different this semester.

Harrison: Trust me, I am painfully aware of the last time I saw you, Sunshine.

Me: I don't know what you want me to say. I have been busy. I am running late for girl's night, gotta run.

I hurry and power off my phone before he can reply. Even more disappointed now, I begrudgingly grab my purse and head up to Janes. We used to just walk into Jane's apartment but ever since she started dating my overprotective brother, who insists on her always having her door locked, we now have to knock. Jane opens the door with a giant smile on her face and throws her arms around me. "Hey girl, I have missed you so much. Come on in. Stella already started pouring the margaritas, you need to catch up." Jane says as she leads me into her living room.

I find Stella and Emma sitting on the floor with drinks in hand.

"Yay, you came! I was worried we would have to come find you." Stella adds with an over-the-top smile. I wonder how many of those drinks she has already had.

"Sorry, I was late. Class got over late tonight."

"Here ya go, drink up" Emma hands me a pink drink that reeks of more alcohol than fruity concoction.

"Umm, thanks, but I probably shouldn't drink tonight. I need to drive home tonight." I leave out the part that the smell alone will probably cause me to get drunk.

"No worries, the guys said they will come get us and be out DD's," Stella adds.

"Girls, you promised no guys tonight," I say way whinier than I mean to. Trying to prove I am an adult will be hard if I use that whiny voice again.

"Maybe you just tell us why you are avoiding the guys then," Emma adds, sounding less drunk than a minute ago.

Oh, I see, this is a trap. Well played, girls, well played. "Fine ask your questions so I can go home and put my pajamas on and heat up a frozen pizza."

Jane pipes up, "We are worried about you. Why are you avoiding us?"

Jane sounds hurt, which makes me feel like a first-class jerk. "I am sorry, girls. I am not trying to avoid you on purpose. I am trying to prove that I am not the kid you guys all refer to me as." The small truth slips out.

"Oh, Ginger, I am sorry if us referring to you as kid hurt your feelings. That was never our attention. I have known you your entire life, and it has been a privilege to see the woman you have grown into" Stella adds with a tiny slur still. She might really be drunk.

"Is there any other reason you are avoiding us, mainly the guys?" The ever-astute sister-in-law of mine strikes again.

"Ok, Emma, there might be another reason. But it is so pathetic, it barely warrants mentioning it."

"It's about Harrison, right?" Jane asks quietly from her spot on the couch.

"Fine. Yes, I am avoiding that man with everything I have in my being. Happy now?"

"I would be happy with more details" Stella perks up with the chance at group gossip. I swear she and Bubba are worse than the old ladies in the quilting bee down at the local church.

"What do you want me to say? Want me to tell you that I have had a serious crush on that man since my Jr. year in high school? That I compare all the guys to him that I go on dates with. That I wish he saw me as a woman not a kid. That when he calls me Sunshine it does weird things to my stomach. When he touches me, my skin feels electric. He feels like the only man that will make my heart feel whole. Is that what you want to hear?" I look at the girls, who are all wide-eyed and speechless. "Pretty pathetic, right?"

"So, I clearly don't pay that close of attention. I just thought you were bored with Larry, and you were entertaining a summer fling with Harrison," Stella states.

"Oh my, okay, well, I had no clue about 95 percent of that info either," Jane admits.

"Ginger, why haven't you said anything to us before now?" Emma looks like she is treading carefully like I am about to bolt.

"I mean, what is the point? Nothing can come of it. He clearly looks at me as a kid. I am not even his type. You have seen the women he has always gone out with. I am nothing like them. And I seriously doubt he would ever go against my idiot brother's wishes that I die a single nun."

"You don't know that. Maybe Noah might take some convincing, but I think Max would be on your side without much convincing," Jane says as she looks toward Emma for conformation.

Emma agrees with Jane but offers, "I think Noah will always see you as this little girl that needs protection. He would just need a minute to wrap his mind around it, but if Harrison is the one that makes you happy, then go for it, girl. Your brothers will catch up and get on board eventually."

"That does not solve the issue of the age gap. Harrison will always see me as a kid and not a woman he is attracted to."

"Okay, can we talk about him calling you Sunshine? When did he start calling you Sunshine and, I don't remember the last time I heard him call you kid. So maybe the age gap is just an excuse you are using to avoid putting yourself out there." Weird half-drunk Stella seems insightful tonight.

"The Sunshine nickname started this summer around the time I broke up with the ex, who shall not be named. He would text me or find me when no one was around. At first, I really liked it but then it started to feel like a dirty little secret that he was embarrassed of. I decided I needed to put up some walls and put space between me and him. As a bonus, my somewhat annoying, overprotective older brothers have also been banished behind the wall of defense."

"You might be wrong about some of the conclusions that you have made about how Harrison feels. I think you are wrong about his type, too. We have all noticed the way he stares at you. I can't explain why he went out with those other women who are your opposite in every way, but he really hasn't dated in forever. I would guess that might have to do with you," Emma adds.

It feels so good to share some of my secrets with the girls, but I cannot give in and believe that maybe they are right and maybe Harrison might share my feelings. "I am sure it doesn't even phase the guys that I am not tagging along anymore. But I do promise to make more of an effort for girls' night and see you all more regularly." I promise them.

"Ginger, we just want you to be happy, but you should know that I think it is affecting Harrison. Max was telling me the other night that Harrison has been in a mood for a while, and the guys can't figure out what his problem is." Jane says as she starts putting the Mexican feast on the table. Homegirl has out done herself tonight. I immediately go for the guac and her homemade chips. Everyone joins in loading up their plates.

Stella says, with a mouth full of food, "I agree with Jane. Bubba has been worried about Harrison, too."

"I don't know what to say. I am sure it is not me causing his sour mood. But can we change the topic? I have done enough confessing for one night. Plus, you all need to fill me in on what is happening with you" pleading for a topic change.

The girls give me the much-needed reprieve I needed, and Jane jumps in. "I have been trying out some new breakfast menu items. They seem to be a big hit. Oh, I am also thinking about entering a holiday baking competition. Max won't let up on me applying."

"I volunteer to be a taste tester," Stella says before taking another large gulp of her margarita.

With a smirk on her face, Jane replies, "I never seem to be short on those volunteers."

"Well, Lola and I are bored. I have come to hate the end of summer. Lola and I are missing having Noah around more often."

"You don't get to complain, you get unlimited snuggles to the cutest baby all day long," Jane whines. Even though my brother, Max, and Jane have only been dating a couple of months, I wouldn't be surprised if he puts a ring on her finger, staking his claim sooner rather than later. Jane has been baby-hungry ever since Lola was born, so my money is on the soon-to-be fact that I will be an auntie again very shortly.

"Nothing new with me. I think Zane and I are over again, probably for good this time." Stella adds to avoid the baby topic.

"What? What happened? I thought things were going better this time." I focus on Stella. Stella and Zane have been on again off again for over a year now. It feels like they spend more time fighting and breaking up than happy and together.

"Not worth talking about anymore. But the short version is he didn't like some of my friends, and we were unable to find a compromise that we both could live with," Stella says it like it's no big deal while shrugging her shoulders and reaching for another taco.

If I had to put money on it, the person Zane has a problem with would be Bubba. What I really want to ask Stella is why she doesn't make a move on Bubba, but I know her too well, and she will shoot me down fast. Both Bubba and Stella claim only to be best friends and nothing more. But anyone with eyes can see how much that is a big fat lie. They both want more with each other. But as someone who is unwilling to voice what I want, I am not sure I am in the position to ask the same of my friend.

The heavy feeling that has fallen on girls' night is unusual for us. Normally, it is all fun, food, and endless laughter. Feeling partially responsible for the heavy mood, I try to change the topic again, telling the girls about my tiny dancer class. It seemed to do the trick. The rest of the evening passed, and we avoided boy topics, and by the end of the night we were laughing and were back to our normal selves. Emma and Stella were arranging rides home, this was my cue to head out before the guys showed up to claim their women or the leftover food. It is a toss-up which reason they would be showing up for.

I say my goodbyes and promise not to disappear again. When I got home, I hurried to get ready for bed. I was tired before girls' night started, and now I am way past exhaustion now. Wanting to crawl into bed and give into my exhaustion, I remember that I turned my phone off before going into Jane's tonight. I grab my purse off the kitchen counter and climb into bed. I am digging through my purse, looking for my phone and locate it at the bottom of the never-ending pit.

I turn it back on with the intention of setting my alarm and then going to bed. Once it was powered back up, it started to ping with notifications of unread text messages. If I was smart, I would ignore them and set my alarm and go to bed. But, big shocker, I have never been accused of being smart when it came to matters of the heart.

I open the text app and see that the new messages are from the one and only Harry. I reread the conversation from earlier tonight that led to the new ones he sent.

Harrison: So you are not dead.

Harrison: Glad to see you are not ignoring the girls anymore. They have been worried about you.

Me: I am not ignoring anyone.

Harrison: Then why have I not seen you since the last time we went out on the boat this summer?

Me: You are being dramatic….You have seen me. Plus, I told you I would be busy with my internship and nothing would be different this semester.

Harrison: Trust me I am painfully aware of the last time I saw you Sunshine.

Me: I don't know what you want me to say. I have been busy. I am running late for girls night, gotta run.

This is where I so maturely turned off my phone to avoid him, but apparently, he kept texting.

Harrison: I want you to say you hate this distance between us too.

Harrison: I want you to say that you miss me as much as I miss you.

Harrison: Really, Sunshine, I just want you.

Sweet mother-less goat…I am in trouble. Where do we go from here?

Chapter 6
Harrison

She must have turned her phone off. I am staring at my phone, and the last few messages that I sent went unread. What was I thinking sending those messages to her. She is going to hate me when she sees them. Probably tell her brothers that a dirty old man is harassing her. I am sitting in a bar, alone, nursing my beer. Did I mention alone? I should have never texted Ginger tonight, but when I heard that Ginger had finally agreed to hang out with the girls, I couldn't help myself.

The guys were trying to get me to go out with them tonight and I am man enough to admit I have been in a funk the last few weeks. My company lately has been complete crap. I haven't seen Ginger since the night that she announced she was staying in town. After texting some of the guys and them giving me advice to man up and make a move, I thought it was finally my time to prove to this woman that I was the man for her.

I thought that it would happen naturally the next time everyone got together to hang out. I could make a move and ask her out, but she has been avoiding all of us like the plague. Let's be honest, she is avoiding me. After that realization I couldn't bring myself to make a move. Maybe this was one sided and I should just move on and leave her alone. Except the thought of Ginger with anyone else drives me crazy.

"I thought we would find you here, but I was hoping you wouldn't look so pathetic." A big hand slaps me on the back, grabbing my attention.

"Bubba, what are you doing here?"

"Not just Bubba, we all think you need an intervention," Henry pipes up as I slowly turn on my bar stool to find Henry, Bubba, Ralph, and Max standing there. There is a mixture of expressions all have different degrees of pity weaved into them.

"How did you guys know where to find me?"

"Umm, that is insulting Harrison. Not only am I the Chief of Police and can find anyone, but we also have all been best friends for most of our lives. Finding you was not that hard," Ralph adds like the know-it-all that he is with his arms crossed over his chest.

Still not buying that explanation, I look over my shoulder and spy Gus, the owner, pouring drinks. I knew immediately that the old man turned me in. "Really, Gus, you traitor. You called them. I wasn't even causing any problems."

"Listen, son, you look pathetic now. Take your beer and go find a table and let these boys fix your problem so you can get over it faster," he huffs out at me, then returns to the other side of the bar to pour drinks.

I turn back to the wall of friends staring down at me. "I am not in a sour mood; I am just fine." Even to my ears, I sound like a little kid about to throw a tantrum.

"Let's grab some food and drinks, and we will discuss the problem that is not causing your sour mood," Henry adds.

Before I know what is happening, I have been relocated to a table. A food order has been placed, and everyone is staring at me like a firing squad.

"Might as well spill your guts. You are stuck with me until Jane tells me I can come over. Have I mentioned to you guys how much I hate girls' night? Such crap." Max huffs out. Max has always voiced his dislike for girls' nights since he and Jane got together this summer. And secretly, I agree I like having the girls around too.

Oh, NO!! I can feel the color draining from my face and panic setting in. Why is it just now dawning on me that Max is one of Ginger's overprotective older brothers? I can't tell him what is bothering me. The other guys must have picked up on my panic.

"Okay, let me help you out, brother," Ralph starts, but I do not feel like this will be helpful. "So, Max, the reason our boy here has been in the worst mood ever is because he has been carrying a torch for your sister."

"It is true, he so far gone for Ginger. It would be funny if he wasn't such a mopey, pitiful excuse for a man with no mo-jo to get the girl I have ever seen," the next not-helpful soon-to-be ex-best friend, Bubba, chimes in. At this point, I think I actually let out a whimper. I didn't see this night getting any worse, but I am rarely right these days.

"Calm down, Harrison. Max can't kill you in public," Henry strikes next.

Right then, the waitress brings out the food. All the guys start digging in. I am just sitting there waiting for Max to lower the boom and end the friendship, punch me, or bury me where no one will ever find me.

"What's the big deal, Harrison? Ginger is a great girl, and she has had a rough go of it lately in the love department. I have known you almost my entire life. She would be lucky to be with a guy like you," Max says around a mouth full of cheese curds. "And for the record, I missed cheese curds so much. You would never get something this cheesy with the right amount of grease served in California."

I don't know what to say. I am literally sitting here speechless. Struggling to form words being totally blindsided by Max being ok with me and Ginger being together.

"Harrison, pull it together. If you don't dive into this food, we will not save you any. You know the rules" Bubba adds with his mouth stuffed full of nachos.

"Wait, I am confused…"

"We know that is why we tracked your pitiful butt down tonight to get you out of the funk. You clearly didn't take our advice a few weeks ago when we told you to make your move, so we had to resort to plan B," Henry chimed in with his two cents on the matter.

"Wait, I am scared to ask what plan B is?"

"It was obviously bringing Max to talk some sense into you. Moody, sad Harrison is not so much fun. So, whatever we can do to help you get your girl, we are in," Ralph adds like it was a no-brainer what plan B was.

"Max, you really don't care if your sister and I were to start dating each other?"

"Harrison, you are one of the best men I know. I have been gone the last few years, but when I moved home, I could see that there was something between you and Ginger. I feel bad if you thought I would stand in your way. You have the wrong twin. Now, Noah will be a pain in the buttocks about it at first, but he will get over it when he sees what the rest of us already see."

"I don't know what to say, man."

"You could tell me that you are going to figure your crap out and ask my sister out."

"I am pretty sure that she does not feel the same way. I think I am the reason she has been avoiding everyone. Lately, anytime we talk or text, I seem to put my foot in my mouth and make her mad or push her further away. Plus, I am pretty sure she is still in love with Lawerence."

"Geez, it is worse than we thought, gentlemen. Not only has he lost his mo-jo and is on the longest dry spell ever, but he is also at risk of losing his man card with all this whining." Ralph states with the most annoying smirk plastered on his face.

"You know, I am sure there is a reason we are friends, but I am struggling to find a reason right now."

Everyone starts to laugh and throw in with their own brand of insults that only endear these men to me more. I don't have a memory that doesn't include one or all of these guys. It strikes me that Noah should be here. "Where is Noah tonight? I feel bad that he is the only one that is out of the loop now."

"He is on Lola duty tonight with the girls doing a girl's night. He was going to try and sneak her in, but she apparently is teething and is not loving her life." Max says.

"Not sure that her teething should be the reason he does not bring his baby into a bar. Maybe being the local principal and, responsible for young children and a pillar of the community should also be a deterrent. I admit I know nothing about being around kids but even I know bringing kids into a bar seems like a bad idea." Henry pauses, devouring his wings to give his opinion.

"I would like to say my twin is thinking of the welfare of his baby or his status in the community, but in reality, he is afraid of his wife, who would kill him and enlist the help of the girls to bury his body if he ever brought Lola to the Thirsty Moose, let alone think about doing it." Max shrugs like the death of his twin would be justified.

"I should probably talk to him and let him know my intentions with Ginger. I feel bad he is the only one out of the loop."

"How old are you, man? Your intentions? Out of the loop? Gotta say, kind of starting to think maybe you are too old for our girl Ginger," Bubba states deadpan serious.

I wadded up a napkin and threw it at him. "Always the helpful one, Bubba!"

"What you need is a plan to get the girl. And maybe this time you follow our advice" Ralph looks in full sheriff mode now. It is somewhat intimidating, not that I would ever let on to him he could strike fear in a grown man.

"Well, I might have an idea," Max chimed in. My mind is still blown that not only is he okay with me dating Ginger, but now he is scheming with me to get my girl, who is also his sister.

"I am man enough to admit that I am desperate and need a plan because any of my attempts are failing."

"I have a photography friend who reached out and asked me if I knew of any hotties that worked at the fire department."

"This is taking a weird turn," Bubba adds.

"I agree and am not sure if this is helpful. You clearly know no one that would fall into that category. And even if you did, how does that help Harrison get the girl." Typical Ralph, always so helpful.

"Focus men. She is doing a calendar for a charity project for fallen heroes. All the proceeds go to the families of the men and women who died in the line of service."

"Max, it is hard to make jokes when you say things like that," Henry adds.

"Not sure where you're going with this, Max, or how it is supposed to help me convince your sister to give me a chance."

"I told her that you would be Mr. December. I already cleared it with your Chief at the station. I am coming this week to take your photo at the station."

"What?!"

"Not sure what part you are struggling to understand?"

"How about where you agreed to make me Mr. December without asking, or talking to my boss, or more importantly how does this get me Ginger." How does this night keep getting worse?

"This is going to be so hilarious. I need to know the time and place so I can show up and support our local Mr. Hottie." Bubba can't even get it all out without bursting into laughter.

I start to rub my temples not sure when my life became this side show joke. "I ask again how this gets me the girl?"

"You have that little faith in me. Well, that just hurts more than I expected."

"Ok, Max, better put our boy out of his misery and fill him in before he strokes out," Henry chimes in.

"It is simple. I am coming to take your photo on Thursday morning; your boss already approved it. I will get Ginger to show up and ask her to be my assistant with the photo shoot." Max sits back in his chair with a satisfied grin on his face as he crosses his arms over his chest like this plan magically gets me the girl.

"How does Ginger witnessing my very public humiliation convince her to give me a chance? Or, better yet, how are you going to convince her to even come within 500 feet of a place that I will most likely be? She has been avoiding me."

"Ye of little faith, man. I will get her there, and I will set you up for success, but you are actually going to have to man up and make a move." Max is supposed to be the nice one. But I see his point.

"I can freely admit that I am skeptical about how you are going to get her to show up." Ralph leans in like he is now turning his interrogating skills on Max.

"Well, clearly, we will need to enlist the girl's help in this matter. It is definitely going to have to be a team effort to get the two of them together." Max growing in confidence in his plan.

"I like how you are thinking, Max. The girls will be our secret weapon in operation 'Get Harrison the Girl.'" Henry is beaming with the stupid name of the operation. Ralph and Bubba are trying to keep their amusement under wraps but are failing in spectacular fashion.

Even though I am approaching 30, I apparently have lost any and all skills to get the girl. Desperate times call for desperate measures. "I can do this. You get Ginger there, and I will shoot my shot."

"You better because if we enlist the girls and you fall on your face, I am not going down with you. I can't live without Jane, and I really hate when she is mad at me."

"Pretty sure both of you have lost your man-cards. If this is what happens when you fall for a girl, then count me out. I will keep with my bachelor status quo." Henry looks seriously nervous that his man card is at risk of being lost.

Max phones phone starts to vibrate. Then Bubba's goes off. Then, like clockwork, Henry and Ralph's go off. Mine is deafening quiet. Max reads his text first. His face lights up like it is Christmas morning. He starts pumping his fist in the air. "Yes, freakin girls' night it over. I am out of here. Harrison, be ready Thursday morning to get the girl." He is standing and getting ready to leave before I know what is happening.

"Stella and Emma need a ride home. They let Stella mix the drinks, or at least I think that is what the text says. Stella is well past the legal limit if that text is any judge of her sobriety." Bubba has a smirk on his lips of pure adornment when he talks about Stella. Why does he not get more crap from everyone about his lack of getting the girl?

"Why did you two Yahoos get a text?" I turn to ask Ralph and Henry.

They both look a little guilty but not guilty enough to turn down the offer that was texted to them. "Let me guess, Jane offered you leftovers if you guys wanted to go grab them?"

"Sorry man, but they had homemade guac and chips tonight," Ralph adds, even though he already devoured a truckload of food tonight.

"And Jane might have made ice cream cookie sandwiches for dessert. Plus, you have to prepare for Thursday morning. We don't want to get in your way. See ya, man." Henry barely tosses a wave behind him as the four men exit. I can't really blame them. If I had a girl or really good food to run to, I would be there just as fast, too.

I need to commit to giving this my all, and at the end of it, she doesn't want what I am offering I think I could walk away if that is what she really wants. I think.

Chapter 7
Ginger

After returning home from girls' night on Monday evening, I went over Harrison's last text to me over and over again. He really couldn't have meant those words. That man has me all tied up in knots and in a constant state of confusion.

On Tuesday morning, I woke up to even more texts, adding to the confusion.

Harrison: Morning Sunshine. I hope you were able to get some good rest last night. I hope you have a good day. I will be thinking about you.

I chickened out and didn't respond. What does he want me to say? I still kind of feel like his dirty little secret. I am sure he is just being nice because he has known me my entire life, or he is afraid my brothers will beat him up. I juggled with emotions throughout my day, getting through work but always having Harrison on my mind. Then the jerk ends the night with a text: like I can take anymore.

Harrison: Sweet dreams, Sunshine. I hope I get to see you in my dreams tonight. I have missed you so very much.

I want to reply. I want to go to him and tell him not to care about all the barriers between us. I miss you so much, too. I want you to, Harry, but of course, I don't text any of that. I'm a coward. I crawl into bed, knowing I'll be dreaming of the one man who constantly fills my thoughts, day and night.

Wednesday is more of the same, and I wake up to a good morning text wishing me a good day. During the day, he sends a text with a silly selfie. The smile it brings to my face lingers throughout the day. The way this man makes me feel should be illegal. Then, before I head to bed, my phone vibrates with an incoming text message. I hate that I have been waiting for his message, no needing this message to arrive in my inbox. I am craving any contact with this man that I can get.

Harrison: Good night, Sunshine. I hope you had a good day. I know I haven't always said the right thing or done the right thing when it comes to you, but I promise you I am trying to be the type of man that you deserve. I hope you get a good night's sleep. I will be dreaming of you again, sweet dreams, my Sunshine.

What in the actual name of all that is holy! How am I supposed to respond to that? He has always been the type of man that I have wanted and deserved. How can he not see that? I know I should respond, but how? I can't find the words. Sleep eventually takes me.

Thursday morning, I drag myself from bed. The lack of sleep is starting to take its toll on me. I head downstairs to find something to do to keep myself busy. I keep checking my phone for my good morning text, but there is nothing. I busy myself with cleaning the reception area where the parents wait for their dancers. After vacuuming, washing windows, and straightening up the lost-in-found area there is still no good morning text. I hate that the disappointment stings more than I want to admit.

I move to the reception desk with plans to stop avoiding the monthly paperwork that needs to be done. Someone knocking on the front door grabs my attention. I look up to find the unexpected appearance of a young guy, probably around my age, holding a brown paper bag and a bouquet of beautiful flowers. I slowly make my way to the front door, unsure what is happening. When I reach the front door and unlock it, I push it open.

"Can I help you?" Feeling nervous all of a sudden. Little Falls is a small town where nothing bad ever happens, but I still have never seen this guy before.

"I hope so. Are you Sunshine?"

"What? What did you call me?"

"Oh, crap!! Please don't tell him I called you Sunshine. He is going to kill me. We all hear him constantly talking about his girl, and he usually refers to you as Sunshine, but I am pretty sure he will kill me or at least make my life miserable for the next month for messing this up."

The guy is in full-on ramble panic mode. "Whoa, calm down. Who are you and what are you talking about?"

"Are you Ginger?"

"Yes. Now answer my questions."

"Captain Stone wanted me to drop off breakfast and these flowers for you."

Still confused over here. "Why did Harrison ask you to bring me flowers and breakfast?"

"Listen, I would really appreciate it if you would take your breakfast and flowers and avoid mentioning that I called you Sunshine to the Captain. I would really appreciate it. I am the new guy, so I get

assigned all the grunt work as it is. Please take the food and flowers?"
he says as he thrusts the items in my face.

"What is your name?"

"Tony."

"Well, Tony, it was very nice of you to bring me this surprise this
morning, and your secret is safe with me. No need to worry." I am
trying my best to ease this guy's worry as he has broken out in a light
sweat on his forehead from the stress.

"Thank you so much, Ginger! I really appreciate it. I hope you
have a great day." And just like that, Tony's gone, and I'm just
standing there, holding this gorgeous bouquet of wildflowers with pink
roses mixed in—my absolute favorite, by the way! Plus, a bag of
something that smells delicious. I lock up again and head back to my
desk, which has items spread out everywhere. I open the bag to find a
breakfast sandwich and my favorite juice. I did not realize how
hungry I was until the smell of bacon wafted toward me. I hungrily
unwrap the breakfast sandwich and take an un-lady-like bite, and it is
heavenly. With my cheeks puffed out like a chipmunk my attention is
brought to my phone vibrating on the desk.

Harrison: Good morning, beautiful. I hope you enjoy your
surprise. I will be thinking about you all day.

He is definitely trying to drive me crazy. What is up with the new
Harrison, who is not hiding and saying all the right things? I don't
know what to make of Tony saying that Harrison talks about me all the
time and that I am his girl. Before I can think about responding, my
phone is vibrating with an incoming call. When I look back down at
my phone I see Jane is calling. I can't let it go to voicemail after
promising to be more available to the girls.

"Hey Jane, how's it going?"

"Terrible! I need a favor any chance you can help a girl out this
morning?"

"Sure, what is going on?"

"Tiffany called in sick, and I am slammed."

"Well, I can't cook worth anything, but I can come to work the
counter. My first class isn't until 3 o'clock this afternoon."

"Oh, that is sweet of you to offer. I can handle this beast, but I do
need you to run an errand for me that is time-sensitive. And before
you say no, hear me out."

"That does not sound promising."

"My annual fire inspection just came up, and they came out and checked all the sprinklers and did all the other stuff that comes with an annual recertification."

"Okay well, what is the problem if they already did your recertification?"

"I was supposed to go by the fire station to pick up my paperwork at the beginning of the week and I totally forgot. My insurance states it must be posted, or I could lose my business insurance. I am totally freaking out. I know that the chances of them popping in randomly right now are not high, but I can't lose my insurance. I would ask Max, but he is on a photo shoot."

"I have to go the firehouse to get it?" She knows why I am asking and why, of all the places, I am avoiding that place.

"I know what you are thinking, and he is not working today. Please, I wouldn't ask if it wasn't important. You are lucky you don't own the dance studio, or you would have all this stress piled on you, too."

It dawns on me that I do own this building. One of the many lies or half-truths that are floating out there that I haven't shared with anyone yet. I never even thought about scheduling a fire inspection for certification. Maybe I can ask about my certification while I am down there picking up Jane's paperwork.

"Sure, Jane, I will go grab your paperwork and bring it over to you. Try not to worry. See you in a little while."

"You are the best!! I owe you big. Bye, girl!"

And just like that, she hangs up, and I am dreading agreeing to this favor.

Chapter 8
Ginger

As I pull up to the fire station, my nerves kick in. I try to keep telling myself that he isn't working today. I will be in and out so fast that this feeling of nerves is me being silly. As I get out of my car and stand there staring at the fire station, I am starting to regret that I didn't get ready for the day. I am wearing yoga pants and a fitted crop top that I was cleaning in this morning. My hair is pulled on top of my head in a messy bun. I am wearing my oversized black sunglasses. Who am I kidding? I look like a hot mess not a business owner. I still have a long way to go before I figure it all out. I push down my nerves and head toward the entrance.

When I enter the building, I push my sunglasses up on my head like a headband, completing the hot mess look. I am not prepared for what I walk into, though. Harrison is standing in the middle of the room shirtless. Is that an 8-pack or a 6-pack? No matter how many packs this man has, he is beautiful. I have always thought he was the perfect height at 6'3." He normally wears his blonde hair in a clean-cut style. It has been a few weeks since I have seen him and his hair is a little grown out and wild, in a good way. His lean, muscular build has always filled out his clothes perfectly.

He is currently only wearing his uniform pants that he wears out to fires with the suspenders dangling off the back of his pants. I am pretty sure I stopped breathing; I might have even swallowed my tongue. What I am 100% positive is I am staring. I can't help myself. This man has the body Greek God. This is silly because I have seen him so many times before out on the lake, but this feels different. At his work, half his uniform on, he is holding an ax and posing. Wait, why is he posing? Then, I start to take in the bigger picture. There are cameras and a few lights set up. Before I can process what is happening, I hear someone calling my attention.

"Hey, sis, what are you so mesmerized by?" Max is standing right in front of me with an annoying smirk plastered all over his face.

I shake myself out of my hot fireman stupor. "What are you doing here? Jane said you were busy at a photo shoot today."

"I am at a photo shoot right now. I am doing a shoot for a charity calendar to help a friend out. And lucky me, I could really use a favor. Your timing is perfect!"

"Well, seeing I am regretting the last favor I said I would do, I am not sure I am willing to be helpful," I say as I cross my arms over my chest, looking like a toddler in full pout.

"Please I could really use the help, and you never know when there will be an emergency around here and the shoot will get shut down." Max must feel like he is winning the battle, so he puts the nail in the request coffin. "All the money goes to help families of fallen heroes."

"Ugh, fine. What do you need help with?" These are my famous last words. Not in a million years can I have imagined what my brother could have possibly needed help with.

"Great! You are the best sister ever. I just need you to rub this oil all over Mr. December's chest and abs. I need him glistening for the shot." He is thrusting a bottle of massage oil into my hands as he heads past me toward the offices. "I will be right back, I need to chat with the chief."

I turn to face him as he is walking away from me, and I yell after him, "Wait, are you kidding me? Who is Mr. December?"

"That would be me, Sunshine."

Oh, garbage! You have got to be kidding me. Why does the sound of his voice send a shiver down my spine? I try to hide the shudder, but I am pretty sure he notices. I have no words right now. I can't believe my best friend set me up, and her boyfriend, my freakin brother, wants me to rub oil all over his best friend. Did I hit my head? I don't remember. Maybe this is a dream.

"Sunshine, I need you to turn around and look at me. Please."

It is the please that is my undoing, and I can't refuse him. I slowly turn around. Still unable to make eye contact, my gaze is locked on the floor. Harrison slowly lifts his hand to my chin and raises my chin until I can only see him.

"Hi."

"Hi, Sunshine."

"Thank you for breakfast and the flowers this morning. They made my day. I can't remember the last time a man gave me flowers." I have no idea why I am sharing that with him. There is something about Harrison; there has always been something about him. I have always wanted him to know all my truths. He looks away and mumbles something under his breath, that sounded like him cursing out the male species for being idiots.

"Sunshine, you deserve all the good in this world. I am going to prove it to you." He turns his full attention back on me with his green eyes holding me in place. I could get lost in his eyes and the feelings they are bringing to life in me right now. We are momentarily lost in our own little bubble.

"Mr. December, uhh?"

He almost looks like he is embarrassed before he recovers "Yeah, not my idea of a good time, but now that you are here, I am warming up to the idea. I could use some assistance; I am starting to see the benefits of the gig." His confidence is growing. "What do you say, Sunshine? Are you going to rub oil on me for my big debut as a model?"

"Harry, are you really trying to tell me you can't rub this on your own chest and abs and other rippling muscles that seem to be everywhere all of a sudden…" I know I am 5 seconds away from drooling as I am now focused on the muscles. He clearly finds this amusing with that stupid grin covering his face.

"Sorry Sunshine, this is a job only you can do. Please help me. This is my first modeling gig, and I am nervous. Please, Sunshine?" He is standing there with his bottom lip pouted out so far that he might trip over it, and his stupid puppy dog eyes. Then he added the stupid 'please,' and I am a goner for this man.

"Fine, I will help you. Let me put my keys and phone down." I walk over to a table with some of Max's equipment spread out on. As I slowly turn around, Harrison is standing right behind me, his expression unreadable. I go to open the bottle of oil and find my hands shaking. I am mortified that he has a front-row seat to this embarrassment. Before I can come up with an excuse to ditch out, Harrison is placing his hands over the top of mine, instantly calming me.

"Sunshine, it is just me and you. Why are you shaking? You don't have to help if you don't want to. I never want you to do anything you don't want to." There is a gentle kindness in Harrison's eyes. He has always shared this part of himself with me.

"I think the problem is how much I want to do this," I mumble under my breath.

I start to unscrew the cap. I pour some of the oil into the palm of my hand. I set the bottle down on the table. I start to rub my hands together, all while avoiding eye contact again. I take a deep breath and proceed to move my hands in a circular pattern over Harrison's chest. After years of dancing, rubbing sore muscles is second nature to my hands. I get lost in the movements. I have never touched Harrison like this before. What was I thinking, I should not have put my hands on him. If I was honest with myself, his daily texts were already wearing me down. Now, this, I will not survive Harrison Stone.

"Um, Sunshine…" Harrison pulls me out of my thoughts.

I look up at him with my palms still pressed up against his abs. I clear my throat, hoping my voice doesn't betray me. "Yeah, Harry?"

"What is going on up there? You look like you are about to combust with whatever you are thinking about," he says as he taps gently on the side of my temple.

"Honestly?"

"Always. I always want your truths, Sunshine." Now, he has his palm holding tight to my cheek as his thumb barely moves over my cheek in a soothing stroke.

I lean into it. "Harry, I miss you. I want things with you that I have never wanted before. I hate this distance I put between us, but I don't know how this works with all the barriers in front of us. So, I thought if we had some space, it would hurt less when you do find a girl that fits in your life." We just stand there for a moment, staring at each other. Pretty sure I freaked him out. I am about to backtrack and try to salvage whatever is left of my tattered pride when we are interrupted.

"Hey, Ginger, it's good to see you again. Did you enjoy breakfast?" Tony walks up without a care in the world, not realizing what he just interrupted.

"Read the room Probie. And don't talk to Ginger. Forget you know her name" Harrison doesn't take his eyes off me as he scolds Tony like a toddler. I step back and remove my hands from him. I grab a towel off the table, wipe my hands off, and turn back toward Tony.

"Hey Tony, good to see you again. And yes, breakfast was very delicious. Thank you for delivering it to me this morning." Tony's head bobbles between Harrison and me. He ultimately chooses self-preservation in the workplace and, ducks his head and takes off without another word.

"That was not very nice, Harry. He is a nice guy who, by the way, did you a favor this morning that was not in his job description. And why can't he know my name? Would it kill you to be a little nicer to him?"

"He is a Probie that is literally in his job description to do whatever I tell him. And I can forbid him from knowing your name," he says as he moves closer to me. I take a step back.

"You forbid him from knowing my name? I didn't take you for the caveman type, Harry. You are being ridiculous; he would never give me a second look if you hadn't sent him to my place of business this morning bearing gifts," I huff out as I cross my arms. Immediately, I feel like the child I am trying so hard to prove I am not.

I'm not sure which emotion is taking over more right now, all I know is I need to get out of here. "I should go get Jane's paperwork and get it back to her; she seemed pretty stressed about it."

"Wait, we are not done talking."

"Yes, we are," I say as I turn to head to the offices.

My brother, for once in his life has good timing and comes walking out of the offices I need to escape into. "You guys done? We need to get these pictures shot."

"Sunshine, wait!"

A little gasp escapes from me. "Harry, Max is right there. He can hear you!" What is Harrison doing calling me Sunshine in front of Max, has he lost it? I am sure Max heard him. By the looks of it, though, Harrison doesn't look all that bothered by Max knowing. What is happening? This morning has been so bizarre.

"Fun! You guys already have cute pet names for each other already."

I just stare at my brother with my eyes wide open in shock. Did he really say that? Who is this guy? Ever since he fell head over heels in love with Jane, who, by the way, he calls Cupcake, he has been weird. I guess part of his new weirdness is he thinks pet names are the new normal.

Not sure where to go from here. All I know is I need to get out of here before Harrison feels the need to continue the conversation to nicely let me down easily in front of everyone, including Max. "Well, I wish I could say this has been fun, but I am leaning more toward weird. I should get going, I need to get back to work. Jane is also expecting her certification paperwork so we can avoid her stroking out." I am slowly backing up hoping that is the end of it and I can make my escape.

"Wait up, kid, I haven't seen you since you started your internship. I was hoping to catch up with you" Max pleads with those puppy dog eyes that he thinks every girl is powerless to resist.

"Max, those eyes only work on Jane. Now that I have seen them in action, I am not quite sure why they work on her." Trying to make light of the situation. "I really do need to get back to the studio and work on my teaching plans for the afternoon."

"Ok, if you can't hang out now, how about hitting up Ralph's BBQ on Friday night this week? I haven't seen your reply to any of the group texts about it."

"Umm, Ralph's BBQ…". I know exactly what he is talking about. I have been ignoring the group thread with the BBQ details for a while now. I look between Max and Harrison, wishing the fire alarm would go off so Harrison would have to leave for an emergency. Fairly certain that makes me a sociopath wishing for an emergency to avoid this question. "Yeah, sure, I could probably go, it should be fun." I did miss everyone, and it was getting harder and harder to come up with believable excuses.

"Yes!! This is awesome. Everyone will be so excited to see you." Max pumps his hand victoriously in the air like he won an Olympic medal instead of what he actually does, which is convincing his kid sister to hang out with family and friends.

"Okay, well, I really do need to go. Bye, boys." Without another look at Harrison, I throw a hand in the air to wave goodbye and head for the door, hoping and praying I can make an escape. I stop by the secretary's office and grab the paperwork. Funny how she was confused that I was picking up a copy since they mailed it out a few weeks ago, and Jane should have already received a copy. I try not to think that my best friend just set me up as I think of ways to get her back. I also checked and made sure the certifications on the dance studio were up to date. Relieved to find out that mine were not due until the spring.

"Well, Miss King, this is a pleasant surprise. You are on my list of people to call today." The Fire Chief emerges from his office. Chief Johnson has been chief for as long as I can remember. Although I want to run from the building to escape another run-in with Harrison, I can't bring myself to be rude to the Chief.

"Hey Chief! Good to see you. And what did I do to warrant being placed on your to-do list today?"

"Well, I need your help, a favor really."

What is happening today? Does everyone want a favor from only me today? As much as I want to say no thank you without hearing what the favor request is, I can't bring myself to turn the Chief down. He looks too much like the typical grandpa. His bushy eyebrows and white caterpillar mustache make it nearly impossible to turn him down.

"Color me intrigued. What can I do for you, Chief?"

"Well, I called Mrs. Hannigan this morning. You see, she normally helps me in the fall on a committee that is comprised of local business owners. She is one of the co-chairs. We put on the fireman's ball every year. You might say I was a little surprised when she told me she no longer was a small business owner in town. That she had, in fact, sold her business to you."

I can just imagine that all color has drained from my face, and I am standing there in shock that he so casually drops one of my big secrets that I have been neglecting to share with anyone. The look of shock on my face doesn't seem to deter him, and he continues.

"I think it is great that you are continuing with the school. Mrs. Hannigan has been wanting to retire to Florida for years. And I can't think of anyone better to be a role model for our young dancers here in town."

"Umm, thank you, sir. That is a very nice vote of confidence that you have in me. I haven't really told anyone that I am the new owner of the dance school quite yet. Could you be persuaded to keep this between us for the time being?"

"Of course, kid. I am not here to start trouble for you. I was just curious if you are interested in taking Mrs. Hannigan's place on the committee as a co-chair. We could really use some fresh perspective. I think you are exactly what we need to make this event the best we ever had."

"Well, flattery usually works like a charm on me, but I really have no idea what I would be doing, and I don't want to let you or the department down."

"Don't you worry. I will pair you with another co-chair from the community who will be your partner in crime. I wouldn't ask if we didn't really need the help." The chief is borderline begging. Even the bushy eyebrows are raised in a hopeful manner.

"Okay, sir, I will give it my best. I really hope I don't let you down. Who is the co-chair I will be working with?"

"I need to talk to them as well. When I have my concrete plans, I will have them reach out to you. Does that work for you?"

"Of course. I look forward to making this event one to remember. It was good talking to you. I hate to run off, but I really do need to get back to work."

As I say my goodbyes to the chief and his secretary, I sneak out the side door and make my way across the parking lot to my car. I replay the conversation with the chief in my head. Even though it is overwhelming to be helping with such an important event in town, I can't escape the excitement of doing something that will help prove that I am capable of this adulting thing. Before I get to my car my phone dinged with an incoming text message.

Harry: Please don't change your mind about coming to the BBQ. If me being there will keep you away, I will stay away. Everyone misses you.

Why is it, that I wish he had texted that he was the one that missed me instead?

Me: I said I would go.

Harry: Great!

Harry: PS, we are not done talking, Sunshine.

Oh crap, I am back to wanting to kill Jane.

Chapter 9
Harrison

I must look like an idiot just standing here half-dressed staring at the door that Ginger just exited. Did I mention that I am covered in a nice layer of oil that is leaving me with a glistening shine that is covering my chest and abs. I would probably be prone to want to kill Max for coming up with this stupid idea if the memory of Ginger's hands on me weren't so fresh in my mind.

"Well, that could have gone better, but it could have gone worse so I am taking it as a win" Max says way too pleased with himself as he is slapping me on the back.

"You have got to be kidding me. She practically ran out of here, couldn't get away fast enough."

When Max initially explained his master plan to me, I thought it had merit. I mean, how could you go wrong with your girl rubbing oil on you. In hindsight there was quite a few glaring issues in the plan. His plan never included Ginger practically running from the building like it was on fire.

"What are you talking about man? That went perfect! You even have glistening pecks to prove it. Now hurry up and clean up. If we hurry, we can grab a bite to eat before I need to report over at Jane's for a very important job."

"Let me stop you right there, I don't want to know what this important job is you are doing for Jane. Plus, are we done with pictures? What was the point of Ginger spreading oil all over me if you had all the shots you needed?"

"Okay, you might be a lost cause. If I need to explain to you what the point of a girl you have been drooling over for who knows how long is rubbing oil on you and you can't see the point to this, than I wash my hands of you. You might never get the girl."

"Don't say that!"

"When did you start calling her Sunshine, by the way? Better yet why did she freak out when you called her Sunshine?" He starts to pack up his equipment, he stops abruptly and looks at me with a horrified look on his face. "Wait if it's something freaky I don't want to know. She is still my sister, man."

I laugh, I can't help myself. "How is the name Sunshine freaky? It is way better than Cupcake, by the way". I throw the last comment in there just to poke the bear. When Max started calling his girlfriend,

Jane, Cupcake we all rolled our eyes and teased him mercilessly but now it seems second nature to hear him call her that.

"If you still want my help then you will not use the mocking tone in reference to my Cupcake, and the plan was not a huge fail. Were you not paying attention when she agreed to come hang out this weekend at Ralph's BBQ?"

"Are you seriously trying to take credit for Ralph buying a new grill and wanting an excuse to use it this weekend?"

"Umm, yeah I am. Now stop trying to point out the obvious and focus on part two of my master plan."

I hate that I am intrigued by what this idiot will come up with next. I grab the last clean towel off the table and start to wipe away the oil off my skin. "Okay genius one what is part two?"

"Although, I think you are being sarcastic I like the title so let me continue. It is clear by the way you two make goo-goo eyes at each other that you are both crazy about each other."

"Even if that was true, I think she is worried about some of our obstacles in her way."

"She is just over thinking it. You will have all your boys there on Saturday to act as your wingman. Jane is going to help get Emma and Stella on board with convincing Ginger to come around to the idea of liking you." Max looks pleased with his plan, even though it really doesn't sound like a plan.

"Great, so what you are saying if we can't brow beat her into liking me with peer pressure maybe guilting her will work" I say with a straight, non-impressed face with his stupid plan.

"You are making it sound somewhat illegal at times but yeah that is the gist of it."

As Max packs up the remainder of his gear it hits me that Ginger will probably try to back out. I pull out my phone and shoot off a quick, a borderline pathetic text pleading for her to come this weekend.

Me: Please don't change your mind about coming to the BBQ. If me being there will keep you away, I will stay away. Everyone misses you.

I am to big of a coward to text her the truth, that I miss her.
Ginger: I said I would go.
Me: Great!

Me: PS we are not done talking, Sunshine.

55

Chapter 10
Ginger

I pull up outside of The Cupcake Shack. I have too many emotions running through my body; Excitement that the chief thinks I am capable of chairing a town event. Annoyance with the misguided matchmaking attempt on Jane's part. I am not sure I can come up with words for the emotion that I feel when I think about my interaction with Harrison today. I need to dance this out. Whenever life becomes overwhelming, I head into the studio and let the rhythm of the music take over my body. By the time I am done, I always feel peace washing over me. I crave that feeling right now.

I head inside the bakery, and to my surprise, I see Tiffany behind the counter restocking the displays with something that smells divine. With how this morning has been going so far, why am I surprised? I should have expected Tiffany to be here and not at home, sick.

"Hey, Ginger! How's your day going? Stopping in for a sweet treat?" Tiffany is so happy and always welcoming.

"Well, actually, I stopped by to chat with Jane. Is she around?"

Speak of the devil, "Tiffany, do we need any more of the…" Jane stops mid-sentence when she sees me standing there with my arms crossed over my body, hoping she can pick up on the irritation that is coming off me in waves.

"Oh, hey, Ginger. Didn't expect you so soon." Jane fumbles to find the right words. Tiffany is clearly in the dark about what is happening.

"I am happy to see Tiffany is no longer sick," I say looking between Jane and Tiffany, not letting Jane off the hook.

"What are you talking about? I am not…" Tiffany tries to talk but is cut off by Jane. "Okay, thank you, Tiffany. Why don't you finish up the restock? I just need to chat with Ginger really quick in the back and then I will be out to help with the ordering list." Jane motions for me to walk around the counter and follow her. I really want to call her out and make her squirm more in front of Tiffany, but honestly, that is not my style. No matter how misguided Jane's actions were, I still love her, and she is one of my best friends. I begrudgingly head around the counter and follow her into the back.

Before I can get a word out Jane starts in on what becomes an epic rant. "Ginger, I didn't mean to lie to you. I am so sorry. I hated doing it. I thought I was helping. This was not my fault. You must know this was not my idea. Ginger, you have to say something. Please forgive me. I should have stood my ground and told him no to his plan. I told him it wouldn't work. Unless it did work and then you have to forgive me. Right?" Jane finally takes a breath.

"First of all, I thought Emma was the misguided matchmaker in the group. And who is the "him" that you are referring to in that rant? What was the plan after I showed up at the fire station and saw Harrison was there?" I have lots more I want to ask, but those questions are at the top of my list.

"I know I should have left Emma to the matchmaking business. That is a little tricky, though, because Noah is the only one who doesn't know about you and Harrison."

"WHAT?! What are you talking about? There is nothing to know. What are you talking about?"

"I am making a real mess of this. Let's go back to the other questions. The "him" I was referring to was Max. This was his plan. When he asked me to help, I originally said that I was absolutely not going to help, but then he wore me down with his powers of persuasion. Before I knew what was happening, I had agreed to his stupid plan."

Not sure where to go from here or how to respond, I just stand there rubbing my temples. How has this been the longest day of my life, and it isn't even noon yet? "I beg you with every fiber of my being not to go into more details about my brother's power of persuasion. I might lose what is left of my sanity if made to endure those details.

"Ginger, I really am sorry. Don't be mad. Max really thought he was helping, giving you a gentle push in the right direction."

"Did he tell you what his idea of gentle push entailed?"

"Not exactly. And by the look on your face not sure I want to know."

"He asked me to rub oil all over Harrison's chest and abs for some dumb photo shoot."

We stand there staring at each other for a minute, and then Jane cracks and is bent over laughing like I have never heard before. She is gasping for air as she wipes the tears rolling down her cheeks. When she finally collects herself enough to get a few words out, all I can make out is, "And you want me to feel bad for you because you got to rub oil all over the boy that you have been crushing on for years."

When she puts it that way, sure, it could have been worse. "Fine, I will begrudgingly agree that part was not too bad. Can you explain how my brother got involved? Does Harrison know about all this?"

"Anyway, I can convince you to just go with the flow the next little while and just be open to whatever happens will happen?"

"Nope. Need more explanation now. Or I will be forced to go back to ignoring all of you again." It is an idle threat. I can't go back to ignoring the girls, but Jane might not know I am bluffing.

"I really don't know the intricate details of Max's plan to get you and Harrison together. I just know how he wanted me to help this morning."

I put the certification papers on the prep table, I had almost forgot that I was holding them. "I need to go dance. This day has me on overload. I have no idea how I am supposed to react to everyone, knowing I am carrying a torch for my brother's best friend. It is so embarrassing, and I bet you all had a good laugh at the kid sister crushing on the town playboy." Feeling like a fool, I just want to escape.

"Don't say that! Ginger, no one is laughing at you or Harrison. We all love you both and want you guys to be happy." Jane has stopped the laughing fit and looks concerned that she might have truly hurt my feelings.

"No worries. I need to get back to work. I need to get my lesson plans together for the afternoon classes. I will see you around, okay?" Needing to end this conversation and escape.

"I will for sure see you at Ralph's this weekend, right?"

Clearly, my brother has already texted his girl. "Yes, of course. I was planning on going." I smile at her, trying to reassure her that everything is fine. I turn to go, not quite sure how this is my life. How I came to star in a real-life version of the 'Young and the Restless'.

Chapter 11
Harrison

Yesterday has been playing repeatedly in my mind. I want more of Ginger's truths; the one's she is reluctant to share with anyone. I am not sure if I am worthy of that honor, but I want to be the one she goes to share all her secrets with. I ended yesterday with another good night text. I started this morning with a text to wish her a good morning. With every step forward we make together, it feels like we take five steps back, apart.

I had to come into work today for some paperwork that has been collecting dust on my desk for far too long. Okay, I didn't have to, but I needed the distraction. I love everything about my job, almost everything. The paperwork has never been my thing, though. The Chief has been trying to stress the importance of staying on top of it. He often informs me that he can't work forever and retirement is coming soon. I dread that day. I know it is expected that I apply for his position when that day comes. I never aspired to be the boss man. I enjoy going out, fighting fires, and helping people. Even rescuing the occasional cat from a tree is more appealing than sitting behind a desk pushing paperwork.

As if thinking about my boss could conjure him, he pops his head into my office. "Hey, son you have a minute?" The Chief has always treated me like the son he never had. He and his wife, Estelle, were never able to have kids. My parents are great, don't get me wrong but they were always too busy for the little everyday things that raising a child brings. Being an only child was often lonely growing up. If it weren't for my friends, my life would have likely turned out very differently. I couldn't complain about my family situation, especially when I had friends who had it much tougher growing up than I did. Bubba and Stella had it far worse.

When I started at the academy, the chief was the opposite of my parents in every way. He took the time to explain things and teach me. He listened when it was a hard day of training. He took a chance when I came out of the academy and took the time to mentor me. I am not sure where my life path would have taken me if the Chief hadn't seen something in me when we first met.

"Hey, Chief. Of course, I have time. What's up?"

"It is more like a favor I need help with."

"Name it, and it will get done."

"You might want to hear what the favor is before you are, so Johnny on the spot to agree to it," he says with a smirk forming.

"Too late for that now; how bad can it be?" Famous last words.

"You know how I co-chair the Fireman's ball every year with Mrs. Hannigan?" He pauses but I do not want to make any sudden movements even though I am not liking where this is going. "I find myself unable to fulfill that obligation this year. I was hoping you could stand in for me and be the co-chair. You wouldn't have to do it alone. You would obviously have a co-chair to help you. The community really loves this event and has shown great support for the event in the past. The event really plans itself."

I don't want to protest. After all, the man is my mentor, but he is really selling this, maybe a little too much. "But, sir, I am not sure I could fill your shoes. That event is the talk of the town all year. Everyone looks forward to it. I would hate to let you down." I am overconfident, thinking that I could weasel my way out of this and still stay in his good graces.

"Okay, son, I understand. You have a lot of extra duties already on your plate. I am going to ask Tony if he would be willing to step in and take over."

"Seriously, you want Probie to co-chair the event?" I have to stifle a chuckle thinking about Probie working countless hours with Mrs. Hannigan. I have nothing against her, but she was old when I was a kid, she is ancient by now. This seems like a win-win for me. It might make me sound a little petty that I am still annoyed that Ginger was sticking up for Probie yesterday.

"I would prefer you, of course, but I understand."

It should feel victorious winning, but with the chief sitting there with a smile on his face saying he is the victorious one, I proceed with caution. "I am sure Mrs. Hannigan will show Probie the ropes, and it will be a great event."

The Chief stands to leave. He turns when he gets to the doorway. "Oh, Mrs. Hannigan will not be co-chair this year. She also has some scheduling conflicts as well. Tony will be working with someone else on the event." He turns to go again.

"Wait! Chief who will Tony be working with on the event?" The twinkle in his eyes should have prepared me that I was not going to like his answer.

"Ginger King has graciously volunteered to co-chair this year. I think she and Tony will hit it off. They are the same age. Both bring a lot of energy to the project. I am so looking forward to this event this year." And just like that, he turns and heads down the hallway.

Why it took my legs so long to catch up with my brain, I will never know. My brain is screaming; get up and go after him! In what world would it be okay to allow Probie that much time alone with Ginger? Finally, my legs get the message to get up and move. I am up and out of my chair and make my way down the hallway. "Chief, wait! I think there has been a misunderstanding. It was unfair of me not to give more thought to your request. I don't mind stepping into your shoes this year to plan the event."

"That's okay, son. I know I ask a lot of you, and I don't want to take advantage and make you feel obligated to step into my shoes," he says, throwing the shoe comment back in my face.

"No, no, you are not taking advantage. This event is so important for the firehouse, and I would find it a privilege to be involved."

"If you insist, son." The Chief has now moved on from a smirk to a full-blown 'I won the war" smile.

Well played, sir, well played. "Hey, if you don't mind me asking what is the scheduling conflict that came up?" Dreading, he was going to say it was more paperwork that I would have to look forward to if I decided to pursue his position one day.

His smile drops and he looks to panic, momentarily. "Oh, well, it's Estelle."

"Wait, what is happening with Estelle? Is she okay?"

"Please don't say anything to anyone, but she has some health concerns that have come up. I want to free my schedule up so I can be there for her. You understand, dontcha son?"

Suddenly, feeling like a first-class jerk for not immediately saying yes. "Of course, sir. I won't say a word. Will you please let me know if there is anything you or Estelle need?"

"I knew I could count on you son. Now, I need you to get together with Ginger and start working on the plans for the ball. I will have my secretary have all the files ready for you and Ginger to go through. I can't wait to see what you two come up with."

He walks off, leaving me standing there feeling conflicted. On one hand, I am worried that the Chief is downplaying how sick Estelle could be, but I am excited I have a legitimate reason to spend time with Ginger. Lots and lots of time with Ginger. She is done running from me, from us.

62

Chapter 12
Harrison

After the chief left my office, all I wanted to do was run straight to Ginger, but through some creative but very legal stalking, I found out that she was teaching all afternoon and wasn't done until 6 o'clock tonight. The grown-up thing to do would be to conquer the mountain of paperwork on my desk. I did try to focus on the paperwork that was cluttering my desk but ultimately failed at that. Instead, I ran errands that I also had been procrastinating, but that didn't hold my attention long. I wanted the guy's opinion on how I should approach working with Ginger on the Fireman's Ball but thought better of it. I'm not sure they have really been any help in the Ginger department. I also thought I should stop by and chat with Noah, but I also chickened out on that conversation.

That is how I find myself loitering outside of the dance school, waiting for her last class to leave so I can go in. Her last class of the day must be a teen class. Teenage girls start spilling out the doors, huddled up, laughing without a care in the world. I wait a few more minutes thinking Ginger will come lock the doors after the final girls leave. She never comes. I am hesitant to enter not wanting to interrupt her working with a student.

The front lobby lights had been dimmed, and I could hear music coming from one of the back rooms. I make my way toward the music with the takeout I just bought, dangling in one hand. Hoping she might be willing to have dinner with me while we talk. I know how hard she has been working and probably puts off taking care of herself. I want to be the one to take care of her. That thought popping in my head when I was dating other girls would have terrified me and had me running for the hills, but not with Ginger. I cannot deny how much I want to be that person for her.

When I get to the room, I expect to see her working with a student or two. Instead, I find the most beautiful scene unfolding before me. Ginger is gliding through the air. She is in a black jumpsuit thingy with a see-through flowing pink skirt. The way her body moves with the music is graceful. I am rendered speechless. This is the first time in days where my mind isn't racing. I feel a calming peace watching Ginger in her element.

This is the Ginger I fell for so long ago. She is confident and exudes power with every move. Whatever happened between her and

Larry did a real number on her. I was worried that part of her would always be affected by his careless acts. In this moment watching her do what she loves, it is like he never existed, that he never broke her.

I am lost in the moment when a blood-curdling scream rips through the studio. Jumping out of my own skin, unsure what is happening, I end up dropping the bag of food. I see Ginger holding her chest like she is having a heart attack with a sheer look of panic painted across her features. It is then that it occurs to me that she might not be able to see me clearly. I step out of the shadows with my hands up, trying not to frighten her more.

"Sunshine, it is just me. You are safe, and it's just me," I say in a calming voice as I approach with my hands up.

"What are you doing lurking in the dark, Harry? You scared me to death," she says, rubbing her chest, looking less terrified and more pissed.

"I am sorry. I brought you dinner and thought we could talk."

"How did you get in? And I don't want to talk. Can we just pretend yesterday didn't happen?"

Hurt that she was dismissing what could be happening between us but not wanting to push her for more before she was ready. "I know; that is why I am here to talk to you about something else. Don't forget I brought dinner. I think you will like it…" trying to coax her into hanging out with food was a genius idea. Also, kind of pathetic I need to bribe the girl to hang out with me with food, but desperate times call for desperate measures.

"You left the front door unlocked. I know we live in a safe area, but I don't like the idea of you being here at night with the doors unlocked by yourself."

"You sound like Max. He lectures Jane all the time about locking her doors, but I can currently see your point. I really needed to let go of some tension, and dancing is the way that I clear my mind. I guess I forgot to head up and lock the doors after class ended, I was desperate to dance."

I smile at her. I know she would hate hearing me say this, but there is an innocence to her that is hard to ignore. I know she worries everyone sees her as a kid but that is not what I see when I look at her. I see a strong, capable woman who is stealing my heart piece by piece. I reach up and tuck a piece of hair behind her ear that has slipped out of her messy bun. Ginger looks up at me and we are locked in a moment together.

Ginger whispers so quietly I can barely hear her, "You mentioned something about feeding me?"

I let out a laugh. The way she started to whisper, I was expecting something intimate to be spoken, nope not my girl, she wants to be fed. "Yes, Sunshine, I brought you food. How does a Juicy Lucy from the diner with a side of cheese curds sound."

"Ahh, you know my love language." Ginger is making her way toward the discarded bags at the entrance of the studio.

"What? Feeding you is your love language?"

"No, silly man! It is cheese. What I wouldn't do for cheese" the carefree Ginger is back with her teasing and smiles that make me want to fall to my knees for her.

"Anything for you, Sunshine, anything at all."

We move back into the lobby area. Ginger proceeds to pull the curtains and lock the door. She then turns on some lamps, bathing the area in a soft yellow light.   I am surprised she doesn't turn on the overhead light. This feels more intimate and cozier than is normal for us. You won't find me complaining. I have thought about nights like this with Ginger for longer than I care to admit. We head toward the couches. I sit first and am pleasantly surprised when Ginger sits right next to me instead of opting for another seat.

I start to unpack the food while Ginger gets back up to go get some drinks. I noticed on the reception desk the flowers I sent her. She returns to find me smiling like a crazy person. "Want to explain what put that smile on your face, Harry? Heaven help you if dug into the cheese curds without me." she is teasing, I think; her tone is scary, but there is a smile on her face.

"I would never dream of starting without you," I say after popping open the container and offering up the first cheese curd. She pops one in her mouth, and a groan escapes her.

"Please explain why something so bad for me tastes so good. Life is hard, Harry, and then we all die of clogged arteries but happy" she says as she pops another one in her mouth.

"I was smiling because you put your flowers out. I wasn't sure if you would keep them after yesterday."

"Of course, I would keep them! They are beautiful, and I love them. All the students are super jealous of the mystery man sending flowers to me. Apparently, according to the older girls I teach, chivalry is dead, and boys don't give flowers anymore," Ginger explains as she unwraps both burgers.

She places my burger before me like she is serving me a fine dining experience. "Well, actually, those are my words. They explained that boys are dumb and only text flower emojis." She smiles and takes a bite of her burger.

"Well, glad to see this old guy hasn't lost all his game yet." I bump her shoulder with mine and then dig into my burger. We eat for a few minutes in silence. It is a comfortable silence with us. When I have been out with other women, I have always felt the need to fill the silence, but not with Ginger.

Ginger picks up a napkin and wipes her mouth. "So, if we aren't talking about yesterday, what did you need to talk to me about?"

"I am glad you asked. You will never guess what happened at work today."

"If you tell me that you rescued a litter of kittens from a tree and they need a home, I am going to stop you right there. My plate is already very full, and yesterday filled my quota on favors. Then there is the small detail that I don't need the extra title of cat lady at my age. My best guess for the sucker in the group that would help you out is Bubba. He has always struck me as a closet cat guy."

This girl is adorable, and I want to keep her forever. I am aware that makes me sound like a weirdo that belongs on Dateline, but I can't help it. I let out a chuckle. "You know, now that you mention it, I can see the closet cat guy thing being Bubba's thing. Sadly, though, we can't test the theory because no kittens were rescued today."

"Ok, what happened then?"

"I was asked to be the co-chair of the Fireman's Ball this year," I say as I glance out of the corner of my eye, trying to gauge her reaction to the news.

She has the burger halfway to her mouth when she freezes. I continue on, "I might have heard that you were the other co-chair, small world, right? I guess this means you will have to stop ignoring me. We have a lot of work to get done."

"Are you serious? You and I are the chairs for the ball?"

"Yep," I pop the P, unsure what else to say at this point.

"What was the chief thinking? Isn't this event a huge money maker for widows and orphans fund, as well as the department to purchase items for the firehouse? Has he lost his mind putting the both of us in charge?”

“Some might be hurt by the lack of faith you have in us. The event practically plans itself. I have files from the previous years and what vendors they used that were successful. I have been so many times. What is the big deal? We can do this.”

“Glad to see one of us is confident in the process.” She appears to lose interest in dinner and slumps back onto the couch. “I was really hoping this event would be a success and people might start to look at me differently.”

I take her lead and, lean back on the couch and scooch in closer to her. Our shoulders are touching. “How do you want people to see you, Ginger?”

She looks down like she is unable to tell her truths and keep eye contact with me. “Every one of you is seen as a pillar of the community. Responsible adults that people can turn to. You have all nailed the adulting game to a tee. I want people to stop thinking of me as Max and Noah’s little sister who tags along with big kids. I don’t want my failed relationships to define me. I want it to be okay if what I choose for my life is different than the original plan. I want to have a happily ever after. I don’t know, maybe I want too much.” She peeks up at me, nervous energy running through her eyes as she searches my face. “Or maybe I am totally cheese drunk and said too much. Pipe dreams of a silly girl.” She starts to pull away like she is shutting this conversation down. Seems to be a pattern with us. One of us shows the slightest bit of vulnerability and then turns and runs.

I don’t want us to continue with that pattern; no more running. I grab her hand and pull her back down toward me. She was not expecting it, and it threw her off balance with her landing against my chest. With her one free hand, she places it on my chest. The touch is electric, reminding me of yesterday when she had her hands on me. Her eyes are wide with surprise, but I don’t see any hint of fear. I release her other hand. I move my hands up to cup both sides of her face. We stay like this for a moment, both of us taking in the other. When I don’t think I can take anymore and I want to close the distance between us, it is Ginger who makes the first move.

Ginger lunges forward, our lips making contact. There is a split second of hesitation on both our parts then Ginger takes over. She is timid at first. My brain is having a hard time catching up with what is

happening. I have wanted to kiss this girl longer than I care to admit.
The nerves of this first kiss between us melt away, and Ginger
becomes more confident in taking what we both want.

I am not sure how long we sit there making out like we lust-crazed
teens before she pulls back. She doesn't go far. She is resting her
forehead against mine. We are both out of breath. I don't want to say
something that will spook her and ruin the best kiss I have ever
experienced before.

"Wow," she speaks first in a hushed whisper.

"Agreed. That was better than anything I have been thinking
about."

Ginger pulls back slightly so she can see me clearly. "Y-You have
been thinking about what it would be like to kiss me?"

"Yes." I keep it simple, so I don't freak her out.

"I don't understand. Why have you never made a move or said
anything before?" Ginger asks, looking hurt.

"For a lot of the same reasons you never said anything or made a
move." She does not look satisfied with my answer. I decide that this
is the moment to lay it all out on the line, and then we can figure out
how to move forward. Hopefully, it will all come together. "Sunshine,
you have meant more to me than I would allow myself to admit for a
long time. At first it was our ages that stopped me. I am too old for
you. You should be with someone your age. Someone young and fun.
Then you came home this summer with a boyfriend. You were in love,
and I hated everything about it. I was so jealous and miserable that
Lawerence was the one who got your kisses and time. Another big
obstacle has been your brothers. Your brothers have been more like
brothers to me than friends. My family was always too busy for me
growing up, but your family let me be part of it, no questions asked." I
have more to say, but I also feel like I said too much.

"Oh, Harry, we are quite the pair. I want to be older you want to
be younger. Let's never talk about the ex that shall not be named. He
is not worth my time or yours. That leaves us with my brothers. Max
seemed okay with the idea of us as he was instructing me to lather you
up with oil."

I don't know if she is aware of it or not, but she is dancing her
fingers around my chest in a circular pattern like she did yesterday.
"Max is so over the top in love that he wants everyone to jump off the
love cliff with him, but I do agree he has been supportive. Noah, on

the other hand…" I trail off, not wanting to say out loud that Noah will not be accepting of whatever is happening between Ginger and me.

"I know. I think Noah is having a hard time separating the little girl in pigtails running around in a tutu from the woman I am today. He is still upset with me that I chose to stay here this semester. I think he was more upset that I did it on my own without consulting him first."

"He loves you, Sunshine. You are a hard girl not to love. Noah is just being the overprotective older brother who wants the best for his little sister." Ginger looks totally deflated like the Noah issue is a deal breaker for me.

We sit there in the quiet for a while. At this point she is sitting in my lap with her head on my shoulder. Our hands are intertwined, and I am rubbing my thumb mindlessly against the back of her hand when she softly asks, "What do you want, Harry?"

Isn't that the million-dollar question? What do I want?

I must be taking too long to answer her. She starts to squirm in my lap, and I tighten my hold on her.

"You. I want you, Sunshine." Relieved she doesn't push me away or run from the room screaming 'no thank you", I try to lighten to conversation.

"What do you say about the Fireman's ball? Think you and I can team up and make it a year no one will forget?" I look down at her and notice for the first time all night how exhausted she looks. The hours that she is putting in the dance school for the internship must be taking its toll on her.

"Yeah, Harry, I think we will do great. My mind has been going non-stop with some new things to try this year that might generate some new interest in the event." she gets the last part out around a yawn.

"Sunshine, you need sleep. If I wasn't holding you, you would probably fall over."

"Hmm, I like you holding me."

"Ok, that is not helpful. I like it too. I need you to kick me out so you can go get some sleep. You teach in the morning, don't you?"

She sits up and stretches her arms over her head. "Fine, be that way. Be a grown-up, Harry. Be careful you are starting to show your age." Even though she is acting all sassy, the smirk on her face lets me know that she is only teasing.

I help her clean up our dinner mess. "Promise me you will lock up right when I leave. I need you safe." I tuck the loose hairs that have fallen free behind her ear.

"I will, don't worry. Thanks for dinner tonight. It was exactly what I needed before I even knew what I needed it."

I lean over to kiss her on the forehead. I don't dare go in for a real kiss, and I really will change my mind about leaving then. "Goodnight, sweetheart. Talk to you soon." I turn to leave and exit through the front doors. I stand outside in the brisk fall air and wait until I hear Ginger activate the front door lock.

I continue to stand there, staring at the front of the school. The lights go dark, and I assume Ginger is making her way to the apartment above the school now. Everything has changed tonight. No matter what obstacle or challenge is put in front of us, I need to find the solution. The alternative of not being with Ginger is no longer an option for me.

Chapter 13
Ginger

After turning off all the lights and making sure all the doors were locked and secure, I made my way to my apartment. Before Harrison came over tonight, I was planning to heat up some SpaghettiOs in the microwave and go to bed at an obscenely early time for someone my age. The exhaustion from earlier was still lingering, but the high from spending the evening with Harrison in his arms outweighed the exhaustion, not to mention the kiss that somehow still lingered on his lips. Oh man, he can kiss a girl stupid! It is not like I am new to the kissing game, but I have never felt anything close to what I felt when Harrison and I were kissing.

I start to get ready for bed, wash my face, brush my teeth, change out of my dance clothes, and put on hoodie and sleep shorts to sleep in. I crawl into bed and stare at the ceiling. Even though my body is exhausted and begging for sleep, I can't seem to turn my mind off from the racing thoughts. Even though Harrison said he wanted me, what does that really mean for us? What if Noah is never okay with us dating?

I knew little pieces here and there about Harrison's family life growing up. I didn't realize how much he came to rely on my family to be his family for support. I could never be the reason that is taken away from him. As I spiral with the what-ifs, my phone starts to vibrate on the nightstand. I reach over and see I have a text message from Harry waiting for me.

Harry: I know we spent all evening together, and you are probably already sick of me but I really like starting my day and ending my day texting you.

Normally, I just read his texts without replying to them. I thought all the reasons for not replying were valid at the time. Now, I think they were just excuses of cowardice to avoid what was happening between us.

Me: Did you make it home safely?

Harry: You replied?!

Me: Did you not want me to? Want me to go back to not replying?

Harry: NO! I am just surprised.

Me: What can I say? I am full of surprises.

Harry: I know you need your sleep. I just want you to know that tonight meant everything to me.

Me: I am glad you are not here to see me blushing.

Harry: I am not. I love seeing you blush, especially when I am the one making you blush.

Me: Tonight meant everything to me, too.

Harry: Are you still coming tomorrow to the BBQ right?

Me: About that….

Harry: You promised.

Me: Everyone will be there.

Harry: Yes, kind of the point.

Me: I want to explore whatever this is between you and me without everyone else's opinion being loudly expressed.

Harry: Did I just become your dirty little secret, Sunshine?

I am screwing this up. I don't want to make Harrison feel like I am hiding him. The truth is I just don't want to share him with anyone. I want to be selfish, and I keep whatever this is that is happening safe and protected against everyone's opinions. Knowing them all like I do, they will all have opinions.

Me: NO?! Of course not.

Harry: I am teasing, Sunshine. I am fine keeping us quiet for a little while. It will give me time to talk to Noah about us, too.

Me: SO you can see why I should not go tomorrow?

Harry: Nope, I do not see.

Me: We are not that good of actors. All our friends will figure out that something is up in the first 5 seconds.

Harry: Speak for yourself. I have had feelings for you a longer than I care to admit and no one figured it out.

Me: So, what you are saying is that you can hang out all afternoon and not look at me like you want me, not touch me, not kiss me?

Harry: Are you trying to kill me? You don't play fair.

Harry: Challenge accepted. I want you to start hanging out with us again. Something has been missing the last few weeks and I will do whatever it takes to have you back hanging out with us all.

Me: Ok, I will come. I do miss seeing everyone. I always hated when school would start back up, and I didn't get to hang out regularly with you guys.

Harry: Sunshine, you need to get some sleep. Sweet dreams, or better yet, dream of me. I know that I will be dreaming of you tonight.

Me: Good night, Harry

I place my phone back on the charger and I snuggled up under my blanket with a huge smile on my face. Even though there are more unknowns in my future than sure things, the one thing I am very sure of right now is that I am happy. Genuinely happy and content. As I relax into my bed and feel like sleep could take over me when my phone buzzes again. How was I supposed to get to sleep if he didn't stop texting me? I grab my phone, not at all annoyed with the conversation between us continuing. I look at the screen and immediately tense up when I see the name from the incoming text. The EX.

The EX: Hey Ginger. Long time no talking. We need to catch up. Call me we need to discuss some things.

I read it a few times hoping this is a nightmare and not really happening. Why would Lawerence be texting me after all these months, acting like he didn't blow up my world the last time we spoke? What could we possibly need to discuss? Do I care what he wants or needs? All questions I am not sure I really want the answers to. The smile that was plastered on my face moments ago is now long gone, and sleep escapes me for hours as I lay here worrying about the ex that shall not be named.

Chapter 14
Harrison

I wake up energized and ready to get a start on the day. The sooner the day starts, the sooner I can see Ginger tonight. Ginger's concern about being in the same room without being discovered might be a valid concern, but I am willing to risk it to see her again.

I need to find a way to talk to Noah about Ginger before it goes any further between us. I open up the guy's text thread.

Me: Morning men. Who is ready for the day?

Bubba: Why? Just WHY?! Any idea what time it is, Harrison?

Me: I can see Bubba woke up on the wrong side of the bed this morning.

Henry: Seriously, do you know what time it is? Why are you awake?

Ralph: I vote we have a new rule: no texting of any kind before noon.

Max: Agreed.

Me: You all are a treat this morning. Is it so bad to rise early and welcome the day with a smile and text lifelong friends?

Bubba: Ralph, can you drug test Harrison? I have concerns.

Henry: Maybe his dry spell is over?

Me: You all suck.

Noah: I, for one, welcome Harrison's positive attitude on the day. Thank you, my brother, from another mother. I have been up since 5 am with Lola, who is not thrilled to be cutting her molars.

Henry: You really talk up this parenting thing and make us jealous that we are not in your shoes.

Max: Are we going through with the vote or not? I am sleepy. It's sleepy time.

Ralph: Max, your man card was already called into question when you started saying snugglefest, but now you say sleepy and sleepy time like a toddler looking for a sippy cup. I definitely move to revoke it for good.

Ralph: And yes, a drug test for Harrison can be arranged.

Noah: I miss this. We need more guy nights. I hate being an adult and working full-time.

Max: No to any nights the girls are not there.

Henry: We have lost Max to the dark side of love and relationships. WE should just cut our losses and let him go.

Bubba: Someone remind me why we are texting this early and not sleeping??

Me: I am bored. Want to hang out this morning.

Bubba: No, I am sleeping

Henry: I need to go check on Bubbles.

Ralph: To early to talk about your pregnant stripper

Bubba: LOL, that never gets old…

Henry: Bubbles is not a stripper name. Where is the respect for the West African Hippo?

Max: Sorry, I can't hang. Jane needs some help this morning. We are planning to head to the BBQ this afternoon, though.

Bubba: Anyone else gets the feeling that is code for something that will make us all gag?

Noah: I am out, too. Emma gave me the "honey-do" list from hell. My one day off and I have a list longer than my arm to get done.

Ralph: Brave man posting that on the group chat. Emma is going to kill you for speaking against the "honey-do" list.

Noah: WHAT!? Babe, they tricked me. I love working together on the list on the weekends.

Henry: LOL, like I said dark side of love.

Bubba: Dying over here. Actually, wiping tears from my eyes.

Ralph: Calm down, Noah. I was just kidding. We are on the guy thread. Good to know you are whipped and scared of your wife.

Me: I'm not saying this was a complete waste of time, but pretty close.

Bubba: You're welcome

Henry: Maybe try to text during business hours next time.

Ralph: Thanks for the wake-up call, Harrison. Expect one of my deputies to stop by with that drug test.

Noah: See you guys later.

Max: Ahh, finally, sleepy time.

Chapter 15
Harrison

I texted Ginger good morning and she never replied. I thought maybe she would, but I also realized she had classes this morning that she was in charge of. Her internship seems a little intense. I would have thought she would teach two or three classes, but from what I can tell, she teaches every class.

After not hearing back from her and the ridiculousness that was the guy's text thread this morning, I was anxious to get to the party to see her. That is how I found myself to be on Ralph's doorstep forty-five minutes early.

"You're early," Ralph says after answering the door. No time for pleasantries or even a hi; that is Ralph.

"Thought I would give you a hand. Being the host can bring stress, and I thought I would come to alleviate that and help."

By the look on his face, he is not buying it. "Does your acting weird have anything to do with a little Miss Sunshine agreeing to come tonight?" He stands there with his arms crossed over his chest in his interrogation stance.

Freakin Max, I mumble under my breath. "I had heard she was coming."

"You can only come in if you spill and tell me what is up with you and Ginger."

"You seriously are not going to let me in?"

"Correct." Short and to the point, that sums up Ralph.

"Fine, you win. I need this to stay between us. I am counting on Police Chief-friend privilege."

"That is not a thing." He moves to the side and lets me in. I step into his home and even though I have been here a million times, I always chuckle to myself. Ralph's design sense could only be described as non-existent. He has a mix of cowboy meets hunter meets bachelor. I can't wait to meet the woman that he falls for. It would be helpful for the success of their relationship if she was blind and couldn't see this hot mess.

"Okay, spill, or I will kick you out." If I had not known this man all my life, I might have taken offense to his gruffness, but he struggled to get the last part out with cracking a smile.

"Fine, you big bully. What do you want to know? It appears that Max already shared plenty with you."

"Max has always been the blabber mouth in the group. Do you remember the time we got caught toilet-papering the preacher's house in high school because he refused to let his daughter go on a date with Henry?"

"Of course, I remember, we got stuck doing the yard work all summer at the church because we were caught."

"And you never wondered how we were caught?"

"Never really crossed my mind, I guess. I just remember that summer sucked, and the punishment seemed way harsh for the crime."

"It was Max."

"No way. Why would he sell us out?"

"Ralph grabs two beers from the fridge and, pops the tops off and hands me one. "I don't think he intended to sell us out. He let something slip at dinner one night, and his mom took five seconds to put it together. Max crumbled with a mild interrogation from the parents. Hence, we all were sentenced to the summer of hell."

"Funny, how did I not know any of that?"

"I don't know why you didn't know, but stop staling. Have you made any progress with our favorite ballerina? And what is up with calling her Sunshine?"

"Ugh, where to start? I call her Sunshine because she is all light and joy. Calling her kid doesn't fit her for me. Max had her rub oil all over my abundant rippling muscles. We kissed. She wants to keep us on the down low. Noah is the only one who is in the dark about anything happening between her and me." I take a swing of my beer. "In short, she wants me to pretend like nothing is happening and nothing has changed between us. I agreed, but a big part of me hates it."

"That's a lot. I can't help you unless you are honest with me, buddy."

"What are you talking about? That was all the truth?"

"You said you have an abundance of rippling muscles." he holds it together for less than five seconds before losing it and is bent over, laughing a little too hard for my liking. "Clearly, that is an exaggeration."

I can't help it. I start to laugh, too. Ralph is always seen as the serious, gruff one in our group to any outsiders looking in, but if you really know him, he is a true friend. He always seems to know what I need. This is what I needed. To not take myself so seriously and just laugh. "I bet I have more than you, jerk."

"Harrison, you have to give Ginger a little time. I am guessing that ex of hers did a real number on her. She just needs a little time." I hate that he is making sense. "And with regards to Noah. That is a Band-Aid you need to rip off. Probably sooner than later. Max was cool with it. My guess is Noah will blow some older brother protective steam at first, but he will come around, though."

"Thanks, Ralph. You are a good friend."

"If you start tearing up or want to braid my hair, I will kick you out."

I start to chuckle. "You got it man, no tears and no braiding hair."

"Okay need details on the good stuff. You kissed her, did you? Max did not share that detail with us."

"With us? Are you kidding me?   He told Bubba and Henry, too?"

"Jane and Stella too," he shrugs as he says it is like it is a no-brainer that of course, they would know too. "What is the big deal? Can't keep it a secret forever."

"Apparently not. I can't wait for the time when you fall on your face in love with a girl. I will be there with so many not helpful tips."

"Not going to happen, man. Not in the cards for me. I like my life just how it is. Never really saw it in the cards for me to be the family man. I am content with how my life is. I like protecting this town. I have you all. I get to be the fun uncle to my niece and nephew. Life is pretty perfect as it is. Don't see any need to change that."

I want to call him on his bull that he just spewed out, but the doorbell rings, effectively putting an end to the conversation.

Within a few minutes, the house explodes with laughing and lots of people. As I stand in the kitchen listening to everyone, trying not to fixate that Ginger is the only one missing, I wonder if we have always been this loud. I want to text Ginger and make sure she didn't bail last minute on coming tonight. I want to give her the time and space that Ralph said she probably needed, but I am worried that time and space will give her time to run.

"What's up with you tonight? You look like you are a million miles away, lost in thought," Stella says as she bumps into me with her shoulder.

"Nah, I am here, promise. What trouble have you been up to lately?"

"I am hurt that you think I am up to trouble," she says dramatically, with her hand clasping her chest to add to the dramatic effect. "I am the good one in the group."

"Yeah, right, sorry, Doll, that title goes to Jane or maybe Ginger now that Max has corrupted Jane," Bubba says as he slings his arm around Stella and pulls her in close.

Not at all offended by what Bubba said, she relaxes into him. "You are probably right. Hey, speaking of Ginger, where is my girl? I had it on good authority that she was coming tonight."

Out of nowhere, Ginger enters the kitchen. "I am here. Just running late, sorry. The door was cracked open, so I just let myself in. Hope you don't mind, Ralph."

"Of course not, kid. You are always welcome anytime. Glad you could make it."

"I couldn't miss the inaugural first-time run of the new Superman grill, could I?"

Everyone laughs and crowds around Ginger to say hello. She is doing and saying all the right things, but something is off with her. She looks even more exhausted than when I left her last night. I thought a good night's sleep would have helped. Sadly, she is avoiding eye contact with me, and I want to march up to her, pull her into my arms, and ask her what is wrong. I have almost talked myself into this plan when Noah comes into the house from the back door.

It is no secret that it has been strained between Ginger and Noah since she announced she was doing the internship. We all stand there, and our heads bobble between Ginger and Noah. Noah is the first to crack and breaks the silence. "Hey, kiddo. Glad to see you could make it."

"Wouldn't have missed it for anything. It is not every day Ralph gets a super grill off Amazon. Had to check it for myself."

"That might be true. This is the first super grill he has ordered, but we all know that Ralph's true love is Amazon and their two-day shipping," Henry says causally. Everyone busts up laughing, taking turns trading insults with each other. And just like that, the tension is gone.

"Make fun all you want, but there is not one of you that doesn't benefit from my wise purchases on Amazon," Ralph says with his chest puffed out.

"Of course, old man. Now, can we stop talking about the super grill and use it? I am starving," Bubba says as he heads toward the refrigerator to grab the burgers and brats.

"Bubba, you better not even think about trying to be the first to use my grill!" Ralph yells after him. All the guys pile outside. Clearly, it takes six men to supervise grilling operations. I am the last to join the men outside as I linger in the doorway going outside and the kitchen. I wanted to try and catch a moment with Ginger. I know the greeting that I want to give her is off the table right now, but I still want to check on her and ask her what happened to put the worry in her eyes.

"Harrison, hurry up. We need a fire expert out here to supervise in case these idiots can't handle the power that comes with a super grill," Noah yells at me when he notices I am lingering in the doorway into the house.

"You are all idiots, and you know that, right? What even makes this a super grill?" I ask, only half invested in the grill.

"What happened to happy Harrison, who needed to be drug tested this morning? You remember him, Mr. Happy Pants, that woke us all up?" Henry said, jumping into the conversation.

I catch Ralph's eye and realize I am doing a crappy job of hiding that I would rather be inside with Ginger. Damage control time. "Still happy. I just have a lot going on at work, but I will put that out of my mind for the night. What does make this a super grill, Ralph?" I am asking but not really caring about the answer that will be coming. But my deflection has worked like a charm. Everyone turns to Ralph as he proceeds to give his review of the super grill that any Amazon product would be proud to have posted. I glimpse over my shoulder and see all the girls laughing and talking in the kitchen as they prepare the rest of the food.

Chapter 16
Ginger

I almost bailed tonight. After a sleepless night and a full morning of dance classes, I am more than ready to crawl into bed. The bigger problem that came out of nowhere is the dreaded Ex. He has continued to text me multiple times today. He even called after my morning hip-hop class, and he didn't leave a voicemail, halleluiah. I don't want to tell the girls about this new development. I am a little worried that it is a real possibility that Stella might murder him, and Emma will help hide the body.

I don't feel like I can tell Harrison about it. I don't even know what we are to each other. What I am sure of is no one wants to deal with drama from a past ex. That is why I found myself sitting outside Ralph's house tonight, unable to go in. I cannot handle keeping one more secret in my life, but I feel I have no other options. The only reason I dragged my butt out of my car and into the house was purely selfish reasons. I wanted to see Harrison. I know how pathetic it sounds, seeing I just saw him last night, but I missed him. I missed the feeling of calm we had last night together, curled up on the couch.

The guys all piled outside to start grilling while the girls stayed inside to prep everything else. I keep trying to steal glances at Harrison. He looks really enthralled in whatever Ralph is going on about. As sneaky as I think I am being, I am clearly not because I got caught sneaking peeks.

"Ginger, girl, we need details now" Emma grabs my attention away from Harrison and back to them.

"What? Sorry, I missed what you said. Details on what?"

"We have limited time before the guys come back in here, and we are forced to listen to the pros and cons of the super grill's perfected meat. For the love of all that is holy, we need details on how it's going with Harrison" Stella does not appear like she is willing to back down.

"There is nothing to tell. Besides the fact that Jane tried to steal Emma's job as the group matchmaker," I say, trying not to smirk. There is no way Emma will like the idea of being replaced as the match maker. This will hopefully distract them until the food is ready.

"Nice try, Ginger. I am in a sticky place, trying to pretend I know nothing but dying to want to know and help. I pushed Jane to help Max because I need to hold back until you and Harrison talk to Noah. Trust me when I say getting Jane, the rule follower, to mislead you a little took way more work than setting the plan into action." Emma looks quite proud of herself as she dips a carrot in some hummus and takes a bite.

"I should have known," I say, rubbing the sides of my temple. I love these women more than anything in the world but they sure are busy bodies. I worry for their future kids; they should be warned. "So, everyone knows what exactly?"

"The photoshoot with glistening pecks was the last I heard about. I have been slammed this week at the salon, so I might be out of the loop," Stella says around a mouth full of pickle she just grabbed.

"We agreed to keep whatever is happening between us to ourselves for a little while. One reason is Noah. We both feel bad that he is the only one who apparently is in the dark."

"What are you keeping to yourselves? Did something else happen?" My blessed sister-in-law would make a great interrogator for the police department if Ralph ever needed the help.

"Emma, how are we supposed to keep it to ourselves if I blab it to you girls? Stella will blab to Bubba. Jane has no prayer of keeping it from Max. You will feel guilty knowing and Noah not knowing. Bubba will then blab to the others."

"She is not wrong," Jane, the voice of reason, agrees.

"Of course, she is not wrong, but I need to know what else is going on. Needing to know the whole story is my own personal genetic defect I was born with; I have to know. You know we will all find out eventually. Just spill the goods." Stella is borderline begging.

I blame it on the lack of sleep and the growing hatred I have for secret keeping as the reasons I cave. "Fine, he came over last night. He brought takeout. We talked. We made out. We snuggled. Now you know all. Can we get back to prepping the food? I am getting a little hungry."

"In what world do you think you can skip over all those details like you are reading off a grocery list and not expect us to freak out for you!! You made out?! Yes, girl, it is about time."

"Emma, you need to keep your voice down. The guys will hear you" I try to use a tone that would convey that I mean business, but it was an epic fail on my part. All the girls start jumping up and down, screaming. Yeah, sure, girls, this won't draw attention to us at all at this rate.

"Yay!! I am so excited for you, Ginger. Isn't being in love just the best?" Jane says with a sigh.

"Calm down, and no one said anything about love, Jane."

"I knew you were going to be more difficult than Jane when it comes to the love stuff," Emma adds in a somewhat annoyed tone.

"Rude, I wasn't difficult." Jane folds her arms over her chest and looks five seconds away from full-on pouting.

"I agree with Emma. Ginger, you finally have what you want in front of you; don't let fear stand in your way." Stella jumps in with her two cents.

"Very good point, Stella. Jane don't be offended; it is Stella that will be the hardest nut to crack in the love department. I am saving my efforts on her love life until my toddler stops cutting her back molars before I can concentrate any energy on her love life."

The three of us stand there staring at Emma. I am sure Stella wants to say a big no thank you for any help in the love department. Jane is still on the fence whether the full pout is warranted or not and then there is me. Regretting getting out of the car. The few glances I have gotten of Harrison hardly seem worth the twenty questions about my intentions and love life that I received.

"Girls, I love you all so much. I want you to find the happiness I have found. I might come off as pushy sometimes, I am just trying to help. I am sorry."

It is hard to be annoyed, pout, or regret anything when you have a friend who just wants you to find the same happiness she has found. Simultaneously, we all move toward each other and join in an awkward group hug. We are all giggling when we break apart except Emma who is crying.

"Why are you crying? What is the matter?" I ask, genuinely concerned that I am missing something.

"Your stupid brother knocked me up again. The hormones are real and way worse this time. I am surprised you guys haven't noticed before now." Emma is trying to talk around the sobs.

We are all a shell shocked momentarily. Then we are all hugging and crying together. This is how the guys find us. The four of us sobbed while embracing each other. I wish I had a camera to capture the looks on the guy's faces. They all look horrified and unsure how to approach us. Noah is the last one to enter the kitchen. He looks around at the scene and is the first one to speak. "Seriously, you told the girls, didn't you? What happened to waiting?"

"Waiting? Waiting on what? Can someone explain to me what is going on? And why is my Cupcake crying? I hate when she cries, it is the worst," Max speaks next.

"Your stupid brother knocked up my best friend again, and the hormones might be killing her or making her mean in the love department. I am not sure, and you guys interrupted us before we could get the big picture," Jane sobs out.

Max slowly approaches Jane. "Come here, sweetie."

"Nope, no touching. I don't want to end up like that." Jane points over her shoulder at Emma.

Max lets out a little chuckle, not a smart move if you ask me. "Babe, pretty sure you can't catch pregnancy with a hug." He gently pulls Jane into a hug. She puts up no fight and melts right into him. I can vaguely hear her mumble something about Noah being stupid. Max chuckles again.

Bubba heads toward Stella and starts to comfort her. Noah makes his way over to Emma. "I am sorry, babe, it just came out," Emma explains halfway through a hiccup fit caused by the sobbing or the baby. Who really knows?

"It's fine. You know how I feel about secrets anyway. It is better this way. Besides, when you end up throwing up all the food that was prepared on the super grill, Ralph won't take it so personally." Noah beams at his attempt to lighten the mood.

Ralph moves past him to put the food down on the counter. "You are an idiot, but congrats on the new tax deduction" Ralph says behind a giant smile.

"When are you due?" Henry asks.

Emma pulls back a little so she can answer him, "I am due in the spring, May 8th."

"Awesome, you and Bubbles are due right around the same time. Lots of babies this spring."

"Isn't Bubbles your hippo at the zoo?" I can't tell what Emma is thinking, and with her last emotional outburst, people should approach with caution.

Bubba pipes in, "He swears it is not a pregnant stripper that he is secretly dating."

That grabs the girl's attention all of a sudden, and we are staring at Bubba. The guys try to hide their amusement at the comment but fail when some laughs escape from them. Henry just shakes his head, certain this is not the first time the guys have given him a hard time about a pregnant hippo.

"Bubba, are you comparing me to a stripper or a hippo?" Emma straightens her back and crosses her arms over her chest.

Bubba is the biggest of the guys. He is a mountain of muscles and tattoos. I don't think I have ever seen him speechless or turn white like he just did. Out of nowhere, Emma bursts out laughing. "Bubba, you should see your face. I am just giving you a hard time. Lighten up! Let's eat, I am starving, and now that you all know I am eating for two, there is no judgment about how much I pile onto my plate."

Pregnancy hormones are weird. The way Emma just sailed through the full gambit of emotions in a matter of moments is terrifying. You don't have to tell this crowd more than once to dig into the food, so no one stops to analyze the emotional roller coaster. I am the only girl just standing there without someone to lean on. I look up to see Harrison staring at me. I want him to come to me and be my person. He looks like he is sharing the same thought as me. Before either one of us can act, I feel my phone vibrating in my back pocket. It is enough to distract me from breaking eye contact. I don't need to look at my phone to know who it is. Anyone else that would call or text is already in the room.

I chose to ignore my phone and grab a plate. There are serious perks to hanging out with the adults instead of the college crowd, the food is significantly better. The food spread that covers the kitchen island is impressive. I am so focused on what to grab first that I don't notice Noah come up beside me.

"Hey, kid." He seems more timid than normal when he is speaking to me like he is afraid I will bolt.

"Hey, brother. Congrats on baby number two. I can't wait to see Lola as a big sister."

"We went out and bought her a baby doll for her so we can practice being gentle before the baby comes."

"That is a cute idea. I bet Lola snuggles the baby doll and is the best little mama in training."

"That was the hope, but sadly, you would be wrong if that is what you are picturing. Picture her dragging the doll around by the ankle and hitting the head along the way. I even found the doll hanging halfway out of her diaper genie the other day. I didn't even know she knew how to open it."

I can't help but laugh at this point. Ever since Max babysat Lola once this summer, and it did not go well for anyone involved, Max has lovingly referred to her as the Spawn of Satan.

"Emma got the idea from one of her baby books, and as you saw earlier, questioning her is not an option."

"Don't worry. I won't tell anyone that you are afraid of your pregnant wife."

He looks part relieved and part amused by the thought. "Listen, I am glad you came tonight. I have been meaning to reach out. I owe you an apology. I am sorry about how I reacted when you told us about your internship. I really hope you haven't been avoiding everyone because your older brother was a jerk. Please tell me you forgive me, and you will start to hang out with us again."

He seems sincere, and honestly, I could never stay mad at him. "There is nothing to forgive. I should have told you all sooner than I did instead of popping it on you last minute." I grab his forearm, hoping he is really listening to this next part. "Noah, I need you to try to understand that I am not a little kid anymore who needs her big brother to step in and save the day. I am going to make mistakes and fall flat on my face. I promise I will pick myself up and keep going. But these are my mistakes to make and learn from."

"When did that happen?" Noah asks, almost in awe.

"When did what happen?" Now, I am confused.

"When did you grow into this independent woman who is taking the world by storm? You are going to leave us all in the dust now that you have figured out how to soar." He lifts his arm up, and I slide into his side. "How about this? I will work on being less bossy and overbearing in the brother department."

I look up at him skeptically. "What is the catch?"

"No catch, Ginger. I don't want to be the one that clips your wings and stops you from going all the places you are destined to go."

"What if I am destined to be right here, and I never leave Little Falls?" I am testing him and his resolve to really allow me to make my own life decisions.

"Ginger, if that is what you want, then choose that. I know I am a little slow to show support, but all I have ever wanted was for you to be happy. If Little Falls makes you happy, you won't hear a complaint from me." He gives me a final squeeze, then releases me. "Plus, call me crazy, but that would mean we have a built-in babysitter that we trust. Let's be honest: Max is not allowed to be alone with my children without Jane there to supervise."

Did we just really have this heart-to-heart conversation in the middle of the chaos that is our friends and family? From the living room, we hear Emma yelling for Noah to bring her another cookie because the baby wants one. We both let out a little chuckle. "Duty calls, kid. You sure we are good?"

"We are better than good, big brother," I say as he grabs a handful of cookies to bring to his wife. Smart man, of course. When she says she wants one, that is not what she meant. I feel a huge burden lifted from my shoulders after talking to Noah. I finish loading up my plate, and by the time I am done, everyone else has found a place to settle in and enjoy their food. I notice Harrison is off on his own. I know I said I wanted to keep this thing between us on the down low, but I can't help but be drawn to him.

"Is this seat taken?"

He looks up. "Yeah, sorry."

Wait!? What. I stumble a step back. He reaches out and gently pulls me closer. "I am kidding, Sunshine. I was hoping if I looked pathetic enough over here all alone, you would take pity on me and come sit with me." That stupid, sexy smirk is plastered across his face again. If I didn't like it so much, I would be tempted to smack it off his face.

"You did look kind of pathetic over here." I return with a smirk of my own.

I place my food on the table, remove my phone from my back pocket, and place it on the table. I go to sit down in the chair as Harrison moves the chair closer to his chair. The only way I could get closer to him was if I was sitting in his lap. I don't say what I am thinking out loud because I don't want to give him any ideas.

Chapter 17
Harrison

After moving her chair to be as close to me as possible so I don't have to lean in that far to be able to whisper in her ear. "Hi, Sunshine. I missed you." I know I am playing with fire, but I can't help myself. I am also very aware that we are not alone, and if our friends were not so content with stuffing their faces, we would have an audience gaping at us.

She lets out a little shiver, then turns her face slightly toward me. "I might have underestimated how hard it would be to keep this a secret."

"Does that mean you want me to stand up and make an announcement to the group?" I put my hands on the table like I am pushing myself up to stand. "I think we could even get more shocked reactions than the baby announcement tonight."

Ginger yanks on my arm to pull me back firmly in my seat. "I doubt we can out do the baby announcement. No one knew that secret. Everyone except Noah knows our secret."

"What are you talking about? No one knows anything about us."

"I am pretty sure I know everything that has been happening with our meddling friends. What I don't know is what your part in the match-making scheme was?" She looks over at me, expecting a confession.

"You are making it sound worse than it is. It all started with me trying to get some helpful advice from Ralph, Henry, and Bubba. After not following through fast enough on their advice, they brought Max in for further consultation. Max came up with the photo shoot idea and enlisted Jane to help get you to the fire house." I have never been a religious man, but this is what I imagine confession would feel like.

"What was the initial advice the guys gave you that you didn't take?" She asks.

"They told me to man up and ask you out on a date."

"But you never did. How come you did not just ask me out? We might have avoided being the center of our friend's fascination the past few weeks."

"I was planning on it, but that is when you started ghosting everyone. Well, ghosting me. I got it in my head that I had made up the chemistry that I was feeling between us."

"Ugh, I wish we could get do-overs in life. I would have handled this differently. I would have handled so many things that have been happening in my life differently. Sorry, I made you feel that way." She places her fingers gently on my leg in a reassuring manner. "Tonight has been full of heavy conversations. First with the girls, then Noah, and now you. I will need a nap after this party. Do you think that is a sign that I am finally adulting when I am so exhausted I need a nap to recover?" She smiles at me, trying to lighten the mood.

I want her to tell me about all the heavy conversations and all the secrets that have been weighing her down, but Rome wasn't built in a day, and tearing her walls down won't happen in a day, either. "I saw you chatting with Noah. It looks like you guys were able to work things out?"

"Yeah, it was a really good talk. It seemed like a turning point for us."

"Do you think he would be cool with us now? Or do you think he will still break my nose if I brought it up with him?"

She lets out a little giggle. "We can't allow him to break anything on the money maker." Her expression sobers a little. "I know this really bothers you that he doesn't know, and I don't like it either. It's just we are finally on solid ground, me and him after months of not being. I was hoping to ride out this peace for a little while. Is that okay with you?"

I want to tell her, no, it is not okay with me. I want him to know so I don't have to hide my feelings for Ginger any longer. I hated that she was the only one of the girls in the kitchen that no one ran to comfort when they were all having a moment. It feels selfish of me to not give her the time she needs. "Of course, Sunshine, whatever you need."

"Thank you, Harry," immediate relief floods her delicate features. "So, tell me, was the super grill really that super?"

"Good thing you asked me and not Ralph that question. I will give you the reader digest version instead of Ralph's version." I briefly pause "It was cool."

She is full-on giggling without a care in the world. My new life goal is to find ways to keep her always giggling and happy.

"What is so funny, Ginger?" Stella comes from the living room and joins us at the table.

Ginger composes herself enough to get out, "Harry-ison, umm, yeah, Harrison was just explaining the finer points about the super grill to me." Ginger turns a shade of pink right before my very eyes. She slipped and called me Harry in front of Stella. She tried to cover it up, but judging by her face, she didn't feel like it was a successful recovery. Stella momentarily looks between the both of us, takes pity on Ginger, and lets it go.

Slowly more and more of the group joins us at the table, dragging stools and other chairs up so we can all be together. Desserts have been set out on the table, and everyone is welcome to indulge in a caloric feast. I dread the day when I will have to be mindful of what I am eating and can no longer stuff my mouth with whatever I want. That day is not today, though, so I grab another cookie and shove half of it in my mouth.

"Harrison, I heard you are keeping a secret from us all, and I, for one, will not stand for it," Stella announces, grabbing the attention of everyone. She takes a bite of her cookie like she did not just set off a huge bomb in the middle of us all. Ginger is frozen in place when I glance at her direction.

"Not sure what you are talking about." I am hoping I am coming across as more confident and less terrified about the bomb she just dropped. It doesn't help that I am talking with a mouth full of cookies.

"Sure, you do." she leans into the table away from Bubba, who looks like he is trying to pull her back. I am hoping Bubba can stop her before she continues.

"Harrison doesn't have any secrets; the man is an open book. What can he possibly have to hide from us?" Noah chimes in.

"Glad you asked, Noah. Harrison here has had something huge happen this week in his life. Something that I think is worth noting with everyone."

That's it, Stella is definitely off my Christmas list this year, which she is going to hate. Everyone loves my over-the-top, playful, yet thoughtful gifts.

"Harrison, are you going to tell them, or do you want me to?" She looks at me with this evil glimmer in her eyes. What did I do to piss her off that she wants me to die tonight at the hands of Noah? Ginger lets out a quiet whimper next to me. When I don't say anything, she continues, "or should I address you as Mr. December."

Ahh, cripes she is outing me doing the calendar, not dating Ginger. That I can handle. Ginger slumps back in her seat with obvious relief. Stella looks so pleased with herself. She clearly knew why I was seconds away from a heart attack.

Bubba, also looking a little relieved that this was the direction Stella took it, pipes in, "It's true. I heard something about glistening pectorals."

"Don't get him started on this, his head is already too big as it is. He is also under the impression he has an abundance of muscles." Ralph joins the public humiliation that is my life.

"I already saw the proofs. They are not glistening, and I concur with Ralph; abundance might be a stretch," Noah says casually.

"Wait a minute, how did you already see the pictures? I haven't even seen them yet?" I have no idea why I sound outraged because I really don't care.

"There has to be some benefit to having Max as a twin. He shared them the other night when he and Jane stopped by. Jane needed a Lola fix."

"Gee, thanks, brother. Your kind words overwhelm me" Max says with an unimpressed tone.

"I would say that Harrison has an abundant number of rippling muscles. I bet the calendar sells well this year only because of Mr. December," Ginger says without giving it another thought.

The room is stunned into silence. I can't help but stare at her with my mouth hanging open in shock that she said that in front of everyone. Does she not understand the concept of down low? Commenting on my muscles, no matter how much I liked what she had to say, is not playing it cool.

Noah is the first one to respond, "Eww gross Ginger, Harrison is like a brother to you. Please never refer to his muscles as rippling or abundant again."

It's not great that Noah thinks that Ginger finding me attractive is gross, and he would like her to stop thinking about me. I need someone to throw me a bone here.

"All joking aside, I appreciate your help, man. All the money raised with the sale of the calendars goes to help the widow and orphan funds for first responders," Max said, jumping to the rescue.

"I am going to need a signed copy, Mr. December. The girls that come into the shop will go crazy with all the eye candy," Stella dreamily says. I would say it is odd that Bubba looks like he could murder me, but I get it. His girl, whom he is unwilling to admit is his girl, is talking about another man driving girls crazy. I want to reach over and pat him on the back and commiserate with the poor sap.

"That is a great idea, Stella. We should sell signed copies of the calendar at the Fireman's Ball. Max, do you have access to all the models? Could you help arrange it, so that we get every month to sign a few copies?" Ginger asks with excitement at the possibility of the idea.

"Sure, kid, I can arrange that, but don't you need to ask someone if that is okay that they are sold at the ball?" Max asks, confused that she would suggest the idea.

"Funny you might bring that up. I was asked this week to help co-chair the Fireman's Ball this year. So, I am pretty sure I can get it approved."

"That is a lot of work, Ginger. Are you sure you have the time? You already seem slammed with your internship. We barely get to see you as it is," Emma asks with concern.

Before Ginger can reply to Emma, Ralph jumps in, "The other co-chair is Chief Johnson. He has been putting this event on for years. It practically runs itself. Between his experience and your fresh ideas, it should be a great event."

Ginger looks up at me, hoping I will explain who the other co-chair is. Right then, Ginger's phone starts buzzing from an incoming call. Ginger hurries to silence it and moves her phone to her lap. Ginger looks panicked by the incoming call. Not wanting to throw her under the bus and bring more attention to something she is clearly trying to hide, I throw myself on the sword in a manner of speaking. "I am the other co-chair this year. Chief asked me to take over this year. He has been wanting me to take on more responsibilities at work that usually fall onto his plate. I am worried that he is retiring sooner than I thought."

I was hoping the crowd of vultures would focus on my boss retiring and nothing else I just shared. No such luck; it is not my night.

"You and Ginger are doing the event together," Noah asks. I can't tell what he is thinking.

"I take back my previous statement. Ginger, you have your work cut out for you." Why is Ralph one of my best friends? Why?

Everyone began sharing their thoughts; 99% of them weren't helpful. I look over, and Ginger still looks distracted and worried about that call she just received. I wait until everyone is distracted and not paying attention to Ginger before I lean in and whisper, "Sunshine, who just called you?"

That snaps her out of her funk, and she looks up at me. "I am sorry. What did you say?"

"Who just called you? You look upset and disappear into yourself."

"Oh, that, just a spam caller. Nothing to worry about." She tries to give me a reassuring smile, but it falls short, and we both know it. What I am sure of is my Sunshine just lied to my face. What is she hiding that she doesn't trust me with?

Chapter 18
Ginger

The last few weeks have flown by. I don't think I have ever been so busy in my life. Between my responsibilities at the dance school and planning the Fireman's Ball, my spare time has been limited. I spend my days working on school stuff and my evenings with Harrison.

After a week of constant texts and calls from my idiot ex, I finally wised up and blocked him. Why it didn't occur to me to do that in the beginning is still a mystery to me. With the dreaded ex-banished and out of mind again life slips into a comfortable routine that I am loving.

Hanging out with everyone is back to normal again, too. If this was a normal semester, I would be back on campus by now, unaware of all the fun that I had been missing out on by not being here. I am also rethinking the idea that these people are functional adults. I have strived for so long to be a mature, responsible adult like my friends. I think I was misled to believe that they were all that mature all these years.

A good example of the questionable maturity level of the guys has been the lead-up to Halloween. The Thirsty Moose is holding their annual costume party with prizes being handed out depending on your costume. I have never met a more competitive group of people in my life. The guys all wanted to outdo each other and come away with the title of best costume that was going to be handed out at the end of the night. No one was giving any clues as to what they had chosen for their costumes.

The group text thread is where I started to call into question the maturity level of the guys. I have never looked forward to reading any text messages as much as the ones talking smack about each other costumes. The insane things the guys are throwing at each other are simultaneously hilarious and reeks of middle-school lunchroom banter. My favorite times are when Harry is sitting next to me on the couch, and the text battle is being waged, and they are all trying to outdo each other. I love watching Harry laugh and enjoy himself. He seems so relaxed and carefree in those moments.

Harry looped me in on his costume choice the other night that he had found a Thor costume online. He asked if I could help him with some of the details for his costume. Intrigued about what details a Thor costume would need help with, I agreed. Tonight is the party. We agreed to get ready at his place and then head to the party together. No one seems to be questioning us showing up places together since the night we announced we were working together as co-chairs.

He emerges from the back of his house where his room is, and it is the photo shoot all over again. He is wearing tight spandex pants, no shirt, and a long flowing cape. He has a ridiculous metal helmet with wings on his head. And then there is a hammer clenched in his left hand like he is preparing to head into battle. I can't find any words, at least that would be appropriate for the moment.

"What do you think, Sunshine? With your help on the little stuff, I've totally got this." He spins around to show off.

He was so pleased with himself; I do feel bad for losing it and come close to dying from my laughing fit. "Harry, what are you wearing? I think you forgot some of your costume."

"Sunshine, you could really hurt my feelings if I didn't already know you were a big fan of my rippling pectorals." The ridiculous man is making his pecs dance right before my eyes as he is talking to me.

I shake my head, trying to regain control after my laughing fit. "You are ridiculous, Harry, and I agree I don't hate the view. What do you want me to help you with for your costume? Besides helping you locate the rest of your missing costume that has clearly been forgotten, I am not sure what I can do to help."

"I need you to touch up my abs."

How is he saying this with a straight face? "I am sorry I think I misheard you. You want me to what?"

He walks over to the table, picks up a box, and starts to open it. "I bought this makeup air gun thingy online to highlight my already abundant muscles. It is going to be dark at the Moose tonight and I just want to make sure it is clear who the winner is tonight."

"I have never used one of those guns before." Now starting to get worried he is being serious.

"I found a YouTube video, and it looks easy enough. Please Sunshine. I have to take home the best costume prize this year. There is a lot on the line." He has been reduced to begging.

"Are you guys really this competitive?"

"Yes, of course, we are this competitive, but that is not why it is so important for me to win this year. This is the first year I am bringing my girl with me."

I am pretty sure he is not aware of what he just said. He just threw it out so casually that I was his girl. Fake abs, make-up tutorials, and winning the grand prize are all forgotten as I stand there in his living room staring at him.

"Did you mean it?" I ask, barely above a whisper.

"Yes, I meant it. I need you to operate the gun. I cannot get the right angle doing it myself."

Is he completely clueless, or is he purposely avoiding the 'my girl' comment? "No, Harry, I meant, did you mean what you said about me being your girl?" I hate the amount of vulnerability that is present in my voice when I ask him.

He stops unpacking the make-up gun and abandons it on the table as he moves toward me. He crosses the room and stands before me as he slowly moves his hands up to cup the sides of my face with his hands. I have found when he wants my attention or is trying to anchor us, and this is how he holds onto me. I lean into his touch, craving the comfort that it always brings.

"Ginger, you are my girl. How could you question that? I know you need time and space to figure some stuff out. I have wanted to give that to you, but you need to know that I am in this for the long haul. I am here waiting for when you are ready for the next step together." His thumb slowly sweeps across my cheek.

"Harry…" is all I can get out before looking down at the floor, avoiding eye contact. There is so much I want to say to him, but I am never sure where to start.

"Babe, there is no pressure with how we move forward or at how fast we move in that direction. I just wanted to clarify that you are my girl, so there is one less thing for you to worry about up here." He takes his other hand and gently taps on the side of my temple.

I look back up and we lock eyes. How is this man not married? He is perfect in every way. He leans slightly down, and our lips meet in the middle. Every time we kiss it feels like the first kiss but better. I have read my fair share of romance books, and the way the kissing scenes are described it always seems impossible that kisses like those could really occur. A kiss that is all-consuming and soul-shattering that leaves you complete and whole. That was until Harrison was the leading man in my story, and he kissed me like that. The one thing that I know for sure is Harrison Stone has ruined me in every possible way, I won't survive losing him.

We break apart, both slightly out of breath. "Okay, Harry, I need to see this YouTube video. We need to get going if we are going to have you ready to claim your prize of Best Costume tonight."

He gently kisses my forehead before releasing me. He says almost reverently before turning away from me, "That's my girl."

I need to watch the video a few times, and the first few passes of the air gun are rough. Good thing for make-up remover. By the time I am putting the final touches on Harrison's abs, I want to pat myself on the back for the work of art I created. Harrison is patient with me and looks amused by how hard I was concentrating on his abs and pecs.

"You enjoyed that way too much, mister," I say as I start to clean up the mess I made in his kitchen.

"It was not a hardship for me to endure, that is for sure," he says with a smirk plastered on his face while he moves to grab his hammer. He turns to give me the full money shot, "What do you think? Do you think I will win?"

I walk over to him, stand on my tip toes, and place a kiss on his cheek. "I would have to say you are the best God of Thunder with fake abs I have ever seen."

"Well, thank you, wait, hey, take that back! These are not fake, just enhanced." He is acting offended, but he secretly loves my sassy side.

"Come on, Harry, we need to get going, or you will miss out on winning the big prize."

He grabs my hand and pulls me back into his chest so fast I can't stop myself from slamming into him. "I think I already won the big prize, Sunshine."

I am annoyed that Harrison has the power to turn me into goo with a few simple words. Not wanting to admit this fact to him, I bring up something equally as ridiculous: "Be careful. Your abs are going to be on my clothes all night if you keep holding me this way."

"Worth it."

I gently push him back. "Come on, lover boy. You know the guys will say you chickened out if you don't show up tonight to win the title. Can't let them have the last word, can we?" That does it, a simple reminder that bragging rights are also on the line and we are back on track and headed toward the Thirsty Moose.

I am trying hard not to laugh at Harrison right now. He is so committed to his costume he refuses to wear a coat. Falls in

Minnesota can go either way in the weather department. Nine times out of ten, though, it is freezing. That is the case tonight. The thin spandex pants, no shirt, and a cape doing nothing but flapping in the wind have left Harrison's teeth chattering. He might even be turning a little blue. The Halloween party is one of the most anticipated events of the year at the Moose, which left parking sparse. We had to park a few blocks away.

"I could have dropped you off in front and gone to park the car so you didn't have to walk in the cold."

"You have lost your mind if you think that I would let you drop me off and then let you walk in the dark by yourself for multiple blocks." it takes him longer to get the rant out between his teeth chattering.

"We might have to rethink how we fill out your entry form for the costume contest."

"What do you mean? It is too late to find a new costume now," he says, confused, looking down at his costume.

"Oh, I know. I was just thinking you might be more believable as a Smurf now that you have turned blue." I was impressed I was able to get it all out without cracking a smile.

Harrison growls. He honest to goodness, lets a growl out. My strength in resisting to giggle ends, and one escapes. I hurry and throw my hands over my mouth, clasping tightly, praying it is enough to stop any more giggles from escaping. The effort was futile. The giggles come at the same time I find it in my best interest to run for my life. I take off in the direction of the Moose.

I hear Harrison take off after me. I wish someone were taping what can only be described as an absurd scene. I am full on laughing at this point. A half-naked man wielding a Thor hammer is chasing me. I love how playful Harrison is with me, and he never takes himself too seriously.

I reach the Moose before him. I dart inside and scan the packed room for our friends. I find the girls first and make my way toward them. When suddenly, I am grabbed by my elbow and pulled back a hard wall of muscles. Harrison leans down and whispers in my ear, "I caught you, Sunshine. I will always catch you." Then he releases me and moves past me toward our friends. If we were keeping track Harrison would have won that round.

I start moving through the crowd, following Harrison toward our friends. I die at the comical site before me when I reach our friends. Harrison is standing with his hands on his hips by a large green version of Bubba. I am going out on a limb and going to say that he came as the Hulk. Next to him is Iron Man, aka Noah. Ralph filled the role of Captain America. I am going to have to guess on Spiderman but my Spidey senses are telling me that would be Henry under the mask. The only Avenger that is missing is Max. I wonder which superhero he has chosen.

Emma, Stella, and I just stand there staring at the guys, trading jabs about who did their costume better or who will win. Jane walks up in a beautiful yellow ball gown. She looks gorgeous with her hair curled in a half-up do.

"Jane, what in the world? I thought we all decided to leave the costumes to the guys this year so we could sit back and make fun of them," Emma asks her.

"I know, trust me, this was not my idea…"

Before she can finish her explanation, Max appears in a very legit Beast costume. Jane's dress is making more sense now. They're Beauty and the Beast.

"This is our first Halloween as a couple. We had to go in a couples themed costume. Hashtag couple goals," Max adds like it is a no-brainer while rolling his eyes at us all.

"Max no one says hashtag in a sentence like that unless you are underage. Come to think of it, they don't either." I am glad Stella told him; someone needed to.

"Well, I think you are breathtaking, Jane," I offer the compliment toward Jane.

"Thanks, Ginger." Jane lets out a breath like she had been holding in. Jane hates being the center of attention. She is the original wallflower on the back row type of girl. Max is under the impression that she should be out front and center shining, and somehow, they have found a way to make it work. We all turn our attention back to the band of misfit Avengers for more comic relief.

After the judges make their way around the room and score cards are tallied, it is time for the winners to be announced. They give out a few prizes in minor categories that hold no interest for the guys. They all have their eyes on the prize, the best costume. I am surprised how many awards are given out before we arrive at the time of the night they have been waiting for.

I am having a hard time taking the guys seriously right now. They all want that ribbon and title more than I think they want their next breath.

The announcer steps back up to the microphone. "Quiet down everyone, quiet down. It is time to announce the winner of Best Costume. This year was so hard. So many of you really came to play tonight. But there can only be one winner. Tonight, the judges were unanimous in our decision." The announcer pauses like he is announcing the Oscars instead of a small-town costume contest. They better hurry it up because some Avengers look like they are going to lose it if they have to wait another minute. "Without further ado, the winner tonight is Beauty and the Beast! Congrats! Come up here on stage and claim your prize!!"

Jane looks like she wants to kill her boyfriend right now as he drags her up to the stage. Max, on the other hand, couldn't be happier with his current couple goals being realized. I look over, thinking the guys will be bummed but find them cheering loudly for their friends. I love these humans. They are some of the good ones.

Things start to die down after the results are revealed. Some of the younger crowd leave probably in search of their next Halloween thrill. We all crowd around some tables and enjoy the rest of the evening.

Noah and Emma fill us in on trick-or-treating with Lola. Lola went as an elephant. The pictures of her dressed up in her costume even got an "ahh" out of Ralph. Then Stella had to explain why her hands were stained green.

"How do you think the big guy became green tonight? I took one for the team in hopes of bringing home the win tonight, but apparently, my sacrifice was in vain."

"Wait, you said it would come off with no problem in the shower," Bubba asks with a tinge of panic in his voice.

"Yeah, I thought it would. Don't worry, and it can't last forever. My hands already look better after washing them a few times. Everyone starts laughing and making jokes at poor Bubba's expense.

It is torture to be around Harrison and not reach out and hold his hand or lean into him for comfort. I am tired of the secrets and just want to send out a mass email outlining them all one by one. I can't even remember how we got here or why I started keeping things to myself in the first place. I need to come clean, and the sooner the better.

After an abundance of candy was consumed, we all called it a night, going our separate ways. Harrison and I speed walk back to the car. The temperatures have dropped even more since we entered the bar a few hours ago. We jump into the car, and he cranks the heater as high as it will go. Poor guy must be freezing in his get-up.

Now that we are alone, I reach over to touch him without eyes questioning me "Sorry you didn't win tonight. If it were up to me, you would have gotten my vote."

Harrison smiles at me, then grabs my hand, intertwining our fingers. He brings our joined hands up to his lips, gently kissing the back of my hand. "Sunshine, I did win tonight. I had my girl by my side all night. Nothing else I could ask for."

He is going to kill me with his sweetness.

Chapter 19
Ginger

I was worried that changing my focus from becoming a professional dancer to a dance teacher would not fulfill me in the same way I felt when I was performing. But boy, was I wrong! I have always loved dancing and performing for others, and I suspect that will never change. I am happily surprised by how much I have loved teaching the students. Watching my students learn and grow as dancers is a simple joy that I didn't expect when I started this new path. Things have been going so well that I am going to add two more classes that will start right after Christmas break is over. I need to crunch the numbers, but it is looking good that I could even add on another teacher to lessen the load on me.

I don't want to jinx myself, but everything appears to be falling in place with the plans for the ball as well. We are in crunch time with finalizing the plans for the Fireman's ball. Thanksgiving is next week, and then there are only two weeks before the ball. Harrison is coming over tonight so that we can work on some of the decoration details.

The last students of the night had just left. After a busy day of having dancers and their parents using the front lobby area waiting for their classes to begin or for the dancers to be done, it is always thrashed by the end of the day. I start with clothing and water bottles that have been carelessly left behind and put them in the lost and found. A thought pops into my head: how many times did I forget something that was lost that my parents had to replace for me? It reminds me that I need to stop in and catch up with my parents. I then start picking up discarded trash to throw away in the trash cans. Even though the trash is not full I still decide to take it out to the dumpster to avoid any lingering smells in the morning.

As I am heading back in through the back entrance, I hear the front door open bringing an immediate smile to my face. Harrison had texted earlier, saying he was running a little late, but he was still planning on coming over tonight. I look down at my watch, surprised he is not late but early. I dart into the powder room quickly to wash my hands. "Hey, babe, I will be right out. Want to get takeout tonight? Or are you craving my culinary treat of a frozen pizza?" I dry my hands and, make my way toward the lobby, and stop dead in my tracks when I find that it is not Harrison standing there.

"Glad to see you are not mad anymore, and you are calling me babe again. But I will say blocking me is a little childish even for you, Ginger," Lawerence says toward me. "And have you ever known me to want to eat that frozen garbage that you call food, honestly, Ginger?"

"W-W-What are you doing here, Lawerence? I thought I made it clear that I want nothing to do with you." I hate that Harrison was right and I should have been more careful with locking the front door.

"I have given you plenty of time to have your tantrum, but life needs to move on. I said I was sorry for my indiscretion that occurred this summer. Now, you need to grow up and stop acting like a child."

His words land like a slap across my face. Finding him in bed with another woman is an indiscretion? He thinks I am the one acting like a child. "Lawerence, I would like you to leave. Things between us are over. I have moved on." My voice is shaking, not conveying the strength that I was hoping for.

Lawrence looks around, and the disdain for my dance school is obvious. "You must be kidding me, Ginger, and this place is a dump. What are you even doing here? You need to be preparing for your audition that is coming up in January. You have made your point; you are upset about this summer. You need to get over it, and we need to move forward with our plans."

"It is not a dump. This is a very well-respected dance school that has been a staple in this town since before I was born."

He doesn't even blink at me trying to defend my business, and he just continues on with his rant. "And why did you not return to school this semester? If you delay graduating, I am going to be very disappointed in you. It will look better for me if you graduate and have a degree, even if it is a useless one like dance."

Lawrence was never abusive when we were together. He never hit me or mistreated me in any obvious way that would cause me to be afraid of him. Looking back on our relationship after it had ended, I could see better how he would talk down to me as if I were a child. His words often made me feel small and not worthy of anything better. I vowed to myself that I would never let someone talk to me like that again but here we are, and I am just standing here taking it again from him.

"I think you need to leave. I will not ask you again. My boyfriend will be here any moment. He will not like finding you here."

"Boyfriend?! Right, nice try, Ginger. We both know there is no one else. Now, enough is enough. My firm is putting on a list of social engagements that I am required to be at. Some of the partners have been asking about your whereabouts in the last few months. I can't keep covering for you. When can I expect you to start looking for a place to move up closer to where I live."

Has he always been this thick-headed? Better yet, did I always let him steamroll me into doing whatever he wanted me to do? I don't want to spend too much time, analyzing the answer to the last question.

"You are wrong, Larry" I use the nickname that Stella would call him, knowing he will hate it. "My boyfriend is on his way. Harrison will not like you being here. He was never your biggest fan, if you remember."

"Ah, you are dating the firefighter. What a joke. He is too old for you. He is biding his time with you until something better comes along. And trust me, something will come along that is better for him." The cruel words just flow out of him without further thought of how they will land. "A firefighter is an obvious step down from me, but I guess this will make us even now, and we can move on."

"Even?" Hating the wobble in my voice. I hate how he is speaking about Harrison like he is beneath him.

"I cheated on you with Annie, and now you have cheated on me with the firefighter loser. See, we are even."

I can't believe I spent so much of my time with this man without truly seeing him for what he really is. "I need you to listen very carefully to me, Larry. I do not or will I ever want anything to do with you ever again. You are a first-class jerk that I wasted too much of my time on already. If you do not leave me alone, I will talk to the Sheriff about a more formal understanding between us. How would that look to your partners? Now, please, I will not ask you again to leave."

"Ginger, you have always been so childish. I cannot wait forever for you to grow up and start acting like an adult. Being with me would have elevated your status, but I am too busy to keep pulling you along. This will work out better for me, now I am free to go find someone that is less childish in the ways of the world. It would have been too much work to get you up to the standards for someone of my status in the community." And just like that, he turns and exits through the front door.

I briefly stand there, shaking from the confrontation. His words hit harder than a slap across the face. Words like unworthy, childish, and too much work keep ringing through my head. Lawrence took all my insecurities and threw them back in my face. I move toward the door and lock it. I don't think he will be back, but I don't want to chance it.

I need to do something. A thought enters my mind that I can't get out of my mind. I head up to my apartment to gather what I will need to cleanse Larry from my life forever finally.

Chapter 20
Harrison

If one more thing comes up that delays me leaving work, I might lose it. I was supposed to be at Ginger's an hour ago. Even though I texted that I would be running late, I thought I would have been there by now. I hit send on the last report that was due. I close out my laptop and gather my things to leave. I turn the lights off in my office. I am in the hallway when the Chief comes running out of his office. He spots me and makes his way toward me.

"Harrison, I am glad I caught you..."

I cut him off before he asks for a favor. "Chief, I am already running late. I was supposed to be out of here over an hour ago. Can this wait until my next shift?"

"No, son, that is what I am trying to tell you. We just had someone call in on the non-emergent line that they spotted a fire, possibly in a trash can."

"Okay, roll out the boys. They can go check on it." I am still clueless as to why he is so worried about a trash can fire. It is probably some teens goofing off.

"The fire is reported to be behind the dance school. Ginger lives in the apartment above the dance school, doesn't she?" I take off running for my truck. I don't even give my boss a second thought. I need to get to Ginger and make sure she is safe.

I pull my truck up along the side of the street that faces the entry to the alleyway behind the school. I make it to the scene five seconds before my co-workers join me. I jump out of my truck and see Ginger standing with her back to me, throwing things into a fire. Relief hits me that she is safe and the fire is relatively small. Ginger hasn't noticed anyone's arrival yet.

I grab the fire extinguisher from the back cab of my truck. The guys come running up to me, ready to fight a fire. "Stand down, guys. I have this under control. You guys can head back to the station. If something changes, I will let you know." They turn to head back with no arguments.

I start down the alleyway toward my little pyro, and her trash can fire. "Ya know, just because you are dating a fire expert does not give you the right to start fires on your own." I was trying to joke with her, just relieved that she was okay and nothing worse had happened here tonight.

Ginger looks up at me, and that is when I notice the tears that have stained her face. Her eyes are red and puffy. Seeing me triggers her to start sobbing harder. I pull her in close, trying to soothe her. I whisper calmly in her ear as I hold her, "You are okay, babe. I got you. Everything is going to be okay." I am also attempting to take the pin out of the extinguisher so I can put the fire out. I can honestly say that this is a first for me, holding a woman while trying to use a fire extinguisher.

After a few attempts, I am successful. The fire takes seconds to put out. I still have Ginger locked under my arm as we make our way inside. I put the fire extinguisher down by the door. I turn slightly to engage the lock on the back door. Not being able to take another moment of Ginger's hushed sobs, I bend down slightly to pick Ginger up so she is cradled in my arms. She throws her arms around me and snuggles in. I make our way toward the couch in the lobby. I sit down with her in my lap so I can hold her close.

I am not sure how long we sit there with me rubbing gentle circles on her back. I feel like I am crawling out of my skin. I hate seeing her this way. I don't think I have ever seen Ginger this distraught in her whole life. I wonder if I should call her brothers or maybe the girls to come to fix whatever happened. Unsure what the right thing to say is, not knowing what happened to cause this reaction, I just stay silent.

Ginger's sobs have slowed and turned more into whimpers. I decide to take a chance. "Sunshine, you are killing me. I hate seeing you like this. Do you want me to call your brothers or the girls to come over?"

Ginger lifts her head to reveal her face. She looks ravished by the tears that have been flowing unchecked for the last little while. "No, please don't call anyone. I need you, just you, please, Harry." Her voice is a little hoarse from her sobs.

"Okay, I won't call anyone, but I need you to tell me what happened. Who did this to you?" I don't know why I think it is a person who did this to her. I just can't shake that feeling.

Ginger tries to sit up, but I don't loosen my hold on her. I am unwilling to let her go just yet. She pats my chest, "I am not going far. I just want to be able to look you in the eyes for this conversation." This does not sound good, but I relent and loosen my hold on her. She straightens so she can sit up and we are able to make eye contact but still staying close so I can hold her.

"Harry, I have been holding on to so many secrets for so long, I am not sure where to start." Ginger looks exhausted, and we haven't even started to discuss what is going on. I want to tell she doesn't need to tell me anything and that maybe a good night's sleep will help her, but I know she needs to purge herself of these secrets so we can move forward together.

"Do you trust me, Sunshine?"

Without any hesitation on her part, "Of course I do, Harry."

I smile at her lack of hesitation in her response. "Then trust me to know your secrets and help carry whatever has been burdening you down."

"Not sure where to start." Ginger fiddles with her fingers. I stay quiet, allowing her time to form her thoughts. Finally, she finds the words to start: "I guess it started this summer. I know you know what happened between me and my ex. I am sure the whole group knows. Nothing stays a secret in this group long."

"I have my suspicions about what happened, but I would like you to tell me. I want to hear it from you, in your words."

"Ugh, this is so embarrassing. Fine, I can't hide forever. I want you to know everything so you can make your mind up for yourself."

I want to stop her to ask her what she meant by making my mind up for myself, but I don't want to stop her as she is starting to open up to me.

"I went up to the cities to surprise Lawerence for an unplanned weekend visit. He was always complaining that I did not make enough of an effort when it came to our relationship. I had a key to his place. I let myself in." Ginger stops talking again. She looks like she is going to lose it again. I am seconds away from telling her that she didn't have to tell me what happened when she takes a deep breath and continues. "I found him in bed with one of the law interns that was hired at the same time that Lawrence was."

I had thought that cheating was the cause of the breakup, but the fact she had walked in to catch the dirtbag in the act of cheating makes it worse for some reason. I have questions, but I stay silent.

"This is embarrassing to talk about, but the breakup spurred all the other secrets. I can't do it anymore, Harry; I don't want any more secrets between us."

I told myself that I would let her talk, but I couldn't help myself and cut her off. "Why are you embarrassed by his actions? You did nothing wrong. I understand wanting to keep your private life private and not share the details of the breakup with everyone, but you have to know that your ex is the only one who should be ashamed of his actions, not you." I can't tell if she believes what I am telling her at this point.

"Harry, I wish I could just take those words to heart, but I've always felt like I had something to prove like I wasn't enough somehow. And when Lawrence chose that other woman over me, it only made those feelings worse. I put everything into making it work, but in the end, he still went to her."

I am about to lose it. I want to find the pathetic excuse for a man a teach him a lesson or two in manners. My thoughts are spinning when I hear Ginger let out a giggle. "Harry, you look like you could stroke out at any moment. That vein on the side of your forehead is bulging. Murder is not an option either. We have more to talk about."

I like that she is feeling more lighthearted, but hate that murder is not an option currently. "Keep going, Sunshine. I need more of your truths."

"So, after we broke up, I found myself in a dark place. Found it hard to find joy in the things that had always brought me joy. I figured I just needed to get back into a routine. I called the school to make sure I was set to graduate after this semester." She pauses and looks nervously at me before continuing "Come to find out I had miscalculated my credits, and I had enough to graduate without returning to school this semester."

"What, so this internship is just a bonus on top of what you needed to graduate?"

"Not exactly. What I am doing here is not an internship, exactly."

"Well, what exactly is it then?"

"Ugh, so I decided to graduate without returning to school. The school mailed me my degree before the fall semester even started."

"Congrats, Sunshine! That is awesome. I am so proud of you. I know how hard you worked to graduate, but your explanation just leads to more questions."

"I can probably guess what those questions might be. Let me try to explain better. Mrs. Hannigan approached me probably a year ago with the opportunity to take over the school when she retires. The idea of living full-time back here in Little Falls seemed like a dream come true. I never thought that would be an option for me. Lawrence and I had only been dating a few months at the time Mrs. Hannigan offered me to take over the school. Lawrence was not supportive of the idea at all. He wore me down eventually, and I turned Mrs. Hannigan's proposal down." With every word Ginger speaks, she looks like a weight is physically being lifted from her.

"Fast forward to a month after the breakup, I ran into Mrs. Hannigan again in town. We ended up going to lunch, and she brought up the idea of me taking ownership of the dance school again. At the time, I thought I had another semester to go before graduating. That is what spurred me into calling the registrar's office to figure out if I could take classes online so I could stay here and take over the school. After finding out school was not a barrier to me taking over the school, Mrs. Hannigan came up with a contract that would allow me to purchase the school. The contract benefited both of us but allowed me to proceed without any financial assistance from my parents."

I am speechless. I knew Ginger was hiding a few things, but I never would have guessed what she was hiding. "Let me see if I understand. You have already graduated?"

"Yeah, my degree is hidden in a box upstairs in my closet."

"You are a business owner in town now?"

"Yep" she pops the "p" like she is nervous about my reaction.

"Okay, anything else? Does this mean you plan to stay long-term?" Then it occurred to me her dance audition in New York that is supposed to happen at the beginning of January. I don't give her a chance to reply to my questions before hitting her with more. "Wait, what about your audition? What happens to the school when you leave?"

"That is another secret I have been keeping from everyone. I canceled my audition and withdrew my application from that school."

"Please tell me this has nothing to do with your idiot ex."

"No, but yes. Let me try and explain. I am a people pleaser to my core. I thought this was what my family, Lawrence, and even my friends wanted me to do. Yes, I love dancing. Dancing will always be part of my life in some form or another, but I didn't realize how much I didn't want to move away until I decided to withdraw my application. I want to be here. I didn't think it would ever be an option, but I want to stay in Little Falls and be with you, Harry."

"Sunshine, maybe I owe you a truth in return. I might have been looking for positions in New York to transfer to. I knew you would nail your audition, and I couldn't be selfish and ask you to give up your dreams to stay here just to be with me. So, I thought I would find a job and move with you. Now that I admit this out loud, it is coming out more 'creepy stalker' than 'thoughtful boyfriend.'"

"You would really do that for me?" Ginger looks shocked but not horrified by my forwardness.

"Anything for you, Ginger, I will do anything."

She tears up again. One tear slides down her face. I gently wipe it away. "No more tears, Sunshine. I didn't mean to make you cry."

"Being willing to move for me means more than you will ever know, but I want to stay here. I want to live in Little Falls and run this school. Harry, you make me so happy, I…" Ginger stops herself. I know how I want her to finish that sentence, but I also do not want to pressure her into saying anything before she is ready to.

"Okay, so that sums up all your secrets? Your ex is a royal loser that is not worth another thought from us. You graduated with your college degree, and we need to celebrate. You are a business owner of a successful dance school. Did I miss anything?"

"Nope, you know everything now," she says with a giant smile on her face.

Then, it occurred to me how this whole conversation started. "Umm, how does your pyro act in the alley tonight play into all the secrets?"

Ginger palms her forehead as she had also forgotten about the events that had taken place earlier. "Okay, maybe one last issue. So, Lawerence has been texting and calling me. I never responded, and after a week, I finally wised up and blocked him." Already not liking the direction this is going she continues. "He might have showed up tonight. And I might have left the front door unlocked, knowing you were coming over. He might have let himself in uninvited."

"Sunshine, you keep saying might like it maybe, or maybe it didn't happen that way."

"Okay, it might have happened that way," she says hesitantly.

"What did he want?" my tone is harsher than I meant it to be. I don't mean to direct anger at Ginger, but my mind is racing with thoughts of what he could have done or said that would have provoked her to react the way she did.

Ginger is chewing on her bottom lip nervously. I reach up and use my thumb to free her lip. "Sunshine, what did your ex want?"

"He spewed a bunch of hateful words at me and told me that I should grow up and put an end to my tantrum. He feels like he has given me an adequate amount of time to pout about the cheating episode, and it is time that I grow up. He wants me to move up to the cities so I am more accessible to him when he needs a plus one for his social engagements with the firm."

I am expecting her to break down and start to cry again, but all I see is a resolve in her eyes. What she has resolved to do makes me nervous. Did she decide to give him another chance?

"What did you tell him?" I ask nervously, looking down.

"Harry, can you look at me." She waits until I look up. "I told him to leave repeatedly. When that didn't get through his thick skull, I threatened to get the police involved with a restraining order. He didn't want his precious reputation ruined, so he left then."

"I am sorry I was late tonight, and you had to face him on your own."

"I hated that there was a brief moment of hesitation on my part where I let his words hit their mark. Hence the fire."

"I don't understand. What did he say to you?"

"Lawrence is a master of taking my insecurities and throwing them back in my face. The exact words really don't matter because he does not matter to me. After I got him to leave, and I locked the door I went up to my apartment. I had a box of random crap from the time that we were together. I also have my Julliard's application and acceptance letter. I am not sure why I kept any of it for as long as I did. In that moment I wanted it gone for good. I didn't think that my firefighter boyfriend would have to show up and put the fire out, though; sorry about that."

"I know he hurt you, sweetheart, but it will just take time to heal and move forward." I am trying to be the supportive boyfriend and say the right things to comfort her, even though there is a part of me hating that she still loves him.

Ginger scrunches her nose up in an adorably confused expression. "Harry, you make it sound like you think I still love the idiot."

"You don't have to hide your pain from me, Ginger. When I found you in the alley, you were devastated, barely consolable. It is okay that you still have feelings for him. It would be understandable."

Ginger takes my face in her hands. I want to laugh because this is usually the move I make on her when I am trying to get her attention.

"There have been too many secrets between us. Let me be perfectly clear, so there is no confusion moving forward. I am not in love with Lawrence. I am not even sure if I ever was truly in love with him. I was bored with him, looked forward to time apart, and hated his opinions that he thought I should share, too. I was not crying tonight over Lawrence. I was crying that I allowed so much of the last few years of my life to be dictated by what others thought was best for me. I was finally letting go of the 'yes girl' version of myself. Does that make sense?"

"It is starting to."

"No more secrets. I never want another secret between us again."

"Agreed." Not wanting to burst the bubble of peace that has fallen over us but wondering how we move forward with Noah. "So, what about Noah then?" That is all I have to say, and she moans and falls forward, hiding her face in the crook of my neck.

Her voice is muffled, but I hear her say something to the effect of "How about just one secret?"

I chuckle while I hold Ginger against me. "The truth has to come out eventually, Sunshine. What was your plan when the semester ended or it came time to leave for the audition?"

"I have a better idea! How about we make dinner and watch a movie together? I know I need to tell everyone else about what is going on, but right now, I just want to spend a quiet evening with my boyfriend. Is that okay? Can we just pretend one more night, Harry?"

I can't tell this girl no when the plans of dinner and a movie sound too nice to turn down. I kiss the top of her head. "Sure, sounds great, babe." We make our way up to her apartment, where we dine on frozen stuffed crust pizza and watch a Christmas hallmark. Ginger is out cold before the opening credits are done rolling. I don't mind. I still get to hold her, so I see it as a win.

Chapter 21
Harrison

It has been a few days since the night that I am referring to as the purge. Ginger and I have grown so much closer in just those few short days. I don't think Ginger realized how much the secrets she was keeping weighed her down and put unnecessary distance between us. We have been texting non-stop about anything and everything. I am trying to find a way out of the current situation I find myself in. I really need to find a way to tell this girl no.

Sunshine: HELP!! It is an emergency!

Me: Define emergency. Like trash can fire? Noah knows and is hunting me down? Did you run out of candy corn? Need to be specific.

Sunshine: Wow, ok, you set one fire, and they never let you live it down.

Sunshine: Not ready to address the Noah situation.

Sunshine: Don't joke about the scared fall candy being all gone.

Me: Okay, what seems to be the problem?

Sunshine: The Santa that we hired to make an appearance at the Fireman's Ball called me this morning to cancel. It wasn't very jolly of him if you ask me.

Me: Hardly seems that would reach the emergency level.

Sunshine: Well, it does. Most Santas are rented out a year in advance. I was lucky to find that guy.

Me: What is the big deal? I can rent a suit and fill in.

Sunshine: And you don't mind doing all the things we had our other Santa scheduled for??

Me: I feel like I should have paid attention during our meetings when you were talking about Santa's duties….Starting to regret staring at your lips and day dreaming instead.

Sunshine: Too late you are locked in to play Santa now!! Thank you babe.

Sunshine: Maybe you could come over later and show me how my lips inspired you?

Me: Are you trying to kill me?! You know I am only halfway through my shift.

Me: What other Santa duties will I be required to fulfill?

Sunshine: You will be performing a dance number with my tiny dancer ballet class. The little ones have been working so hard. It will be amazing!!

As I sit in my office thinking of Ginger instead of the paperwork needing my signature, it dawns on me we have never officially been on a date. We have dinner together almost every free night we have but that is either at her apartment or my house. I have never taken her out for fear we would get caught by the small-town gossip and it would get back to Noah. A brilliant idea pops into my head.

Me: I will be the Santa on one condition.

Sunshine: Ok, I am curious; I will bite. What is this condition?

Me: Go on a date with me. In public. A real date.

Sunshine: Umm….

Me: Before you say no… we could drive up to the city and make a day of it. We need to rent a suit anyway, and you don't have classes on Sunday. So, you have no excuses.

Sunshine: Yes! Count me in. I can finally see the town Casanova's moves up close.

Me: I am not the town Casanova…the rumors are highly exaggerated.

Sunshine: I am going to start looking for a suit to rent. Talk soon.

I put my phone down and stare at it, too distracted to think about work right now. How have I not taken her on a proper date yet? Ginger deserves so much better. I need the perfect date idea to make it memorable.

Someone tapping on the door grabs my attention. I look up to find Ralph filling my doorway. "Why does it look like the town's hard-earned tax dollars are being wasted on you right now?" He enters my office without being invited in and makes himself comfortable in the chair across from my desk. He kicks out his feet in front of him, crossing them at the ankle.

"Well, please come and make yourself comfortable, Chief."

"Already did, thank you."

"What are you doing here? Don't you have better things to do than harass a hard-working, courageous hero like me?"

"Right, courageous, you? Did you survive a paper cut from the backlogged paperwork?" Now the jerk is full-on smirking at me.

"Okay, you got me. I am a little distracted. I was texting Ginger, and my mind is elsewhere right now. Now that you have my confession, you can leave so I can continue to stew over my problem."

"Calm down. I am just giving you crap. What is this problem you are stewing over?"

"If you must know, I just asked Ginger on a date. This will be our first official date, and it needs to be perfect."

"Wait, I am confused. Haven't you two been dating for a few months?"

"What!? What are you talking about?" Somewhat panicked that we were not hiding our relationship as well as we thought.

"You know I am the Chief of Police, right? It is literally my job to know what is happening in this town." Not sure why he looks annoyed.

"I didn't realize your job description covered the townspeople's love life." I am just stalling, and we both know it. "Fine, we have been sneaking around since mid-September, but we thought we were being careful. That is why we have not gone on an official date. Trying to stay off the town gossip loop."

"Dude, you know that some of the biggest town gossips are your best friends, right? Bubba and Stella can out-gossip any of the ladies down at church." He has the nerve to start chuckling at this point.

"Who else knows?" I groan as I start to rub my temples.

"Everyone but Noah. I am a little worried how non-observant Noah has been when it comes to you two."

"I want to tell Noah, but Ginger keeps coming up with excuses. Her latest one is that next week is Thanksgiving, and she doesn't want drama on the big day."

"The longer you wait, the worse he will react to the news, especially if he realizes that we all knew. You're in a tough spot, man."

"Don't remind me. Why don't you be helpful and help me think up the most perfect first date idea."

"I am not really an expert in this area. Plus, you already got the girl. You could take her to McDonalds and only order off the value menu, and she would still be happy because she is with you."

I think about it for a minute. "You're right. You are not an expert. That is a crappy suggestion for a first date."

"We can always open it up for debate on the guy's text thread."

"No way! Last time they all had an opinion, I ended up half naked, dripping in oil."

"If you think that plan was not a success, we cannot help you. What is a total mystery to me is how you came to hold the title of Town Playboy. Where is your game?"

"Well, this has been a pleasant visit, but I need to get back to work. Unless you want to delve into why you are not a dating expert. When was the last time you went on a date?" Ralph has always been quiet about his love life. I know he goes on dates, but they never seem to go anywhere.

Ralph seems amused with the conversation. Nothing rattles this man, which I also find to be very annoying. "No need to get all riled up, Harrison. All I was trying to do is point out that no matter what you plan Ginger will love it. It is obvious to everyone how that girl feels about you. You know her on a different level than the rest of us. You are the best one to plan something that will be a memorable first date for her." He takes a quick breath as he stands and heads for the door. "And as for me. Maybe I am just built a little different than you all. I am content with my job, my friends, and the way my life is right now. I don't feel the need to add anyone to it."

"Sorry, man, I am being a jerk. I appreciate your advice. I don't like keeping things from Noah. I want to be able to shout from the rooftop that Ginger is my girl and stop hiding it." I briefly think about what Ralph just said and he is right, which I will not be saying aloud. No one knows my girl better than I do. "I think an idea just popped into my head that might be perfect if I can make it work. Want to catch a bite to eat? My treat for putting up with my cranky self."

A sheepish grin crosses Ralph's face, "Raincheck. I just stopped by because your chief and I are heading over to a meeting with the mayor together. Good luck with the date. Let me know how it goes." Just like that, he is heading down the hall to my boss's office. Ralph has always been the "old dad soul" of the group. It makes for a perfect Chief of Police. When he first took the position, there were some in the town who thought he was too young for such a responsibility. It took barely any time at all for those with doubts to see Ralph was born for that position.

<h1 align="center">Chapter 22</h1>
<h2 align="center">Ginger</h2>

It is Sunday morning, and Harrison will be here in a few minutes to pick me up for our first official date. I am standing in the middle of my studio apartment with the entirety of my closet emptied out on my bed. Why am I freaking out? It is not like we haven't seen each other almost every day. On the days we don't see each other, we text non-stop during our free time. I would really like someone to explain why I am freaking out right now. I don't have time for this distraction, but I find myself opening up the girl's text thread.

Me: Help!! I need help.

Stella: That is the first step, admitting to it.

Jane: Why do you need help on the only day a week I get to sleep in?

Emma: What could possibly be going wrong this early in the morning?

Me: I have a first date, and I am freaking out about what to wear.

Stella: I am going to need more explanation….

Jane: I do not think Harrison will like that you are going on other dates with other guys.

Emma: I must agree with Jane.

Me: I don't have time for this girls. I need help with an outfit pick. He will be here in a few minutes, and I am standing here half-naked, freaking out about what to wear.

Stella: Calm down kid. We will help you.

Jane: I will help too, but I really am confused about who you are going on a first date with.

I unleash the emoji that is rolling their eyes and the girl face palming herself.

Me: Harrison asked me out on a first date, and I want to look perfect for him.

Emma: As someone who is pretending to know nothing because my husband is still in the dark. I am even more confused. Haven't you two been carrying on for months in "secret" together? How is this your first date?

Jane: What she said.

Stella: Dito.

Me: Even though we hang out all the time and make dinner together, he has not taken me on a date yet. WE can't go out around town with all the gossips watching. We are running an errand for the ball up in the cities. He asked if he could take me out on a date after our errands. No one will recognize us up there.

Me: Are you content with this explanation? Now, please help me! It is freezing today, and leaving the house half naked will not work.

Jane: What are you doing for the date?

Me: He wouldn't tell me. He just told me to dress warm.

Stella: That man is an idiot. It is Minnesota; dressing warm is a given.

Emma: I agree with Stella, he didn't give you any other clues?

Stella: I would like to pause to take note that pregnant Emma agreed with me. I count that as a win!!

Me: That is a rare thing, but I still need outfit help.

Jane: Without further info on what you are doing, go with layers. You can never go wrong with that.

Emma: You can't go wrong with your skinny jeans paired with your brown ankle boots.

Stella: What about that red sweater you grabbed last time we went shopping? It looked amazing on you.

Jane: Do you still have that brown pea coat that you had last year?

Me: See, was that so hard…Thank you for the help!!

I hurry and grab the pieces that they mentioned. I throw the clothes on. I hurriedly add some hoop earrings and a tiny snowflake pendant necklace. I left my hair down in big curls that were hanging down my back. As a dancer, my hair is always up in a tight bun, it is nice to have it down today. I take a photo in my floor-length mirror and send it off to the girls.

Jane: Perfect!

Stella: Harrison will definitely approve!!

Emma: I am tearing up over here. Stupid pregnancy hormones. You look beautiful, Ginger and all grown up.

Stella: You weren't kidding about needing help…it looks like a bomb went off in your place.

I look at the picture I sent them and realize that they can see my bed and all my clothes thrown haphazardly everywhere. The downside to a studio apartment is that I can't hide this from Harrison either.

Jane: Do you have any cute mittens, scarf, and a hat that all match? That will complete the look and keep you warm.

What a silly question, I was born and raised in this frozen wasteland of course, I have multiple matching sets. While I am digging through, looking for the right set I hear a knock at the door. Seeing you can only get to my apartment through the studio, I gave Harrison a key to the building so I could always keep the building locked and secured, but it still allowed him access to come over to see me. I holler that I am coming. Knowing there is nothing to be done about the hot mess that is in my apartment, I abandon any effort to fix it right now. I grab my phone to quickly shoot off a quick text to the girls.

Me: He is here! Thank you girls!

They quickly send texts back with emojis from hearts to thumbs up. I love these girls!

I move to the door and grab my purse off the table. I crack the door open. The new plan is to try and slip out the door hoping Harrison does not catch a look at the current state of my apartment. That plan is quickly thrown out the window when I find Harrison standing in front of me with a bouquet of the most beautiful pink roses.

"Sunshine, you look beautiful, well, at least the parts I can see of you. Why are you hiding behind a cracked door?" he asks, a little amused.

"There was a small…" I briefly pause, trying to find the right explanation for what happened behind me that would not make me come off looking like a silly girl. There happens to be no right words, leaving me with this lame explanation: "Problem in my apartment this morning."

Harry's face turns from amused to concerned within seconds. He places his hand on the door and pushes it open. "Sunshine, whatever happened, let me come in, and we can fix it…" He stops mid-sentence when he takes in the state of my apartment. His eyes are open wide now. He is really making his way through the full gambit of emotions today. Great start to a first date, I think to myself.

"Umm, would you believe that my apartment was broken into and left in this state?"

Harrison turns his attention to me. He now has one of his eyebrows up and the other turned down. I know he doesn't believe that story, but I am getting distracted by his face.

"Okay, I can see that is a no. Would you believe that I found a squirrel in the closet, and I tried to catch it so I could free it outside and, in the process, needed to empty my closet of all my clothes?"

He is back to looking amused with me. "Sunshine, what really happened in here?"

"Ugh, fine, I might have been a little nervous about our first date. I wanted to look perfect for you. Nothing I tried on felt right. Hence, the entirety of my closet is on my bed. I didn't have time to clean up the mess before you got here."

"You are nervous about our date?" Harrison places the flowers on the table and then proceeds to move closer to me.

Feeling like making something up other than the truth would be futile at this point. "Yeah, you are Little Falls OG playboy, and I was nervous I couldn't live up to other girls you have dated, alright? Happy now?"

"Sunshine, want to know a secret?"

I nod my head.

"I am nervous, too. My room back at my place looks similar. I want everything to go perfectly. I was so nervous that I almost texted the guys for advice on what to wear but thought better of it. We already threatened to take Max's man card with the ridiculous things he says ever since he started dating Jane. I knew they would have my man card revoked if I asked for help picking out clothes for a date."

I let out a giggle. "We are quite a pair, me and you." He reaches up to tuck my hair behind my ear.

"I agree, Sunshine. Let's try to let go of the nerves and enjoy the day. It's just me and you, and we have all day to be together and just have fun. I never meant to put pressure on us by making this an official date."

Relief pours through me. Harrison always knows the right thing to say to me to calm me. I reach past him for the flowers. "Let me put these flowers in water then we can get going."

"We have time. Do you want me to help hang your clothes back up?"

"Absolutely not! I don't want to waste one moment of our date cleaning up a mess that will be here when I get back." I place the flowers on the table by the kitchen. "Thank you for these beautiful flowers. Did you know pink roses are my favorite flower, or was it a lucky guess?"

"I bought you some pink roses after your spring showcase that you performed about two years ago. We all drove up that weekend to watch you perform. I thought it was weird if I gave them to you so I had Stella give them to you and leave my name out of it. I might have overheard you tell Stella that they were your favorite flower as you were gushing about them. You were breathtaking that day. Happiness radiated off you in waves. The memory stuck with me." he shrugs like what he said was no big deal.

I lean into him and place a soft kiss on his cheek. "Ever think they started being my favorite that day because of who gave them to me?" He looked surprised by the revelation.

"I saw you in the auditorium waiting with everyone. You looked nervous and were holding the flowers. I am not sure how I knew, but when Stella handed me the flowers, I knew they were from you." I pull his hand toward the door. "Let's get out of here, Harry. I can't wait to see what this day has in store for us."

Chapter 23
Harrison

The drive up to the cities goes by fast. We used the time to go over some of the final details for Fireman's Ball. Ginger remembered last minute to grab her binder that she had been keeping to organize all the details. She hates it when I point out how I find it adorable that she color-coated the sections. I think she looks at it as an insult to be adorable. That is not how I see it at all. We agree to disagree on the topic.

"Let's go over the sponsored Christmas trees. I have a confirmation from twenty-five local businesses that are in the town and in surrounding areas that they will be willing to donate the tree to the silent auction." She is close to bouncing up and down in her seat as she talks about this element of the night.

"Which tree do you think will be your favorite?" I ask, loving her enthusiasm for this project.

"It will be hard to pick. I clearly want to be biased and pick one of our friends that agreed to help. Stella has the beauty shop, Ralph with the Police station sponsored tree, Bubba has his mechanic shop, Henry the zoo, Jane the Cupcake Shack, Noah and Emma are heading up the tree for the elementary school. Even Max offered to do a photography-themed tree." Ginger taps her lips with her pen, giving this a lot of thought, "I don't know—the tree the diner is sponsoring could be really cute too. Oh, wait, I forgot about the library! I do love a good book. See, I have too many options."

"Sunshine, I am hurt that you did not name off the tree the Firehouse is sponsoring. You really know how to kick a guy when he is down." I say with a smirk plastered on my face, so she knows I am teasing.

"Oh, I didn't forget you and your fellow fire experts. I called your Chief this week to confirm the firehouse was donating a tree. He put me in touch with Tony and told me to work with him on that project." She mumbles the last part. I think she is hoping I didn't hear Tony's name.

"Nope, no way. Why would you even call the chief instead of asking me? And no, there is no way you are calling Tony." I am gripping the steering wheel a little too tightly. Is it irrational for me to be bugged by Ginger talking to Tony? Yes. Does that mean I can be rational when it comes to Tony and Ginger talking? No, I can't.

"Calm down, Harry. I don't understand why the topic of Tony brings out your inner caveman. You have been busy at work lately and the chief thought Tony would be great for this project. I don't mind coordinating with him. He is a nice kid, that's all."

"Ginger, he is not a kid. He is 6 months older than you." my voice is rising in octaves.

"When I called him this week to see if he needed any help, he assured me that his G-I-R-L-F-R-I-E-N-D is helping him decorate the tree." her voice is also rising in octaves.

We sit in silence for a moment. I am the first to break, "Sorry, I know it's no excuse, but I hate the idea of you and Tony. He is closer to your age. He is closer to the type of guy I thought you would want to end up with. I have no excuse for my behavior except plain old stupid jealousy." I never feel like my age is an issue for Ginger, but right now I feel so old and out of my league with Ginger.

She sits there for a few minutes, quietly looking out the window. When she finally does break her silence, it is an equal amount of relief that she is talking to me and shock because of what she is saying to me.

"Jealousy looks hot on you, Harry" she says it so nonchalantly. "But I need you to trust me that I would never entertain the idea of cheating on you, never. I think because of how my last relationship ended, I might be a little sensitive to the topic. I was checking things off our list that needed follow-up. That is why I reached out to your chief asking about the tree. He assigned Tony, I didn't seek him out, promise."

I reach over and take her hand in mine. Our fingers clasp together instantly right before I rest them on my leg. "I do trust you, Ginger that was never the issue. You are not the only one with a few insecurities. I will try to think before I react in the future."

"I am serious, Harry..." she pauses then looks at me before continuing, "The jealous caveman is hot." She has her sassy smile crossing her face now. She is trying to lighten the mood again and bring us back to the mood prior to me overreacting.

"That is a good thing, Sunshine. You seem to bring out my jealous caveman a lot."

We continue down the never-ending list of things that need to be reviewed and done before the event can happen. The GPS alerts us that we are nearing the costume shop. I can't believe how many places

I had to call to find a Santa suit. Most people would just laugh at me asking for a Santa suit, and when they found out I was serious and needed a suit, they would laugh all over again.

I finally found this hole-in-the-wall costume shop that had one my size that we could make work. We pull up to the shop, and I start to wish we had brought Bubba for protection. The neighborhood looks a little slim-shady, but we are out of options, and I need that suit. We exit my truck and make our way inside. The costume shop has a gothic feel. If I were in need of Halloween costumes and decorations, this would be the best shop. Christmas cheer, on the other hand, was severely lacking. Ginger and I are just standing there, taking it all in.

"May I help you?"

Ginger lets out a scream and practically jumps into my arms. I whip around to where the request came from. I find a man about my height standing there dressed in all leather from head to toe. He has big, black, chunky combat boots on his feet. He is sporting an impressive mohawk that has been dyed neon green. The next thing that grabs my attention is the facial piercings. I don't think I could count the number of metal things that are sticking out of his face if I tried.

Ginger elbows me in the ribs. I am being rude just staring. "Yes, sorry, you startled us. We were taking in your impressive Halloween decorations. My name is Harrison Stone I called this week about the Santa suit for rent."

"Oh, yes, welcome. Margie told me that you would be stopping by. I am Bert. I am afraid that there was a miscommunication. We don't have any Santa suits for rent this late in the season."

So many things I want to say right now. Like, your name is Bert, really? He does not come off looking like a Bert. And how can they then not have a suit to rent when I just spoke to them this week about reserving one.

But Ginger gets to the punch before me. "What, are you serious? We drove all the way from Little Falls, and we desperately need the suit."

"Sorry, little lady, the best I can do is sell you a Santa suit. It is a little more money, but the perks are that it will not smell like the last Santa, and you will always own the suit."

"Oh, we can do that. Sounds like it is a better deal now that you mention the previous smelly Santa," I say, relieved that we will not be leaving empty-handed.

"Great news. I will go get the gothic Santa suit from the back, and then we can ring you up. I am assuming you will want the fake piercings. I don't see you being that committed to the costume to really get anything pierced. Be right back."

"WHAT?!" Ginger and I cry out at the same time. Bert, doesn't it make it 10 seconds before he is bent over full-on belly laughing at our response? A small part of me was impressed that his mohawk was rock-hard and didn't even move, but a larger part of me wanted to kill him.

"Something tells me you two would not be in the market for a gothic Santa suit. I am just giving you a hard time. My mom says I have a great sense of humor always pranking people."

I think Ginger can tell that the next thing out of my mouth will not be helpful in this situation; she cuts me off, "Oh Bert, you got us good. Your mama is right, you are one funny guy."

"Okay, give me a second to go get your boring normal Santa suit." Bert turns and disappears behind a black curtain.

Ginger turns in my arms which are still protectively around her. "Harry, that vein on your temple is bulging again," she says with a slight smile creeping onto her face.

"You really think we need a Santa for the ball?"

"I am going to pretend that you didn't just say that. Of course, we need a Santa for a Christmas themed ball. Plus, I am dying to see you in your ballet debut with my tiny dancers."

Bert returns from the back room with a large box under his arm, ending our moment. Ginger pulls back, and we follow him up to the cash register to check out. Bert and Ginger are making small talk. She is explaining why we need the suit. Bert seems genuinely impressed by the event. Before I know what Ginger is doing, she is inviting Bert to come to the fireman's ball.

"Can I buy three tickets to the event? I know my mom would love to come and show her support. Her dad was a volunteer firefighter. The third ticket would be for my girlfriend. She gets bent out of shape when I take my mom out, and she ends up having to stay home."

"Of course you can! We would love to have you come. You really saved us on the suit situation. Let's exchange contact info so I can make sure you get your tickets."

I stand there in awe of this woman. She can make anyone her friend. We finish our purchases and say our goodbyes. Ginger tells Bert that she is excited to see him in a few weeks. We make our way out to my truck. I open Ginger's door for her and help her in. I put the suit in the back of the cab. I make my way around to my side and start the truck to get the heat started up.

"Did you really just give your number to Bert?" I ask, just looking at her.

"Are you really going to go caveman on me again?" Ginger doesn't miss a beat with the sass she gives back to me.

I lower my head while shaking it. "No, Sunshine, I learned my lesson. The way you talk about the Fireman's Ball and the cause that it supports means a lot to me. You have never been to the ball before, and you are working so hard to make it successful. I am in awe of you." I want to say more. I want to tell her what she means to me, but I stop myself. I am afraid she is not at the same point, and I don't want to scare her off.

"I was always secretly bummed that I missed the ball every year. When I became old enough to attend I was stuck at college. The ball always would fall during finals week. I have always been curious about the event. How could I not give my all to this event? It directly affects you and the people you serve along with. I know we live in a fairly boring and safe community, but it is not lost on me there is a reason the fund was started and needed in the area. I want to do my part to help. If that means Bert, the local punk rocker has my number so he can buy three tickets to add support, so be it."

"Like I said, in awe of you, Sunshine." I grab her hand and kiss the back of it. "How about we put work out of our minds and enjoy our first date?"

"Now you must tell what we are doing; no more stalling."

"How did I not know you are the worst when it comes to surprising you?"

"Not sure, but I have always hated them. Now give me the goods. What are we doing today?"

"You have a little while longer to wait." She lets a groan out like this might cause her to die prematurely. I put the address into the GPS app on my phone. I turn the Christmas music on, and we head out on our first official date. Nothing could possibly go wrong, famous last words.

Chapter 24
Ginger

I hate surprises. It is sown throughout my DNA. I was the kid who would open Christmas presents and carefully rewrap them so no one knew what I had been up to. I swear Harrison knew this about me. I turn to look at him in the driver's seat. He looks relaxed and happy. I love the Christmas music playing on low over his radio. I have never dated anyone who ever took this much effort to make a date special. Lawrence never in the year that we were together, took the time to make me feel like what I wanted mattered or do something just because it was important to me.

I will never admit this to Harrison, but I secretly love that he planned a surprise for me even though the anticipation might kill me. We drive further out of the cities in the opposite direction of home. "If you are kidnapping me, I know someone in law enforcement who will come to my aid," I say, just to tease him.

"You wound me, Sunshine. I promise I will return you safely to your home sometime before tomorrow," he says with a giant smile on his face.

We drive another twenty minutes or so before we come across a small town called Stillwater. This town makes Little Falls look like a thriving metropolis. We slowly drive down the main street. It is like we are transported back in time. All the shops have their window decorated for Christmas. The light posts have wreaths hanging from them. There is a twinkle-like crisscrossing the street. I momentarily wish we would be here when it gets dark so I can get the full effect. If I could dream up how a hallmark movie would look, this town would fit the bill to a tee.

"It's magical" I whisper to myself but loud enough that Harrison hears me.

He pulls over in a parking lot and finds a spot. I turn to him, and I apparently have a confused look on my face.

"Do you not like it, babe?"

"Are you kidding me?! This place is perfect. It is like a secret Hallmark movie set that we stumbled upon."

"I know you love those movies and watch the Christmas ones year-round. So, I went out on a limb and thought that you wouldn't mind doing some Christmas-themed activities for our first date."

I sit there stunned before jumping across the cab and latching onto Harrison's neck. "Thank you, Harry. This is the best thing anyone has ever done for me. I love this so much." I pull back a little. "What's first?!" Fully aware that I sound like a child on Christmas morning, but I can't help it; this is amazing.

"We have all day. There are booths with homemade items being sold that we can walk through. There is a gingerbread house competition going on this afternoon. I heard rumblings that Santa was also available to take pictures with. There is ice skating in the south of town. Full disclosure though, any respect that you might have had for me would go straight out the window when you see me on the ice with skates on. There is an elf shop where they need help wrapping toys that have been donated that will be delivered to children who are currently in foster care. Dinner is less negotiable because I had to get reservations, but I don't think it will disappoint." He stops to inhale a big breath, and he is full-on Christmas rambling right now, I am loving every moment of it.

I take this opportunity to jump in. "Harry, this is perfect. Thank you! Let's go walk around and find some trouble to get into together?"

"Sounds perfect."

As we make our way down Main Street, hand in hand we stop and look in shop windows. The decorations are giving me so many ideas for the ball that we could easily recreate. We come to the parking lot that has been transformed into a Christmas village. The booths on the outside that are lining the perimeter of the parking lot appear to be selling homemade items. I am dying to walk around and look at each booth. In the middle of the parking lot are food vendors.

"How about some hot chocolate to warm us up?"

"Yes, I think that would be absolutely delicious."

We get in line for the hot chocolate and realize they are also selling freshly made donuts that come straight from the fryer. Harrison looks like he might start drooling from the smell that is wafting our way. We put our order in for two large hot cocoa's and decided to share an order of the cinnamon sugar donut holes. While we wait for our food, I look around, taking it all in. This town has nailed the Christmas vibe. From the music playing throughout the town to the over-the-top decorations that are perfectly placed, I can't get enough of this town. They call our number, and Harrison heads over to grab our food.

We make our way to a seating area that has been set up. No detail has been overlooked. "How did I not know this place existed before today? I grew up in Minnesota, a few hours away, and I had no idea this place was here. I feel cheated." I huff out.

Harrison chuckles at my indigence to being left out of the secret Christmas town. "I am glad you like it here."

"Like it? Are you kidding? I love it! I have always wanted to move back to Little Falls after college, but this town is giving Little Falls a serious run for its money right now."

Harrison shakes his head, continuing to chuckle at my rant. He pops another donut in his mouth. "Well, if you relocate, you will need to bring me with you. I even have the right type of suit now to get the proper street cred that I deserve." Of course, he is referring to the new Santa suit he just purchased.

"Okay, deal. Can I interest you in taking a closer look at some of these booths with me? I am hoping that maybe I can knock out some Christmas shopping if that is good with you?"

"That is more than good with me."

We clean up our mess after devouring it all and make our way toward the booths. Each booth is unique in what they have to offer. One booth had homemade stockings that were knit from yarn. All individuals not one like the other. As we look through them, we point our favorites out to each other. It got me thinking about holiday traditions.

"What is your favorite holiday tradition that you had growing up?"

"That is a tough one. My parents were not big into traditions. They thought that they were a waste of time. I think I was in second grade when they told me that there was no Santa and they were the ones that put gifts under the tree. Now that I am older, and I know them even better, I am somewhat surprised they waited that long."

"Why didn't they like traditions?" My heart breaks a little for Harrison that he missed out on the memories that come with all the things that his parents thought were a waste of time. We continue wandering through the booths.

"They were focused on their careers. That is what they placed worth in. How about you? Any favorite traditions?"

"Where to start? We grew up on opposite ends of the spectrum. Where your family had no holiday traditions, I think my parents went a little crazy. Don't get me wrong, I loved every moment, and I will have to fully warn my future husband that I am nuts about the holidays, but I am sure some think it is overkill." We wander into a booth that makes beautiful ornate candles. I instantly find myself wanting them all. "If I had to pick one tradition, it would have to be anything and everything we do on Christmas Eve."

"Tell me more. What makes it your favorite?"

I love that Harrison is authentically asking questions because he wants to know me and what makes me happy. I stop and turn toward him. "We all would get matching pajamas, and mom would force Noah and Max to wear them, so we all matched. They would whine so much about it, saying they were too cool. We would decorate cookies for Santa. To this day my favorite cookie is a sugar cookie with plain frosting with red hots on top. I even make them during the year when I need a pick-me-up. My dad read Twas the Night Before Christmas before we were all tucked into our beds to wait for Santa's big arrival. We were all together, and I just loved it."

"That sounds nice, Sunshine. I can see why that would be your favorite."

"We still do matching jammies even now that we are adults. I know this will shock you, but the boys still whine about it." I smile up at him.

We come across a booth selling beautiful wreaths. I found two that will look perfect on the front door of the dance studio. Harrison doesn't even complain when I buy them, and he ends up lugging them around while we shop more. One of the last shops we come across is a booth selling t-shirts and sweatshirts with funny sayings. We find one that screams Stella. Her shirts always have a saying on them that makes me chuckle. I find the perfect sweatshirt that has to come home with me for her. The words written on the back say "Son of a Nut Cracker" in a type font that looks like candy canes. Harrison cracks up and agrees that it screams Stella.

Harrison finds a few things along the way, too. We decided to head back to his truck and store the Christmas goodies we bought so we didn't have to end up carrying them throughout town. We hit up the gingerbread house competition next. The houses were insane with the amount of detail that went into them that were all edible. We might have also enjoyed a gingerbread cookie or two ourselves.

Then he convinced me that we needed to make a stop by Santa's village to check in with the big guy about our status and whether we made the good list or naughty. I love every side of Harrison, but the carefree, playful side is one of my favorites.

We are waiting in line to see Santa. There are families with small children in line ahead of us and behind us. I pretend not to see the parents questioning why two adults are standing in line without kids. Harrison is keeping me entertained with stories of his best Christmas-time rescues that he has had to respond to over the years. Finally, it is our turn. One of Santa's elf helpers leads us up to Santa, who I notice is sitting on an impressive throne.

"Ho, Ho, Ho, Merry Christmas, young lady. What would you like Santa to bring you for Christmas this year?" This Santa might be a little too friendly for my boyfriend's liking. I want to laugh at the look on Harrison's face but think better of it.

"Hi, Santa. How about just a picture this year." I thought it was an easy reply: no harm, no foul.

"Why don't you sit on Santa's lap, and we will grab that picture" Santa is patting his leg. He is either brave or has a death wish.

I grab Harrison and wrap myself up in his arms. "Do you mind, Santa, if I stand so we can both be in the picture?"

Neither one of the men is speaking now. The elf moves us to where she wants us for the picture. She snaps the photo, and we move off stage before friendly Santa can make any more comments. We wait a few minutes off to the side when another elf brings us our photo.

I am dying as I look down at it. Harrison looks like he could murder someone, and Santa looks annoyed as well. Then there is me smiling like a loon in Harrison's arms. I bust up laughing. "This is not funny, Sunshine. Everyone is trying to steal my girlfriend. Even Santa is trying to put the moves on you."

I can't help it. I have lost the battle, and the laughing is not going to stop anytime soon. I am distracted when we head through the workshop's exit. I stumble through the door, still laughing. I am not paying attention to where I am going and run smack into the back of another guy who had just passed by. Harrison reached out to try and stop me from running into the other man, but it was too late.

"Oh my gosh, I am so sorry. I wasn't looking where I was going. Are you…" my question to ask if he was okay dies when I see who I ran into. Noah turns around, making eye contact with me.

"Ginger, what are you doing here?" Noah asks, confused by the random meeting. I then notice Emma pop her head around Noah with Lola in her arms. She looks less confused and borderline terrified. Emma knew I had a date with Harrison today.

"Umm, Noah, what are you doing here?" If I am acting guilty, it is because I am guilty. I really wish I would have taken Harrison's advice and spoken to Noah about Harrison before now.

"Emma's parents told us about this town that goes all out for Christmas, and we had to come to check it out." I know the exact moment that Noah notices who is standing behind me. His face changes immediately. "Harrison, what are you doing here? Wait, are you two here together?"

"Sweetheart, maybe this is not the best time for this discussion," bless Emma for trying.

"When is the best time for a discussion on how one of my best friends appears to be sneaking around my back with my kid sister?"

"Noah, this is my fault I should have said something to you sooner. Don't be mad at Sunshine." Harrison realizes his mistake as soon as he says it. Him calling me Sunshine seems second nature now, but I don't think he meant to call me that in front of Noah.

"Sunshine?" Noah repeats. I watch a lot of true crime with Stella to pass the time away. The way Noah said my nickname that Harrison calls me would be worthy of a true crime show where the homicidal guy is being interviewed. Noah sounds a little too much like that guy right now.

"That is enough, big brother. Harrison is one of your best friends. You are really that against me dating someone that you hold with such high regard?"

"Ginger, do you know why we call him the town playboy?"

"He is your best friend! Why would you say something like that." I shoot back at him, not liking where this conversation is going.

"I have known him longer than you have known him. I know him better than you know him. He will tire of you and move on."

"That is enough, Noah. You have no idea what you are talking about. I won't let you talk to her like this." Harrison looks equally homicidal as he comes to my defense.

"Noah, please, can we go sit somewhere and talk about this?"

"No, we can't, Ginger. I am taking my daughter to see Santa and then spend the rest of the day enjoying the Christmas vibe in the town." Noah is shutting down right before my eyes. "You want to be treated like an adult then start acting like one. Sneaking around and hiding big life events is not acting like an adult. Do not come to me crying when he breaks your heart. And mark my words, Ginger, he will break your heart." Noah now looks resigned as he turns to Emma. He takes Lola from her, and he guides them toward the entrance of Santa's workshop.

Emma looks over her shoulder crushed by what just happened. Harrison and I stand there, not saying a word. Both in shock and the harsh words Noah carelessly threw at us.

Chapter 25
Harrison

Ginger and I stand blocking the sidewalk in shock about the words Noah just spewed at us. I knew in the back of my mind he would be mad at first, but I never expected how he acted today. His true opinion of me became quite clear this afternoon. I had no idea he thought so little of me.

"Harrison, I know you said dinner was non-negotiable earlier, but would you mind if we called it a day and headed home? Maybe grab a bite to eat on the way home?" I hate how small her voice is. I hate that Noah thinks so poorly of me but what I can't stand is how he made Ginger feel today. If we could only rewind a few minutes and go back in time when she was laughing and carefree. I don't even mind that Santa was trying to steal her away from me; she was happy.

I grab her hand and pull her to the side so we are not blocking the sidewalk anymore. "Are you sure that is what you want? We can still find some Christmas fun and make our dinner reservations?"

"I am not sure I am feeling very Christmasy right now. I am sorry. I don't want to disappoint you. I know you put a lot of effort into making this the perfect first date. I just don't want to chance running into Noah again. I need some time, and he clearly needs some time to cool off."

She is saying all the right things, but it still feels like she is shutting down and pushing me away. "Whatever you want to do, we will do, Sunshine."

We start making our way back to my truck. I am racking my brain on how I can salvage the evening. I know of an Italian restaurant on the way home that serves the best pizza around. Maybe pizza will lighten her spirits.

"I know you don't want to stay in this town and have dinner, but I know of a place on the way home that might hit the spot. Interested?"

Ginger offers me a tiny smile that doesn't come close to reaching her eyes. "Okay, Harry."

This is not how today was supposed to play out. We reach the truck, and I help her in. I move around to my side and jump in. I look over at her, wishing I had the words to make this right. I see that she is still holding our Santa picture in her hands.

"Did you know that is the first time I have ever gotten my picture taken with Santa?"

That grabs her attention. "You're joking, right? This is your only Santa photo taken, ever?" She waves the picture in between us.

"Yeah, that is what I am telling you. I told you my parents were not into frivolous children's activities. Santa clearly fell into the frivolous department for them."

"So let me clarify. Your only picture with Santa is one in which you look like you want to murder someone, possibly even Santa?"

"That would be accurate."

A laugh escapes her. She hurries to cover her mouth. "That seems like an inappropriate time to laugh. Sorry." Another laugh escapes her.

"Do you think this rises to the level of one of the true crime shows that you and Stella watch together?"

"You are ridiculous, Harry, but thank you for trying to cheer me up." She shakes her head at me. "I think Stella would enjoy a true crime episode where Santa falls victim after trying to steal the young girl away from her hunky boyfriend."

The murder of a fictional but beloved character from childhood helps bring Ginger out of the sad state that Noah left her in. We are careful to avoid talking about what happened today or any topics that would lead back to Noah. The restaurant is about halfway home. I am hoping we do not have any trouble getting a table because it is earlier than the normal dinner rush, and it is a Sunday night.

We lucked out, and the hostess seats us right away. She leaves us with our menus after seating us. Some regrets are starting to sneak in about picking this restaurant. It is on the quirky side. The owner must be straight off the boat from Italy with how he has decorated the place. Lots of statues that are lacking clothes. Every spare inch on the wall is covered with pictures or some type of memento boasting Italian pride.

"Have you been here before?"

I stop looking around at all the décor mishaps. "Yeah, it has been a few years, if I am being honest. I had forgotten about the unique design choices. I promise that the food makes up for it. I highly recommend their Margherita pizza."

"I like it. Reminds me of this dive place where I would grab food and study when I was at college. The weird places always have the best food. Pizza sounds great, want to share?"

Before I can respond we are interrupted by our waitress. "Welcome in tonight. My name is Princess, and I will be your server for tonight. Can I start you off with some drinks?" She is only looking at me, and I have a bad feeling about this.

"Babe, what would you like to drink?" Trying to be obvious that Ginger is my girl.

"I will take a root beer, please."

The waitress writes it down but does not acknowledge Ginger sitting at the table. "That sounds perfect, and I will have the same. We also would like to put in our order now. We will take a large Margherita pizza."

"Okay, great choice, sir I will get your order right in. Flag me down if you need anything else." She collects our menus and walks away.

I look over at Ginger, who has her arms crossed over her chest. She speaks first, "What do you think the chances are that her real name is legally Princess?" She asks straight-faced, not giving away if she is just teasing me or if the night will continue to suck.

"Umm, not sure."

Enter Princess with the worst timing and people skills ever, passing out our drinks. "Sir, do I know you from somewhere? Have we met?"

"No, I don't think so. I have never seen you before in my life. My girlfriend and I are from out of town. Just stopping by." I'm not sure what caused me not to stop talking right after I said no to her.

"I never forget a face. I know we know each other. You look so familiar; why can I not remember how I know you?" Princess just stares at me like the answer will come to her.

I don't want to be rude to her, but I am already on thin ice with Ginger and Princess is helping no one right now with her standing there staring at me.

"Sorry, I can't help. Do you mind leaving us until our food is ready? I want to spend time with my girlfriend."

"Oh, of course. I am sorry, sir. I will bring your food out as soon as it is ready." She finally leaves the table.

More awkward silence fills the air. What are the chances that her brother calls me out for being a playboy who breaks hearts only to have our waitress fixate on thinking she knows me and is openly flirting with me despite Ginger sitting right here? I can't take it anymore. "I swear I do not know her."

"I know, Harry, you look like you're seconds away from breaking out in hives."

"You're not mad? I thought after what Noah said tonight, you would be worried that the things he said about me were truer than not."

"There are a few things in this life that I have complete faith in. You are one of them, Harry. Noah said some cruel things tonight. He also said some things that are true. I should have never kept what was happening between me and you a secret. That is on me. Noah and I will hash out what happened today when he is ready to talk."

Another staff brings out our pizza. Relieved to have a reprieve from the world's worst waitress. We dig in. The pizza is as good as I remember.

"You were right. The food is good."

We hear a screeching scream of delight coming from the area where the servers are gathered. It grabs both of our attention. We find Princess jumping up and down, waving something in her hand. She then looks over at me and starts to make a beeline for our table. Whatever she was waving around across the room was firmly hidden behind her back now.

"I knew it! I knew I knew you!!" Princess is drawing the attention of others who are dining in the restaurant now.

My patience for the day is already shot, and this girl was on my last nerve before she came over here, causing a scene. "Listen, I have tried to be nice, but I do not know you. You do not know me. Please find us another waitress to help us, and do not come over here again."

Princess does not look phased by one word I just said. "Don't be like that. Maybe if I called you Mr. December, it would put you in a jollier mood." Just then, she whips the calendar out from behind her back and shoves it toward me. There I am, half naked, posed with a fire ax. Great, now I want to kill both King brothers. I will be lucky if Ginger doesn't block me and never talk to me again after the train wreck this day has turned into. She has abandoned her pizza at this point and is staring at the nightmare unfolding before us.

The manager finally comes to the table. "Princess, is there a problem over here?" The manager has a thick Italian accent.

"No sir, no problem at all. We have a celebrity in the house tonight. He was just telling me that he wants to sign my calendar."

Princess says all of this to her boss as she thrusts the calendar into my face, batting her eyelashes at me.

The nerve of this woman. "Actually, this waitress has done nothing but harass my girlfriend and me through our entire experience here tonight. I would like the check and a to-go box immediately. We are leaving."

"I am sorry to hear that, sir. Of course, let me get your check and a box. Princess, you need to go wait for me in my office."

There is a small part of me that should feel bad that I got Princess in trouble, but I cannot locate that small part right now. She took any hope I had of salvaging the night for Ginger and blew it up. We are back in the truck now headed home. Ginger has been quiet ever since we left the restaurant. I am racking my brain for what I can say that might turn the night around.

I figure a safe topic to discuss would be details regarding the Fireman's ball. When I gather enough courage to break the silence, Ginger breaks the silence first when a soft snoring escapes from her. I look over to find that she is passed out cold. She looks so peaceful all curled up in my passenger seat. The rest of the drive home is spent with me looking over at Ginger and the inward battle I am having with myself.

The words that Noah said earlier struck a nerve and trying to shake it off has not been easy. Does he really think that I treat women so carelessly, and more importantly, does he think I would ever treat Ginger in that way? I hate that a man I think of more like a brother than a friend has such a low opinion of me. I am so distracted by the war of thoughts that are raging in my mind that it surprises me when I pull into town. The drive flew by with the distraction of my thoughts. I make my way to Ginger's place. I pull my truck into a parking spot and turn off my engine. The downtown area is all quiet and mostly shut down at this time of night on a Sunday.

I look over and hate to disturb her peaceful sleep. I reach over and gently stroke her cheek. I quietly start to talk to her, hoping not to startle her. "Sunshine, we are home. I need you to open your eyes for me."

A smile starts to form on her lips, but her eyes remain closed when she mumbles, "Just five more minutes. I so sleepy."

I start to chuckle, even half asleep, I find her irresistible. I hate having to wake her. I know how hard she has been working the last few months, running herself into the ground. "I know, babe, but we need to get you inside before you freeze."

"Ugh, fine, freezing sounds worse than waking up." She slowly opens her eyes and focuses on my face. "Sorry I fell asleep on you; I didn't realize how tired I was. It just hit me all of a sudden," she says as she stretches out of her curled-up position.

We quickly gathered all the purchases that she made at the Christmas fair today and make our way into the dance studio. We head straight up to her apartment. As we enter her apartment, she seems startled by the scene we are greeted with. "Ekk, I totally forgot I left my place a mess. It feels like this morning was a lifetime ago, not 12 hours."

I put the bags down on the table careful not to stack items on the new wreaths that she bought. "Don't worry, Sunshine. I will help you, and we will have this cleaned up in no time." I start to head toward the closet to grab any hangers, but she grabs onto my elbow, holding me in place.

"Not necessary, Harry. I can clean this mess up; you should head home. You did all the driving today and are probably exhausted," she says as she gently guides me back to the door.

I want to call her out on the fact that she is trying to get rid of me. "Are you sure? I really don't mind."

"I am sure. It looks worse than it is. Won't take me long at all."

"I was hoping we could also talk. A lot of things happened today, and a lot was said that I think we should talk about." I know I sound pathetic as I borderline beg her not to kick me out. I am so desperate to stay that I am willing to help organize a woman's closet. This is new territory for me, caring so much about a woman. I have no idea how to navigate this.

"Harry, today was fun, and there is nothing to discuss. Noah will get over himself. And for you and me, we are good. Please don't worry. We are both tired, and it has been a long day. You should go home and get some sleep. That is my plan after I find my bed again." She leaves little room to change her mind when she heads to the door and opens it for me to exit.

Feeling defeated, I started to leave. I stop right in front of her and we are standing toe to toe right now. I reach up and hold her face between my hands. "Sunshine, do you want to know one of my biggest regrets about today?"

Ginger tries to squirm out of my grasp. I probably worded this all wrong, so I hurry to add what I really wanted to say: "I don't think I told you how beautiful I thought you were when you first opened the door this morning. I know it sounds cheesy, but you take my breath away". She stops trying to get away from me and looks back into my eyes. "I feel like the luckiest guy in the world that you are, my girl." She melts into me as I lean in for a goodnight kiss.

The date started off well; there were parts in the middle that I could have done without, but ending with kissing Ginger good night feels perfect. We stand there for a few moments, just holding each other. I finally let her go. I assure her that I will lock up so she doesn't have to follow me back downstairs.

I get home and replay the day over in my head. Ginger seemed different when we were saying good night versus other nights when I had left her apartment. I try not to think too much about the differences. I send her a good night text wishing her sweet dreams. This is the first text in a long time that goes without a reply from her. I try not to worry as I lay in bed that night, but that proves to be a futile effort on my part. Something is nagging at me that Ginger is pulling away and today affected her more than she led me to believe.

Chapter 26
Ginger

I indulge in something I rarely ever get a chance to do, I slept in this morning. The dance studio is closed all week due to Thanksgiving being Thursday. Mrs. Hannigan advised me when I first took over that there are times that I should consider closing. This week was one of the times she mentioned. So many families take vacations and are busy with holiday prep that attendance has historically been poor. I have never been more grateful for making that decision than I am right now as I am lying in bed, and it is almost eleven in the morning. I couldn't tell you the last time I was still in bed at this time.

After my power nap in Harrison's truck on the way home last night, I hit my second wind. I feel bad for kicking Harrison out last night. I know he wanted to stay, but I needed some space. The energy from the nap helped me to get my clothes all put back in order in the closet. I should have stopped there and gotten ready for bed, but my brain was racing with flashes of moments during the day. To distract myself, I cleaned some more. I scrubbed the bathroom, vacuumed the carpets, mopped all the floors, and dusted the bookshelves. The kitchen even got a proper scouring. I only hung up my cleaning gloves when I started to feel like the bleach smell would lead anyone who might visit to believe I was cleaning up a crime scene instead of distracting myself from the disastrous love life that is always mine.

After getting ready for bed, I climb under the covers. I reach for my phone that I had put on the charger hours ago. I notice I have a text message waiting from Harry. I reluctantly open it.

Harry: Sweet dreams Sunshine. Thank you for the best first date I have ever been on. I hope you get some good rest. Talk tomorrow.

I read it a few times. I go to respond, but for whatever reason, I put my phone back on the nightstand by my bed and roll over without replying. Then, I proceeded to have a restless night of sleep.

I wake up to my phone buzzing like crazy. The text messages are rolling in at a ridiculous pace. I let out a groan of annoyance, knowing the only way to get it to stop is to reply to them. I grab the phone and swipe the screen open. Harrison's text thread is still open. There is a new text from Harrison waiting for me.

Harry: Good morning, beautiful. I hope you got some good sleep. Maybe we can grab some lunch together today.

For reasons that I do not want to examine too closely right now, I closed out his thread without responding again. I push the guilt aside that is crashing over me for ignoring him and click on the thread that is the reason my phone has been blowing up.

Stella: Where are my details? It is a good thing I knew who you were on a date with. I might have been tempted to call Ralph and report your abduction after not hearing from you last night.

Jane: Yep, I need details too.

Jane: Stella, you might need an intervention. Not everyone is five minutes away from being a star on Dateline.

Stella: Oh, Jane, you're cute. A little naive but cute. It is always the quiet ones that you think you know that turn out to be the ones with 27 bodies buried under their pumpkin patch.

Jane: Seriously! Do not ruin pumpkin patches for me. You know I love a good fall festival.

Stella: LOL Sorry, Jane, but knowledge is power.

Jane: Why does it seem like we are the only ones on the thread?

Stella: Good point, Jane. Clearly, my theory that Ginger was abducted might have more merit than you gave it. But that doesn't explain Emma not chiming in??

Jane: Ginger?? Please text back. I think it would be awful if you were kidnapped, but letting Stella be right would be worse.

Stella: Jane, what is Max hearing about the date from Harrison?

Jane: hold on, let me ask…

Stella: I just texted Bubba and he was no help.

Jane: Max, either. He said he would try to get the dirt for us.

I can't take it anymore. If I don't respond, those two will gab back in forth all day.

Me: Girls, it is kind of early for this level of crazy.

Stella: Finally! Took you long enough.

Jane: I agree, but all will be forgiven if you give up the details from yesterday.

Me: It was good.

Stella: You have got to be kidding me. That is all you are going to say? It was good. You are being difficult like Jane was when she first got with Max. You remember how annoying that was.

Jane: Hello, rude. I was not difficult.

Me: He took me to a small town east of the cities. It was all decked out for Christmas. We had a good time.

Is it selfish that I want to keep the details to myself? It really was the best date I have ever been on. That is until Noah blew it up with his very direct honesty about his kid sister and best friend being together. I tried a few different times last night to reassure Harrison that Noah was just blowing off smoke for being blindsided by the news of us, but I am not even sure if I even believed what I was saying.

Me: It was fun until we ran into Noah, Emma, and Lola enjoying the same Christmas festival.

Jane: Oh, cheese and crackers, was it bad?

Stella: I am guessing with Emma's absence from texting this morning it didn't go well.

Me: Yes, to all the above. It was bad, very bad. Noah said some things that were awful and hit their intended mark. The worst part of it all was he might have been right.

Emma: Ginger, take that back right now!

Stella: She lives! Welcome to the convo.

Me: It's ok Emma, no need to pick sides. I never meant to put you in the middle. I should have been the adult that I was trying so hard to prove I was and been honest with Noah about everything from the beginning.

Emma: I am not picking sides. And yes, you should have been more upfront with Noah, but he was out of line with what he said to you and Harrison.

Jane: What did he say?

Me: It doesn't really matter. His words hit their mark, though.

Emma: I love Noah with all my heart, but he is an idiot. He responded out of hurt and anger. He loves you and Harrison. When he calms down, he will see how wrong he was.

Stella: Why does it feel like you and Harrison broke up on your first date?

Jane: This is sad…I was hoping you were going to report back that you had the best time ever.

Me: No one said anything about breaking up and I did have a good time.

Emma: I think we need a girl's night.

Me: You probably should count me out until after the Fireman's Ball. Life is crazy until that is over.

Jane: Well, we are probably going to see everyone at Thanksgiving dinner right? The King's invited everyone to their house this year.

Stella: They host it every year, Jane. Of course, we are all going there for a turkey feast.

Emma: My party of 3 will be absent this year we are headed to my parents.

Me: When did you guys decide that?

Emma: Oh…ya know….

Me: No, I don't…spill Emma. When did my brother decide not to spend Thanksgiving here?

Emma: He is still a little raw about what happened this weekend.

Me: No need to say anything else. I get it.

Stella: Why does it feel like Turkey Day is going to be spicey this year

Me: No spice. Just my momma's delicious turkey. I need to get this day started. I will catch you girls later.

I toss my phone down on my comforter, unable to find the energy to continue the chat with the girls. The longer I lay in my bed, the more the frustration grows. Noah is always spouting the importance of family and has always been so supportive of me. I am not loving this new, unfamiliar territory that we have crossed over into since the run-in with Noah last night.

I throw my covers off me and decide that laying around feeling sorry for myself is getting me nowhere. I get up and get ready for the day. I open my sparkling clean fridge to be confronted with the depressing fact that I need to go grocery shopping. I threw out all the outdated food that was way past its expiration date, leaving me with very few options for breakfast. I grab some paper and a pen from the junk drawer and start the daunting task of making a grocery list.

By the time I finish with my list, I look over the items that I am headed out to buy it hits me that this might be reason 497 why I am not ready for marriage. My list consists of mainly frozen meals, pizzas, and ice cream. I did venture away from the frozen food section but only to add items like chips and, salsa, easy mac, and cheese sticks. I am certain if I oversaw meal planning for a family, they would be malnourished or starve. I grab my keys and my list and head for the store.

I returned a few hours later. The groceries are unpacked and put away. Even though I was berating myself for my lack of culinary skills prior to my shopping trip, I stumbled across a new stuffed crust pizza in my trusty frozen section that looks amazing and is most definitely going to be my dinner tonight.

I spent the next few hours lost working on the Fireman's Ball. I pull out my binder that I have been keeping track of everything that has been done and needs to be done. I spent the majority of the afternoon sending emails to finalize last minute details. Harrison and I agreed we wanted to oversee decorating the main Christmas tree that will stand sixteen feet tall in the center of the room. I start to scour Pinterest for inspiration ideas. I get lost in the endless possibilities of what we can create when my train of thought is interrupted by my stomach growling. I look down at my clock on my laptop surprised to find that it is six o'clock. I have worked all afternoon and lost track of time.

It dawns on me that I haven't spoken to anyone since the girls this morning over text. It hits me like a ton of bricks that I never replied to Harrison about lunch. I am the worst girlfriend ever. I scramble to look for my phone. I finally find it tangled up in my blankets with multiple missed calls: one from my mom, one from Max, two from Emma, and one from Harrison. There are also text messages from Harrison.

Harry: I never heard back about lunch. I am guessing that is a no?

Harry: Sunshine, I am a little worried. Just let me know you are ok, and I will stop bothering you.

Harry: Starting to feel like a first-class clinger here.

Instead of texting him back I call him. The phone rings once before he answers. "Sunshine?!" He sounds nervous and relieved at the same time.

"Harry, I am so sorry." I jump right into my pathetic explanation for my lack of response. "I stayed up cleaning last night, then slept in. I saw your text and was going to reply, but I got distracted by the girls texting this morning. I abandoned my phone in my bed and didn't get your texts or calls until right now. I am so sorry. I didn't mean to worry you."

"That's okay Sunshine. I understand." He is saying all the right things, but I worry that my careless actions might have hurt him more today than he is willing to admit.

"I am sorry I missed lunch with you. Can I get a rain check for another time?"

"Sure anytime. What did you do today? Are you loving the down time with the studio closed this week?"

"You are too easy on my Harrison. I finally got my lazy butt out of bed around noon. Not sure I have ever slept in that late. I went grocery shopping and spent the rest of the day working on last minute things that needed to be followed up on for the ball."

"I see." He sounds hurt again.

"I just sent out emails to the venders that we talked about on the way to the cities. Just some follow up directions that we covered."

"You are amazing, you know that right?"

"It was just emails, Harry."

"Did your conversation with the girls this morning go bad this morning?"

"Why would you say that?"

"You said you were texting with them then abandoned your phone."

Dang this man for knowing me so well and listening the small details that I say that others would skip over. "Well, it is not really that big of deal. Stella and Jane wanted details about our date. Emma jumped in halfway into the conversation. We talked about Noah briefly. Apparently, Noah decided to take his family to his in-laws for Thanksgiving this year."

"You know this is not about you, right?"

"Hard not to feel that way after what he said last night to us."

"Sunshine, you know he loves you and would do anything for you. He is hurt by how he found out. He will get over this and everything will go back to how they have always been."

I don't want to fight with Harrison about this or talk about it anymore. My stomach lets out another loud obnoxious growl right then. The yogurt I had hours ago is no longer holding me over anymore. My thoughts drift to the frozen pizza that is calling my name.

"Your next shift starts tomorrow, right?"

"Yeah. I report at eight in the morning. But I will be off by Thanksgiving morning."

"Ok, sounds good. I was planning on helping my mom with some prep for turkey day the next few days." I hate this weird energy that is between us right now. I feel like he wants an invite over to hang out tonight. I am wanting a little space to let the dust settle on everything that has happened. The silence has become suffocating, so I break it. "Promise me you will be safe the next two days while you are at work?"

"Always, Sunshine, always." He sounds disappointed. "I will text you when I can."

"Okay, sounds good. Good night, Harry."

"Night Sunshine."

I spend the rest of the evening hating that I didn't invite Harrison over to hang out. I don't understand what my problem is. I hate that Noah's words are having this effect on me. Later that night when Harrison texts me good night. I reply with a simple text back.

This is how the next two days go. Harrison will text me. I reply with a simple text back. I fill my days with things that are needing to be done around the studio. I helped my mom a little with prep for turkey day but that was a joke. Who am I kidding I have no skills that would be helpful in the kitchen department. I mainly sat in her kitchen and ate candy corn while she went on about the latest town gossip that she had heard. At times it felt like she wanted to ask me something but changed her mind and kept topics superficial. Which just fine by me. I find myself missing the daily distraction the studio can bring. I have been successful in avoiding other family and friends the last two days.

Chapter 27
Ginger

This brings me to Thanksgiving morning. I love this holiday, well technically, I am a holiday junkie and love them all. Thanksgiving has always been fun because everyone comes over, and we all eat way too much food and spend all day together. The last few years, being away at college and getting limited time with everyone, Thanksgiving was all that more important to have that time with everyone. It makes me chuckle at how, like any other Thanksgiving, I was dying to get home to spend time with my friends and family, and this year, I am hoping for a rare case of bird flu to give me a legitimate reason to stay home.

I find myself sitting in my parent's driveway getting the nerve to go inside. It looks like everyone is already gathered inside. Minus Noah and his family of course. Another unplanned absence is Harrison. He texted me this morning that one of the guys that was supposed to be coming on shift to relieve him was admitted to the hospital last night with appendicitis and is currently recovering from emergency surgery. The open spot needed to be filled on very short notice and Harrison volunteered to take the first day of the shift with another firefighter taking the second day.

A small part is relieved that we can continue to sweep the "Ginger and Harrison" thing under the rug for another day. I also am also starting to wonder if Harrison is starting to feel like our relationship is more work that it is worth and that is why he volunteered to miss today. Ultimately, the freezing temperatures get me out of the car and head inside, hoping for a miracle that my friends and family are not in the mood for a Spanish inquisition on the Harrison topic today.

When I enter my childhood home I am hit with aromas wafting from the kitchen. No matter how proficient I have become at cooking my meals in the microwave it never smells like this in my apartment. I am briefly distracted by the thoughts of what is causing the heavenly smell that I miss the incoming assault from Stella and Jane.

"Where have you been? I was getting close to having Ralph send out a search party for you" Stella says as she slams into my body in a full-frontal assault that is supposed to be a hug, I think.

As she squeezes the very life from my body, I try to reply, "I am only ten minutes late."

"Stella, you are becoming the dramatic one in the group. You know that, right?" Jane pipes in with an amused tone.

Stella releases me and steps back, then turns her glare on Jane. "What do you mean becoming the dramatic one? I proudly wear that title and have for a long time. That is also why I am the fun one. Some might even say the glue that keeps everyone together."

I shake my head at Stella. She has been around since I was born. I don't know life without her loud-in-your-face personality. Maybe it is the time of year for reflecting on life and finding gratitude in the small things, but I am overcome with gratitude for Stella and all she has brought to my life. I start to tear up, surprised by the sudden onset of emotions that come out of nowhere.

"Look what you did, Stella, you broke Ginger," Jane says, horrified after noticing the tears.

I laugh. "No one is broken. Just feeling extra emotional for some reason this fine turkey day. No worries. Ok, I haven't really got to talk to you girls lately. I need the tea, spill. How is life going?" I try to blow it off like it is no big deal that I am leaking.

The girls take pity on me. Jane fills me in on the bakery and some new expansions she has planned for her business. Stella fills me in on some gossip that she heard at the salon this week. We are still in the entryway when Max finds us. I shouldn't be that surprised; he usually has a short attention span when it comes to allowing Jane out of his sight.

"Hey, kid, you are finally here!" He pulls me into a hug. "Mom won't let any of us eat until we have all arrived, and you were the last holdout."

"We better hurry or the guys will have the cheese board demolished before we even make in there" Stella says over her shoulder as she hurries to grab some food.

Jane looks between us before settling on Max. Jane and Max then proceed to have a weird, silent conversation between the two of them. Jane finally speaks first "I am going to see if your mom needs any help in the kitchen," and then walks off without another word.

Starting to put the pieces together, this was an ambush. "So, kid…" Max rubs the back of his neck and looks uncomfortable, unable to find the words to finish his thought.

"Spit it out, big brother. Say whatever you need to. I can take it. I have heard it all lately." Why am I being a brat to him? I cringe at the harsh tone I just took with him. "Sorry, that came out wrong. What I meant to say is, what's up, big brother." This time, it came out a little kinder.

"Ginger, I am sorry about what Noah said this weekend."

"You don't need to apologize for what Noah thinks. He is allowed his opinion." Hating that we are talking about this. This is why I was hoping for the bird flu to avoid conversations just like this.

"Please listen to me. You and Harrison have found something special, and in my experience, that is rare. Noah responded more out of hurt than disapproval of you two. Please do not let his words affect your relationship with Harrison." Max has this pleading tone to his voice that has me close to losing it again.

"Max, I appreciate your kind words, but everything has been way blown out of proportion. Harrison and I have only technically been on one date. There is no need for everyone to get all upset about something that is casual and just started." It is alarming to me how easy it is for me to lie with such ease. What I really wanted to say to Max was something along the line of I am so in love with your best friend, and I am terrified that losing him with destroy me.

"It's okay if you are not ready to be honest with me about your feelings for Harrison but don't kid yourself, whatever is happening between the two of you is not casual. When you stop running long enough to be honest things might start to look different." Max pulls me into a big brotherly hug. Feeling close to the edge of losing the leaky eye battle I try to take a deep breath to calm myself. He kisses the top of my head and pulls back.

"One more thing then I will be silent on this topic moving forward. You are not the only one that will be destroyed if this does not work out. I have known Harrison since Kindergarten. He will not survive losing you."

I let out an audible gasp. Max and Noah are constantly doing that freaky twin mind-reading thing. I have always felt a little left out on their fun party trick. It is like Max heard my inner thoughts and replied to them. Without another word, he walks into the dining room to join everyone else.

I am left standing in the entryway, overwhelmed with too many emotions. Also, was it too much to ask for a case of the freakin bird flu.

Chapter 28
Harrison

The past seven days have been the worst seven days of my entire life. Last Sunday was the start of my bad luck. What should have been the best day of my life was replaced by an awful ending to what was supposed to be a perfect first date. Noah's words hurt more than I want to admit. I couldn't even bring myself to talk to the guys about it. I have just stewed over the words all week. Oddly enough, that was not helpful.

Even though Ginger swears the run-in with Noah didn't affect her, things between us have been off. Monday, she ignored all the calls and texts I sent her. She claimed it was just a misunderstanding that she didn't have her phone. Even though she knew I was going on shift the following 2 days, she made no effort to want to see me that night. I didn't push her, not wanting to put pressure on her.

I then head on to shift for my forty-eight-hour shift. Any texting that occurred between us was always initiated by me, with her responses being short to the point and never furthered the conversations. By this time, I was dying to get some face-to-face time with her. I wanted to call her out on the changes that had occurred between us.

I planned to go to her house as soon as I got off shift Thursday morning so we could resolve whatever was bothering her. I wanted to be able to walk into her parent's home hand in hand. I am tired of the secrets, and with Noah knowing now, I am ready to be done with this secret.

Luck continued not to be on my side when one of the guys that was coming on shift ended up hospitalized after an emergency surgery. With limited options of who could fill his spot, Chief asked me to cover the first twenty-four hours of his shift. I agreed reluctantly, not because I minded helping, but because I really wanted to see Ginger.

There are certain holidays that being a firefighter is just awful and you know you will be going out on calls non-stop. Obviously, the Fourth of July is always full of idiots who are putting themselves in situations that require our help. I would have to say, in my experience, Thanksgiving is the second busiest day for us. From early morning far into the night, we ran from call to call. The majority had something to do with deep frying a turkey and the consequences of not knowing what they were doing. This year, we went out on an alarmingly high

number of calls from people cutting themselves. Those three calls
resulted in paramedics transporting a patient to the hospital for further
medical intervention.

The only good thing about the high amount of callouts was I was
so busy that I had less time to sit around and worry about why Ginger
was pulling away from me. Friday morning came, and I planned to
head straight to Gingers with breakfast in hand, hoping she would
open up to me. Ginger had texted me that she was heading to the cities
with Stella and Jane to look for dresses for the Fireman's Ball and do a
little Christmas shopping. I wanted to scream, throw something
against the wall, and tell her I forbid her to go until we had a chance to
see each other. Grateful for the small sliver of my brain that rejected
those ideas. Instead, I texted her to have fun. Ginger didn't get back
until later than she expected and sent me a 'good night' text instead of
a 'come to hang out text.'

I cannot catch a break to save my life. I had to go back to work
for my regular shift Saturday morning. I have never minded the two
days on four days off rotation before now. I live a low-maintenance
lifestyle that until now was not problematic to make work with that
type of schedule. My personality type has always been easygoing. I
tend to like the downtime the schedule allows for. I have never been
one to hate sitting around the station house.

I am good with a card game or finding a good book to fill
downtime, but that is not the case tonight. After biting off the head of
the third person who asked me an innocent question, I excused myself
for the night. That is how I found myself lying in my bunk, staring at
the ceiling. How has it been a full week since I laid eyes on Ginger? I
know we can fix whatever the problem is as long as we can make time
for each other.

I still haven't heard a word from Noah. I knew he would be mad,
but I have been blindsided by his reaction and words from last week.
The guys clearly know something happened, but I am not sure to what
extent. They have all sent random positive messages to me all week. I
want to tell them to knock it off. Not one of them has made fun of me
or given me a hard time like their normal texts would do. I need them
to tease me or something resembling normal. I just want life to return
to normal, or at least the normal I had grown to crave a week ago.

I wake up this morning resolved that no matter what else I
accomplish today, I will fix things with Ginger. As I started to think of

a plan to woo myself back into the good graces of my girl, I received an incoming text from her. Ginger has not really initiated any conversations in the past week, so I already feel like this is a move in the right direction.

Sunshine: Morning Harry. I know you are coming off a crazy long work week, but I was wondering if I could ask a favor from you?

Me: Good morning, beautiful! Yes, I can help with your favor.

Sunshine: Are you sure you don't want to get more details before you agree?

Me: Does it involve me getting to see you?

Sunshine: Yes

Me: Done deal. You can ask anything of me and I will do it as long as I get to see you!

Me: I just read that, and I sound desperate. Can you pretend you didn't see that and that I played it cool instead?

Sunshine: LOL, not a chance. I have missed you too, Harry.

Me: What is this favor?

Sunshine: I need you to stop by this morning to practice with my Tiny Dancer class. The fireman's ball is less than two weeks away. I need you to get to know the girls, and they need to get to know you. I think the dance should be easy enough.

Me: Ok, name the time, and I will be there. But full disclosure… I have never been a ballet dancer before. Hopefully, the girls can carry the performance, and expectations are set low for my contributions.

Sunshine: Don't worry. I have some secret weapons in my arsenal that I will be pulling out for the performance.

Sunshine: The class starts at 10. Thank you, Harry, see you soon!!

How pathetic does it make me that I don't even care that I will be making a fool of myself this morning, I am just happy that I get to see Ginger. I hurry up and grab my stuff. I kind of want to text the guys that I am participating in a Tiny Dancer dance class. I would normally not want to share something that would bring a countless number of one-liners for years to come, but I also want things to go back to normal. I ultimately decide to hold off on texting the guys about the possible public humiliation that awaits me.

I wanted to arrive early so I might be able to sneak a few private moments with the teacher, but I was held up at the station longer than I thought. I arrive right at ten, and I head straight into the studio. I stop in my tracks when I find a room full of women sitting in the waiting area. Their conversations stop immediately, and they just stare at me like a piece of meat. I am assuming these are the moms of the tiny dancers.

Ginger has shared stories with me about the different types of dance moms that she encounters in her line of work. The dance moms range from terrifying to bored housewives. I always thought that they don't reach the level of terrifying until the dancer is older and has been dancing longer. The way they are staring at me right now maybe my assumptions were wrong. I am a little terrified of these women. Needing a fast escape, I speak first, "Morning ladies. I am here to assist in the Tiny Dancer class. I should probably hurry back." I don't even give them a chance to respond or ask questions before I bolt to the studio that I hear music coming from, but I swear I hear one or two catcalls coming from the lobby area while I am retreating to safety.

I make it to the entrance of the studio. Ginger is sitting on the floor in a circle with six little girls. The girls all have light pink leotards on with pink flowy tutus. They all have pink tights on with tiny pink ballet shoes on their feet. The girls can't be more than three or four years old. Ginger appears to be leading the girls in a warmup routine. Ginger will point her toes then the girls follow her direction. They repeat this cycle a few times with different stretches.

Ginger is wearing similar clothing to the girls. Ginger hasn't noticed me standing in the doorway yet. I cross my arms over my chest and lean against the doorframe. I have always loved watching Ginger dance. She has a grace to her movements that seems effortless. My new favorite thing to watch is Ginger teaching these little girls. She is so good with them. She is silly when she needs to be but can redirect them back onto task with ease.

"Miss Ginger, there is a weird man just staring at you. He is making a weird face at you" a tiny voice says from the circle says.

"Maybe he has to poop. My little brother makes that face when he is making a big poop" Another tiny dancer pops in with her thoughts. Does my face really look the same as a baby poop face? I am not sure if I was horrified or entertained by the tiny dancer's observations.

"My mommy says staring is rude. Miss Ginger, you should tell that man he is rude and to use his manners." Another tiny voice pipes in.

157

Ginger looks over and sees me standing in the doorway. I am gifted a giant smile from Miss Ginger. Ginger rises and heads my way. Once she reaches me, she speaks only loudly enough for me to hear, "Yeah, mister, didn't you know staring is rude." She says it in a similar childlike voice that her students have. She can barely get it out before she also lets out a giggle.

I whisper back, "Does this mean I will need to stay after class for not using my manners, Miss Ginger." Loving that we are being playful with each other, I completely forget six sets of eyes are trained on us.

"Miss Ginger, do you need our help?" Another tiny dancer pipes up.

Ginger turns toward her class. "I am sorry, girls, where are my manners? This is my dear friend, Harry. He is going to help us in class the next two classes."

One of the girls raises her hand and looks like she will combust if Ginger doesn't call on her. "Yes, Lizzy, do you have a question?" Ginger asks.

"Mr. Harry, do they call you Harry because you have lots of hair everywhere? My daddy has lots of hair on his back, and my mommy makes him take it off. She said it was like a rug once. Do you have a rug on your back to Mr. Harry?" Lizzy looks up at me like she did not just overshare.

Ginger looks at me like she is the one who might combust from laughter any moment. She stays quiet, expecting me to know how to reply to that.

"Umm, well, Lizzy, my name is Harrison. I only let my favorite people call me Harry and I can already tell you young ladies are going to be some of my favorites." Not knowing what I should or should not say that would be appropriate in this situation. I looked over to see Ginger clearly liked what I said.

Ginger clears her throat and looks back to her class. "Ok, girls, you know how we have been working so hard on our Christmas dance?"

All the girls start to talk at once. They are clearly excited about the dance. "Girls, would you like to show Mr. Harry our dance that we have been working on?" I wonder if Ginger realizes how good she is with these girls. They all jump up and immediately head for stickers that have been placed on the floor, with each sticker being different. Ginger heads over to the stereo system that is in a cabinet in the wall.

I am trying to keep it together, but the expressions on their faces range from this is the most serious moment of their life to expressions filled with wondering what they will be having for dinner. Music fills the room. It is a song that I recognize instantly. Even though I don't have children, they play this song on the radio during the holiday season. The girls start to move their tiny bodies to the music. A fun voice starts to sing about wanting a hippopotamus for Christmas. By the time the music is fading out the girls strike their final pose.

I start to clap and cheer for them. All six girls start to bow and curtsy over and over.

"Miss Ginger, did you see that we did all the moves without even one help from you!" It is hard not to join in with their excitement and pride for the dance they just performed.

"I did see that, Hazel. I am very proud of you, of all of you." Ginger leads the girls to the area where they had previously been doing their warmups. "Can we all sit back down in our friendship circle? I want to talk to you about something that is so important."

A little hand grabs two of my fingers and gives them a little tug to grab my attention. "Mr. Harry, can you sit by me in da friendship circle?" Not sure how I am supposed to respond I look up to see Ginger watching the interaction.

"Lead the way, tiny dancer. I would love to sit by you in the friendship circle," I say as I look down at my new little friend. She beams with pure joy. We make our way to the circle and join the others.

"Alright, I am so proud of all the hard work you guys have done the last few months to learn that dance. Do you remember when we first started to learn the dance? I told you I needed the hugest favor in the world." Ginger is dramatic and sticks her arms out like she is trying to carry the world. This makes all the girls break into giggles.

Ginger continues, "The fancy dance that Mr. Harry and I are planning is in less than two weeks. I was hoping you girls would be able to perform your dance at our fancy dance party. Before any of you protest or ask a million questions, I need you to listen." Ginger anticipated their reactions before they had time to express them.

"I came up with a dance part for Mr. Harry to do in your dance. So, he will be performing with you guys, but do you want to hear the best part?" Ginger has the girls on pins and needles, anxiously awaiting the best part. She stands and retrieves a box that had been placed against the far wall. She opens it slowly. She dramatically looks between the contents of the box and the girls over and over again. Finally, it becomes too much for the girl who believes her dad has a removable rug on his back: "Miss Ginger, I am surely going to die if you do not tell me what is the best-est part ever. What is in the box?"

Ginger lets out a tiny laugh of her own. "Ok, Katie, I will show you." Ginger reaches into the box and pulls out a red sparkly thing that has more sequins on it than I thought was humanly possible. Fine glitter dust wafts off it every time Ginger swooshes it from side to side to show off the sparkle. I am not an expert on tutus but even I am impressed by the number of ruffles this tutu is sporting. As Ginger holds up the contraption, the room goes dead silent for approximately five seconds before the blood-curdling screams of joy ring out from all six girls as they bounce up and down. To say they were excited by the dance costume would be an understatement.

"You guys don't like these dance costumes, do you? I ordered them just for you girls so you can shine even more during your performance. Would you be willing to dance in these at the fancy dance for me?" She is a master. She has the girls eating out of the palm of her hand, willing to agree to dance anywhere she asks as long they can wear the sparkly contraption.

One of the tiny dancers pops up with a question: "Miss Ginger if Mr. Harry is going to dance with us, is he wearing a pretty costume like ours?" There is no teasing to her comment, she genuinely wants me to be included and wear a sparkly costume, too.

Ginger lets a few giggles free before reining them back in. "Sophia, that is so kind of you to think of Mr. Harry. I thought it would be fun if he dressed up in a Santa suit and danced in that. What do you think about that idea."

"Probably better to cover up his rug with the suit," Katie says, like it is already a foregone conclusion that I am harry beast like her father.

All the girls adamantly agree to dance, and we spend the next 35 minutes practicing. It is harder than I expected it would be to keep a straight face when the girls stop what they are doing to give me direction on my dancing. As the class is coming to an end, Ginger gathers the girls up and hands out a ballerina sticker to all the girls for all their hard work today. She thanks them for a great class. They all start to make their way to the classroom door to leave.

Ginger looks over her shoulder. "Are you coming, Mr. Harry?"

"No thanks, I will wait for you here." I mouth silently, "Mom's scary."

Ginger lets a giggle free and shakes her head as she walks the girls out to their moms. A few moments later, Ginger returns. I walk straight up to her, grab hold of her, and pull her in to hold her tight. "Missed you, Sunshine." That is all I manage to get out.

She pulls back slightly. "I have missed you too, Harry. Thank you for doing this. I think you were a big hit with my tiny dancers today."

"I am pretty sure that every one of them would pick the dance costume over me."

"You might be right about that, but I think you are definitely in a solid second position for favorite things."

"I hate how busy the last week has been. You need to be aware that I am unwilling to go another seven days in a row without seeing you." I take a stance with my arms folded over my chest with my feet spread out a little wider trying to convey that I mean business.

"I know, didn't love that either. And I know you don't want to hear this, but I am not sure it will be much better in the next few weeks. When the Fireman's Ball is over life will get significantly less stressful."

Hating that she is probably right about our nightmare schedules for the next few weeks, I want to argue and tell her that she is wrong, but knowing it will be a losing battle.

"I have another class starting in thirty minutes. Do you have a quick minute so that I can share some emails I received from vendors? Oh, and I want to show you an idea I have for the Christmas tree that you and I will oversee decorating." She takes my hand and pulls me out of the room toward the lobby. Ginger has slipped back into all business mode. I love that she wants the ball to be a success, and by the looks of what she is showing me, I have no doubt this will be one of the most successful years.

The selfish part of me wants us to be focusing on our relationship as boyfriend-girlfriend not as co-chairs of a town event. As I watch her face light as she talks about the tree decorations, I decide that I can put everything I want to say to her about our personal relationship on hold and focus on helping her. It is less than two weeks, and then we can focus on us. I can do this, I think.

Chapter 29
Ginger

It has been a whirl wind the last few weeks. Harrison and I found our groove in completing all the last-minute tasks that have popped up. Any time we spent together has been spent talking about the Fireman's ball or the tiny dancers. He has become quite taken with them. Watching him with the girls during the few rehearsals that we have had threatened to turn me into a pile of goo. I had to catch myself this week as my thoughts were wandering into dangerous territories of picturing him as a dad. I would bet money that Harrison Stone will make an amazing father one day, and I have no business having those thoughts.

I still haven't heard a word out of Noah. If my mom knew about the fight, she would tell me to be the bigger person and just go talk to him. I am not sure what I can say to him at this point. The one time we mentioned Noah this week, Harrison confirmed that he had not heard from him either. I never dreamed that dating me would be a reason Noah would end a lifelong friendship with Harrison. I am the one who asked that we don't talk about the future and what will happen between us until after the distraction of the Fireman's Ball is over. I am finding it hard in the quiet moments alone not to worry that our relationship has an expiration date attached to it.

We finally make it to the day before the ball. I have never been more grateful for the systems that the previous chairs of the event put in place that were so helpful this time. The community volunteers who have shown up this week to transform an old, outdated community center into a winter wonderland are nothing short of a miracle. Harrison was able to take this week off work to be the one that was here to help answer questions of volunteers and direct venders in the right direction.

Walking into the gym area, my breath catches, and I am in awe of what the volunteers were able to accomplish. I am sure I look like a crazy person as I stand in the middle of the room and slowly twirl in a circle.

"I hope you like it, Sunshine, not sure we have time to change it if you don't like it."

Harrison walks up behind me, startling me. I didn't even see him when I entered. I turn to find him walking toward me. This is probably not the most appropriate time for these thoughts to enter my mind, but dang it, why does he have to be so gorgeous all the time? He clearly has been working hard all day, but it is annoying that he can still look this good without trying.

"Hey, Sunshine, if you keep looking at me like that, we will never get this tree decorated." That sexy smirk he sports is annoying and so sexy as it is plastered across his face.

Somewhat embarrassed that I got caught ogling him, I decided to lean into the truth and tell him what I thought about the volunteer attire that he was wearing. "Can you blame me, Harry? You are looking mighty fine walking around in those jeans and a tool belt. Your white t-shirt is pulled across your rippling pectorals in just the right way. We all know that you are a big shot model now, but can you try a little harder not to be so hot." I surprised myself with my flirty reply. I have been all business the last few weeks, and by the look on his face, he is also surprised by my random attempt at flirting.

"Didn't know you had a thing for tool belts, Sunshine. I will keep that in mind." He makes his way toward me and we are now toe to toe. He reaches up and tucks a piece of hair that has escaped my messy bun and tucks it behind my ear. All the other volunteers are busy with their tasks and are not paying attention to us. Harrison still leans in so he can whisper in my ear. "You look beautiful today. You take my breath away. I can't wait until tomorrow night, and I can have you in my arms, spinning you around the dance floor."

The moment that was carefree changed into something more serious. I feel vulnerable and hate myself as I step back from his embrace. Harrison has never been the one who wanted to keep our relationship a secret, that was always me and my stupid justifications. With what he said to me in my ear, he is more than ready to claim me in front of the entire town on the dance floor.

"Well, there will be no dance if we don't finish decorating. Are you ready to get the big tree decorated?" I am a coward. I know it, and Harrison knows it. There is a flash of hurt that crosses his face, and then it is gone.

"Sure thing, Sunshine. I have everything laid out and ready to go." He extends his arm in the direction of the last tree in the room left undecorated.

As we are walking over to our tree, I take in all the trees that are lining the room. The community has outdone themselves this year. I can already pick out trees that my friends did. This is not the time or place to become emotional, so I try to shove the growing emotions down.

"This tree might be a little bigger than I was expecting" Harrison says as he inspects the tree.

"I can't wait to check this off the list of things to do."

"I started to unpack all the decorations before you got here to give us a jump start on the decorating process. I think it will be a showstopper when we are done with it. You should be proud of yourself; the money that will be raised from the event will go to help so many deserving families."

"I think you misunderstood me, Harry."

Harrison looks over at me, confused. "How so?"

"Yes, I am incredibly proud of what you and I have created here, and I do hope it is successful so we can help lots of families...." I trail off, finding it hard to find the right words that don't leave me exposed.

"Sunshine, why is decorating this tree the part you have been looking forward to most?"

"Did you know that decorating the Christmas tree is one of my favorite things to do each year? I have missed out on the last few years being away at college. By the time my finals were completed and I returned home, the tree was always set up and decorated." I pause to gather my thoughts before continuing, "I was just excited that you and I could decorate a tree together. Seems silly to say it out loud."

"Not at all. I haven't had a tree since I lived at home. I have been excited to decorate the tree with you, too. Lights go on first, right?" He moves away toward the table he set up with decorations.

I want to stop him as he heads over to grab the lights and tell him that decorating this tree means more to me because I get to do it with him. I stop myself, though, and follow him over to the table.

Four hours later, after a pizza delivery for a dinner break and countless laughs shared, Harrison and I stand back to take in our work. At some point during the last four hours, all the other volunteers had finished up and left. We are the only ones left in the building. There is Christmas music playing softly on Harrison's phone is propped up on the table.

"It is beautiful" I say in awe of all the hard work that we just accomplished.

"I agree, most beautiful thing I have ever seen."

I look over at Harrison and find him staring at me, not the tree. "Harry, I…" I trail off again. I have spent years imagining what I would say to this man if I ever got the chance to be honest about my feelings with him. Now that I am faced with the opportunity to tell him, the words are lost to me.

"We should probably clean up and get you home. Tomorrow is the big day, and it will be an incredibly long day." And just like that, Harrison lets me off the hook again and does not push me to say things that I am not ready to say.

"Okay" is all I can manage in response.

Clean-up was surprisingly fast. "Are you ready for your ballet debut tomorrow night?"

"I am kind of terrified. What if I mess up? Those tiny dancers are small and cute, but I could see them turning on me if I mess up their dance." Harrison shivers dramatically like he is actually terrified of six tiny girls.

"They all love you so much. Sophia asked if you were going to continue to come to class after this performance. I told her that you probably would not be attending anymore. She started to tear up. I had to give out extra stickers to them to avoid the tears." I shake my head at how ridiculous those little girls are. I can't blame them, though. The thought of not seeing Harrison again would drive me to the same response.

"Those girls have wormed their way into my heart. I might have to continue my ballet training and randomly stop by and check on my tiny dancers after this is all over."

I need to remind myself that he only means when the event is over tomorrow; nothing else is ending, just the event. "I was hoping you would let me pick you up tomorrow?" Harrison says, breaking into my thoughts.

"I had planned to get ready here tomorrow. Stella was going to help me with my hair. I need to be here early to let the caters into the building."

"Okay," I hate how disappointed Harrison sounds with just that one simple word.

We finish cleaning up. We turn off all the twinkle lights and lock up for the night. He walks me to my car. He places a kiss on my forehead and opens my door for me gesturing for me to get in. "Good night, Sunshine. I will see you tomorrow night. Please drive home safely."

I want to blame his hurried goodbye on the freezing temperatures outside, but I worry that I pushed him away one too many times. I might have pushed his patience too far.

Chapter 30
Harrison

I decided that I would arrive early tonight to have a few moments alone before the craziness started for the night. The disappointment of not getting to pick Ginger up tonight is still very much present when I arrive at the community center. I understand her reasoning, but it still sucked arriving without her on my arm.

Nothing has gone as planned today. I was called into the station to help resolve an issue with some missing paperwork that was past due to be submitted. I know that paperwork is not a strength of mine, but I remember specifically filling those forms out and submitting them to the city. That disaster was quickly avoided when I located the needed proof that it was completed and submitted on time. Once people knew I was at the station it was one thing after another that required my attention. I was finally able to get out of work to head home to get ready for the ball.

The next unexpected delay was a call from my parents. Normally we speak every few months, but they randomly called to check in with me. Seeing they rarely show any interest in my life I felt bad cutting the conversation short because I was anxious to see my girlfriend. After the call ends, I am finally able to get ready.

Then, enter the next distraction: the boys start to text, well, at least most of them.

Bubba: I want to go on the record of saying I do not like the dress attire for tonight.

Henry: Did you really say dress attire? Ralph is the old man of the group, not you, Bubba. You are losing your bad-boy edge.

Ralph: Am I supposed to be offended by the old man's comment? Because I am not.

Max: Bubba why are you complaining about getting dressed up? Chicks dig a well-dressed man.

Bubba: I am willing to be the one to say it to you, Max…you are weird since the whole falling in love thing. "a well-dressed man??"

Henry: It really is a head-scratcher how you got Jane.

Max: Agreed, Henry, not sure how I tricked her into loving me. But I am glad I did.

Ralph: How is it that this text chat is always reduced to love talk? We should talk about manly things.

Henry: Like, what is Bubba wearing tonight?

Bubba: Ha ha…I was just curious if there is any wiggle room for another clothing option.

Me: Nope, wear the monkey suit, Bubba, and stop complaining.

Henry: There might be a hippo-inspired surprise tonight. Ginger leaked the possibility.

Max: Why is Henry getting the surprises? I am the only one not complaining about dressing up.

Me: My guess is it will be a treat for you all.

Ralph: Now I am intrigued.

Bubba: Are you saying that something is happening tonight that the great investigator Ralph is unaware of??

Ralph: It was bound to happen that one thing slipped by me. Do you need help tying your tie?

Bubba: What?! Are you kidding? A tie is also required?

Henry: Don't worry, Harrison I will text Stella and have her go over there and make sure the big baby is dressed properly.

Me: Well, as much fun as it is to gab with you idiots about our outfits tonight, I need to get over to the community center to help Ginger.

Me: Ps…Thank you for coming and supporting the cause tonight.

Max: It feels like this moment would call for a group hug.

Ralph: Man card already in jeopardy Max….

I click my phone off. The boys could go all night with jabs back in forth. I focus on getting ready. I pull out my tux from my closet that I rented last week. Most of the guys will arrive wearing suits and the women fancy gowns. Chief Johnson always wore a tux for the event as one of the co-chairs. It only felt natural that I do the same. I am dying to see Ginger. She refused to give me any hints about what her dress looked like.

I arrive at the community center to find organized chaos. The string players are in the process of setting up in the far corner. Ginger had the idea to have some of the high school students perform a few holiday songs throughout the night. When they are not performing, the DJ that we hired will make sure there is no lull in the music for the rest of the evening. Ginger has thought of every detail, no matter how small, and all the hard work is paying off right now as it all comes together.

While I am taking it all in, I see a flash of red hurry by the other side of the room. It hits me like a ton of bricks that the red flash is

Ginger. Ginger can make workout clothes look effortless and is always beautiful in them. I am unprepared for how she looks tonight. She has a long floor, lengthened gown on. She looks like a princess. The top is fitted to her frame perfectly. The skirt flares out at the hip. When she moves the skirt sways with her movement. She left her hair down with soft curls cascading down her back. She has some type of white flower placed behind her ear, pulling some of her hair back. She is gorgeous and left me speechless.

I haven't allowed myself to think about what happens after tonight is over. We will need to deal with the Noah issue and there are also the secrets she is still keeping from everyone else. The one conversation that has me the most scared to approach is where we stand. Is she willing to take a chance on me for more than a secret relationship? Lost in thought, I don't hear the Chief approach me.

"Fine job you have done tonight, son. I am so proud of you," he says as he slaps me on the back, pulling me into a side hug.

"Thank you, sir, I appreciate that. Honestly, Ginger deserves the credit for how the evening will turn out. I just did what she told me to do."

"Smart man! You are already ahead of the curve if you know who is really in charge," he chuckles to himself. "People are already starting to show up. Ginger gave me the welcome intro that she wanted me to read to start the evening. I hear there will be a special musical number tonight that I am very anxious to see. Alright, I won't take up any more of your time. Enjoy your evening, son."

He walks off before I can say anything. I then notice that people are arriving already and still haven't found a moment to talk to Ginger. The next thirty minutes pass in a flash as I welcome people as they arrive. Ralph, Bubba, and Henry arrive together. No matter how much they complained about dressing up tonight, I never doubted that they would show up to support me and Ginger.

"Where is Max?" I don't ask where Noah is. I assume he will not be here tonight.

"I don't know. He should have beat us here. It took forever to get Bubba's tie straight. Ralph wanted to tie two ties together to make it easier to get around his big neck." Henry says between his laughs.

Bubba starts to pull at his collar as if he just remembered he was being strangled. "I would not count on this lasting the entire night."

"Wowzer, you girls look beautiful tonight," Ralph interrupts us, making fun of Bubba when he notices the girls walking up.

Stella twirls in her dress. She has her hair-colored light purple tonight. It is one of my favorite things about Stella. You never know what color her hair will be at any given time. It is always a surprise. She found a dark purple dress that also fits her personality perfectly. It is short and flirty.

"Boys, you all clean up nicely." Even though she says it to us all she is only looking at Bubba when she says it.

Ginger pulls me back by my elbow and whispers into my ear, "As much as I hate to see you change out of this tux, it is time to change into your Santa suit. The tiny dancers are waiting." She pulls away but keeps eye contact with me as she addresses the others. "Sorry guys, but I need to steal Harrison away for some co-chair duties."

"Does this have anything to do with my hippo surprise?" Henry asks with a giant smile on his face.

"It's more like an early Christmas gift I am giving you all. Make sure to have your cameras ready." I say as Ginger pulls me away toward a room that we designated for me to change in.

I feel like we don't have time for any delays, but it needs to be said once we get into the room. I grab her by the hand and pull her back into me, surprising her in the process. I move one hand up to cup her face. "Sunshine, you took my breath away when I first saw you tonight. You are gorgeous in this dress." I let my hand trail down her chin to her neckline and then proceed to trace her arm all the way down to her hand. I bring her hand up to my lips and place a kiss on the back of her hand.

"Oh, Harry, you can't say things like that to me when I am expected to go back out there and act normal," she says breathlessly.

"Sure, I can. I have lots more I am going to tell you tonight, but first, I have six tiny dancers waiting for me. I will change quickly and head to where you wanted me to wait until it is my time to join the dance number."

I hear her mumble under her breath something about a waste of a perfectly good tux as she closes the door when she leaves. Feeling hopeful that Ginger and I are not that far apart in what we want to happen between us. I hurry and get dressed in the Santa suit. I use the staging area to make my way to my entrance spot without being spotted.

The chief is in the middle of giving his welcome spiel. I know that it is almost time as he finishes expressing his gratitude for everyone coming out tonight to support the widow and children's fund. "We have a special treat for you all tonight. I am not sure I can do justice to how special these guests of honor are. I think they have waited long enough. Can you all help me welcome our tiny dancers out onto the dance floor?" The chief starts to clap, encouraging the audience to follow his example. The designated dance floor has the giant tree that Ginger and I decorated last night as a backdrop. There are tables and chairs on the perimeter of the dance floor.

I see Ginger holding Ava's hand, making a train with all the tiny dancers. They weave their way through the crowd until they all make their way onto the dance floor. The tiny dancers are all smiles in there red sparkling costumes. The sequins pick up all the twinkle lights making them sparkle even more, if that is possible.

Ginger gets the girls all in their spots. Ginger nods at the DJ, and their song fills the room. There is no hesitation in the tiny dancers. They start dancing and moving their little bodies to the music. I stand there watching so proud of them that I almost missed my cue. I start weaving in and out of the tables. The audience is oohing and ahhing until they see me. I inspire more laughing than oohing and ahhing reaction. I make it to the dance floor and join in on the dance with the parts that Ginger added for me. There is zero doubt that I will never live this down with the guys but as I look over at Ginger, her expression makes everything worth it. The music fades out, and we all strike our pose.

The entire room erupts in cheers and applause. After an excessive amount of bows and curtsy's the girls turn and run toward me. I crouch down to get on their level, and I am tackled to the ground. I am covered in sparkles and giggling girls. This will always rank as one of my favorite Christmas memories for me. Ginger comes over to save me from the tiny dancers. They all bow again. Their parents make their way to the dance floor to claim their children. The DJ starts some music, encouraging others to take the dance floor.

The original plan was for me to circulate throughout the room as Santa, making the rounds a few times, then change back into my tux. The attendance is turning out to be higher than even we anticipated it would be. Every time I try to exit to go change, I am stopped by someone new wanting a picture or to express how much they are

enjoying themselves. So hence I am still dressed like the jolly fat guy.
Another annoyance is that Ginger and I always seem to be on opposite
sides of the room every time I look for her. At one point, I spot her
with our goth friend Bert. He changed his mohawk to be red and
white striped like a candy cane. Ginger looks overjoyed that he came.
I am worried that she has not got to enjoy herself tonight while
wearing the co-chair hat and playing hostess for the evening.

I noticed that at some point this evening, Noah and Emma arrived.
They were hanging out with everyone at a table in the back. Noah has
made no effort to talk to me or Ginger that I am aware of. I can
understand him being mad at me, but shutting Ginger out is not okay
with me. It dawns on me that Max and Jane are still missing. I go to
grab my phone out of my pocket to text him to make sure he is okay
before I realize that I left my phone in the room with my other clothes.
Frustrated that I am still in the Santa suit I try to make more of an
effort to change but am ambushed by another group of people wanting
to say hello. Looks like I am staying Santa for the unforeseeable
future.

Chapter 31
Ginger

My feet are killing me, and I am exhausted. I am also thrilled with how the evening has turned out. I just got word that all the calendars have sold out. Every one of the twenty-five trees that community members donated has been purchased. We have also received numerous checks from private donors that added to the total of the donations received. The chief pulled me aside and was over the moon with excitement about the money raised tonight. He teared up when he talked about the families that the money would benefit.

All the hard work has paid off and I am going to count this as a success. I have been so busy running from one issue to another or helping volunteers with any problems that arise I have not gotten to spend any time with Harrison all night. There is only an hour left before the night will be ending. Some of the crowd has started to trickle out.

I take this time to find a bathroom. I duck in fast before someone needs something from me. I finish up and am washing my hands when two women in their late twenty's, maybe early thirty's, walk into the bathroom, laughing and talking loudly. They pay me no attention and continue with their conversation.

"Oh, Bella, you are so bad."

"I am sure I do not know what you are talking about. How hard could it be to get him to take me home tonight."

"If anyone can convince him, it would be you, girl."

I know I should not be eavesdropping on their conversation, but now I am curious who this guy is that has grabbed their attention. I am purposely going as slow as possible without drawing attention to me. I need to hear the rest of the story before I leave the room.

"What if he has a girlfriend? There is no way a man that fine doesn't have a girlfriend."

"Who cares? I don't see a ring on his finger. He is fair game. Plus, he was making eyes at me most of the night."

"You are bad." They both start laughing at this point.

I decide that I feel sorry for the guy this girl wants to sink her claws into. I am over the gossip at this point and go to dry my hands. Maybe if I hurry, I can find Harrison for a dance. I stop dead in my tracks at the next thing the mean girl says.

"It is your fault. If you didn't want me to make him mine, you should not have pointed out to me that Mr. December is here tonight as Santa."

A sudden shiver runs down my spine. They are talking about Harrison. What are the chances that I would overhear girls talking about my Harrison in the only five seconds I have had to myself all night? The next question that sends dread through me is, what are the chances that he is really mine?

I find myself walking back into the gym and making my way through the crowd like a zombie. I am so distracted that I run right into the back of someone. That is all it takes me to shake myself out of the fog. Before the gentleman can turn around, I am already apologizing profusely.

"Excuse me, sir. I am so sorry. I should have been paying better attention to where I was going."

The man turns, and I feel like I was punched in the gut by the revelation of who is standing in front of me. Lawrence is there with the woman he cheated on me with and has her hand hooked through his arm.

"Of course, it would be you who would carelessly knock into me. You should be more careful. You could have spilled my drink on me." Lawrence is radiating annoyance.

"W-w-what are you doing here?" My mind is racing at all the options of him being here, and none of them are making sense to me. The last time we spoke, I made it clear that I never wanted to see him again, so why show up now?

"Were you always this articulate? How did I stay with you as long as I did? It was the best decision I ever made when I decided to break up with you."

What the heck is he talking about? I broke up with him. We are off to the side of the room, but somehow, Lawrence's big mouth has drawn attention to us. Out of nowhere, Ralph, Henry, Bubba, and Harrison are on my right side. Stella and Emma come up to my left side. Out of the corner of my eye, I see Noah standing by Emma. I want to cry that he would come to my defense even though we have not spoken in weeks. Maybe there is hope after all.

"Look what trash was drugged in. Larry, we have standards here in Little Falls, and I hate to tell you that you are not meeting them.

You should leave." Stella is fearless in almost all situations in life, especially when it comes to bullies.

"Ironic coming from you, Stella, the literal definition of trash. Look how you came dressed tonight you look ridiculous and out of place with everyone else here tonight that has class." Lawrence takes a drink like he is bored after delivering his hateful words.

Ralph and Henry pull Bubba back as he lunges for Lawrence. I hear Ralph trying to calm Bubba down.

"That's enough, you need to leave Lawrence. I don't even understand why you came. You used to say that these smaller town events were beneath you."

"They are beneath me. I had to come you invited me after all."

I gasp in surprise. My friends all look at me with questioning looks. "You have lost your mind if you thought I would ever invite you. Let me refresh your memory that the last time we spoke, I asked you to leave me alone and not come back or I would have to have the police step in."

"Wrong, sweetheart. You sent an invitation to my firm for this pathetic excuse for a charitable fundraiser. And because I am the low man on the totem pole, I was forced to come to represent the firm."

It is all starting to make sense to me. Harrison and I decided to send invitations to companies in the cities that work closely with our local small business owners. We thought it could boost attendance and possibly bring in additional private donations. Lawrence's firm has helped some of the businesses in town. It never crossed my mind that the invitation would bring Lawrence to the event.

"Do not call her sweetheart," Harrison practically growls. "You lost that right to call her that! She is never going to be yours ever again."

"I will call her whatever I want. And what makes you think I want her back? She dropped out of college. She lost her fancy audition in New York. They probably figured out she is a mediocre dancer at best. Not that being a college dropout without a future is bad enough. She is stuck in this small-town teaching dance to other small-town losers. She has no worth to me anymore. You must be the firefighter who has taken pity on her and has been dating her. You will bore of her too, like I did."

I stumble back as if Lawrence's words were fists that landed their punch. I am trying to find my words while also worrying about which friend might commit homicide with all these witnesses. Harrison acts before I can come up with a plan.

"You are a self-righteous, arrogant loser. You have no idea what you are talking about. Ginger has graduated from college early with honors. She turned the audition down because her career goals changed, which led her to owning the dance school. So, while you are the low man on the totem pole at your job, she graduated early with honors and is a successful business owner in town." I am not even sure Harrison is even aware of everything tumbling out of his mouth. "And PS I love her, so no, I will not grow bored of her. I am going to keep her forever."

"Harry," I let his nickname out on a whimper. Harrison just outed all my secrets and told Lawrence that he loves me. He has never uttered the words to me, but he told my loser ex that he loved me. Everyone is now staring at me. Expecting more answers. I have no words. The silence extends a lifetime it feels like. Out of nowhere Max burst into the center of the awful moment with Jane in tow behind him. Max has never looked happy. Joy is bursting out of both Max and Jane.

"I know we are late! We are so sorry, but we have a good reason. I asked Jane to marry me, and she said yes!! He is jumping up and down with excitement at this point. He grabs Jane's hand, that is now adorning a beautiful princess-cut pink diamond, and thrusts in the middle of the group. Max realizes that Lawrence is standing there. "Oh, I am sorry, I didn't mean to interrupt."

Max never met Lawrence, so he has no idea what he just walked in on. Jane reads the room faster than Max does, and she pulls him back and whispers in his ear. I know the second he is told who the stranger in the group is. His face turns to stone.

"You must be Ginger's other idiot brother. Well, I have had enough fun here in Mayberry, time for me to get back to civilization. Let's go." He pulls on his date's arm to leave without any further recognition.

So many bombs have been set off in the last five minutes, and I have no idea how to navigate it. I start to back up to leave. I can't take the faces staring back at me.

"Excuse me, I need to leave. I appreciate all your support in coming tonight. Max and Jane, congratulations on the engagement." I turn, not waiting for any reply, and take off like the hounds of hell are after me.

Harrison catches up with me with ease. These stupid heels slowed me down. "Sunshine, wait, we need to talk."

"No, we don't. I have already organized all the volunteers with the cleanup responsibilities for when the ball ends in a few minutes." I am still trying to escape at this point.

"So that is it. You are just going to run from me, run from us?"

"Harry, you had no right to tell everyone my secrets. They were mine to tell when I thought it was right."

"Well, someone had to tell them. You were never going to do it. I know Lawrence did a number on you, but ever since you guys broke up, you have been shut down. The old Ginger I knew would have never kept so many secrets from her loved ones."

"Maybe I am not that girl anymore," I say slightly above a whisper. I feel defeated and exhausted. To make matters worse, I start leaking. I wipe fiercely at my eyes, trying to hide the evidence, of tears escaping.

Before Harrison can respond, the awful girls from the bathroom interrupt.

"There you are, Santa. I have been looking all over for you. I am on the naughty list, and I was hoping that you could help me find a way onto the good list before Christmas." She drapes herself all over him. I want to ask if the aggressive mauling technique has proven effective for her in the past.

Harrison and I stare at each other for a moment. I can't compete with girls like these. Maybe I am more broken than I care to admit. I wipe another tear away that escaped and turn to leave again. This time, Harrison doesn't follow or call out to me. He Lets me go.

Chapter 32
Harrison

She left, she just left. It was so easy for her to turn away from me and leave. The ball ended a while ago with no one really knowing of the drama that unfolded right at the end of the night. All the venders are cleaning up their areas currently. All the tables and chairs have been taken down and stowed away. I snagged a chair, and that is where I am currently sitting. In the middle of the room like a first-class loser. To complete the look, I am still in the Santa suit, so it looks like I am a first-class jolly loser.

After Ginger left it took longer than I cared to admit getting rid of the awful girls that wanted off the naughty list. They finally got the clue and left to find the next gullible mark to try their lame pick-up lines on. I left the main room and hid in the back rooms with the clean-up volunteers. I should have gone back to my friends, but I couldn't face them.

So now I find myself sitting in the middle of the room, staring at the giant tree that we decorated together, replaying everything, wondering how I screwed up so badly that I lost the first girl I have ever been in love with.

I hear some banging of chairs behind me. I am too tired to turn around to see what the problem might be. I just keep staring at the tree. Then Ralph is beside me, sitting in a chair he carried over. Then Henry is there. Bubba and Stella follow. Max and Jane are the last to join. Noticeably absent is Noah and Emma. I am sure the run in with Lawrence won me no points in getting back into the good graces of Noah. After sitting here in silence for a while, I speak first "What are you guys doing here? I thought you all left."

"Nope, you thought wrong," Ralph is the first to respond. I can't tell if he is mad, or disappointed in me, or both.

"We were just giving you time to come out of hiding. You disappeared at the end of the night." Henry chimes in.

"I am sorry about how the evening ended." I turn to Stella and focus my attention on her. "Stella, I hope you know how wrong Lawrence was about what he said about you. You are not nothing of what he said. I am sorry he said those things to you."

"Ahh, Harrison. That is very kind of you to be worried about me. But I learned a long time ago that my worth as a person is not dependent on how others view me. Larry is garbage. Always has been and always will be. I am just sorry that the evening ended the way it did.”

“One day, I hope to be as wise as you, Stella.” That earns me a smile in return from her.

“So, are we going to talk about the elephant in the room?” Bubba asks right before Henry reaches over and smacks him across the chest.

“Hey man, you don’t have to resort to violence. I am just saying what you are all thinking.” Bubba rubs at his chest like the swat from Henry actually hurt him.

“Oh, right!! Congrats, Max. I am so happy for you.” I try to muster excitement for the news he shared earlier tonight. “But Jane, if you said yes against your will or he tricked you into saying yes, blink twice, and I will get Ralph to rescue you.”

Everyone laughs except Max, but he is leaning more toward being amused than being annoyed.

“That is not the elephant in the room that Bubba was referring to, but thank you. We are excited and can’t wait to celebrate with everyone when I have better timing.”

“Are you referring to me blurting out all of Ginger’s secrets? Or telling Larry that I loved Ginger before I even told Ginger that I loved her? Or it could be that she walked away from me tonight without another thought, leaving me heartbroken. Or there is the non-Ginger elephant, like how I lost one of my very best friends because I fell in love with his sister, and he thinks I am a womanizer unworthy of her. Which elephant were you referring to, Bubba?” I find a soothing relief in sharing everything with them.

“I never said you were a womanizer,” Noah says, standing behind my chair. I turn and jump out of my seat. Noah and I just stand there staring at each other. Everyone slowly stands and starts to back away. Right before they leave the gym, I hear Henry ask Max if he wants to see a cute hippo dance video.

“If you want to take a swing at me, let me change out of the suit first. I am too cheap to pay for dry cleaning.”

“I not going to punch you, Harrison.” Noah pulls out the chair that Ralph was sitting in and sits down.

“I don’t know what you want from me. You got your way, Noah. Ginger doesn’t want to be with me. You don’t have to worry about her being with someone like me anymore.” I know I am being a jerk to him, but there is so much hurt, and I am having a hard time seeing my way through it right now.

"Harrison, I was wrong. I am sorry it took me so long to see how wrong I was. I am even more sorry for the things I said to you."

"You don't have to say you're sorry if that is truly how you feel about me."

"I have been trying to find the right way to explain this to you. Sometimes, it feels like I chose a different path than the rest of you did. Let me preface all this with I love my family and the life we are building. Emma, Lola, and the new baby are my whole world, and I would not change that for anything."

"Why does there feel like there is a but coming?"

"When Emma and I were first married, you were all off having fun dating a different girl every weekend. Sometimes the pressure of taking care of wife and eventually children, buying a home, and making sure I could provide for everyone's needs felt overwhelming."

"Why did you not ever say anything to us about the pressure you felt?" I look down briefly, realizing that I am trying to salvage my friendship while wearing a Santa suit. How is this my life?

"What was I supposed to say? I have everything I have ever wanted, and it is hard?"

"If that was the truth, then yeah. You should have said that." I pause momentarily, then continue, "I need you to know a few things about me."

"Okay, I am listening. What do you think I don't already know about you."

"First of all, the playboy nickname has been highly exaggerated over the years. Sure, I dated a lot of women while in college, but it was never serious. It was someone to go to a football game with or to hang out with when you all were too busy to hang out. And the last year or two, I really haven't dated anyone."

"Why is that?" Noah asks hesitantly.

"Before I answer that, I need you to know one thing first. I never had these feelings for your sister when she was younger, I promise. We had a moment one weekend when I came home, and she was in high school. That was the first time I didn't think of her as your kid sister. It was just in the last year or two that my feelings grew. After I accepted that I had feelings for Ginger, going out with other girls held no interest for me."

"Well, I have always thought of you as a brother looks like you might become my brother through marriage." Noah leans back and throws his hands behind his back, looking pleased with himself.

"Whoa, how did you make that leap? I know you just started talking to me again five minutes ago, but I told your sister I loved her tonight, and she left. She doesn't want me."

"You didn't tell Ginger you loved her."

"Yes, I did. You were there."

"Sorry, pal, you're wrong. You told Larry you loved Ginger."

"That's not…" I stopped, not knowing how to finish the sentence. "Crap your right."

"Don't worry, she loves you too. I know I didn't respond the best way to the news about the two of you, but looking back over the last few months, there was clearly something going on between you two. I am just sorry I missed out on some of the fun details. I spoke to Max, and he filled me in on the calendar shoot and all the other match-making schemes they have put you two through."

"Wait, what other schemes?" Suddenly confused about what else my meddling friends put us through.

"Oh, never mind. Let's focus on you getting your girl back. I also need to talk to Ginger to make things right between her and me, but first and foremost, what is your plan to get her back?" Noah has the same twinkle in his eyes that Emma gets when she has the match-making bug. It is terrifying.

Chapter 33
Ginger

By the time I am leaving the community center parking lot my face is raw from the tears. It is so cold out tonight that I am worried the tears will freeze on my face. Just as a side note: crying outside during a Minnesota winter is not advisable. I don't want to be alone, so going to my apartment is out of the question. Every one of my friends just found out I have been lying to them for months, so going to them for advice is out of the question. I find myself pulling into my parents' home. My body went on autopilot to bring me home. I am somewhat surprised that there are still lights on with how late it is.

I look in the rearview mirror and am horrified that I look like a missing Kiss band member. I don't know how old I will have to be before I learn that waterproof mascara is my friend. I grab my purse and make a run for the front door the best I can in these blasted heels that I am continuing to regret.

I hurry and close the door once I enter not to let out the heat. I am leaning up against the closed door as the sheer exhaustion, not only from tonight but from the last six months of my life, hits me.

My dad comes around the corner from the kitchen and stops dead in his tracks when he sees me. While he is looking at me, he calls over his shoulder, "Louise, sweetie, it looks like you are going to need to break out the hot cocoa." He doesn't even finish what he is saying to my mom before my sobs start back up. He quickly grabs me and holds me tightly to him.

"William, it is too late for…" my mom takes in the scene that she just walked in on and stops what she was originally saying to my dad. "Okay, definitely a hot cocoa night." She retreats into the kitchen to start the world's best hot cocoa. When I was a kid, we all swore that it was a magic elixir that could fix any problem that we were having.

I don't know how long we stood in the front entrance with my dad just holding me. When my sobs turn more into whimpers, he gently guides us into the kitchen. I take a seat at the island. My dad pulls the stool out next to me. My mom is dishing up the hot cocoa for all three of us. As she hands me my cup and I bring it closer, the smell that wafts toward me brings instant comfort.

"Thanks, Mom," I mumble under my breath. I place the cup down in front of me and move to take my coat off, revealing my beautiful red ball gown. I felt like a princess tonight wearing it. My parents apparently are done waiting for an explanation.

"My darling daughter, do you want to explain why your faces looks like a Tammy Faye Baker make up wipe?" Thank you, mom.

"I was thinking she looks more like a demented panda bear. Because with all the crying she is starting puff up to." My dad added his two cents.

Their descriptions of my face are ridiculous and just what I needed to hear. I am not sure how they did it, but they were able to pull a laugh out of me in a moment that felt hopeless.

"Are you guys saying you don't like my new look?" I say as I frame my face with my hands.

"Well, it certainly is a look. Now I have theories of what is happening, but it will be easier if you just spill the beans." I kind of want to hear my mom's crazy theories, but I am also exhausted, and there is a lot to say before I can find a pillow to rest my head on.

"Not sure where to start." I am clearly stalling, knowing how disappointed they will be in me, threatening to bring the tears back.

"The beginning is a good place. No matter what has happened it will not change how proud we are of you." My dad reaches over and squeezes my arm, encouraging me to go on.

"It started with little white lies that have snow balled into bigger lies. Here goes nothing. I graduated early and received my degree already. I canceled my audition in New York. I bought the dance school from Mrs. Hannigan." I stop as abruptly as I started my confessional.

"Okay, and…" my mom is waiving her hand for me to proceed.

"What do you mean and? That is a lot of secrets to be keeping, Mom."

"I think what you mom meant was, we already knew all that. We thought you were keeping a juicy secret from us."

"What do you mean you already knew those secrets" I asked outraged that I have probably developed an ulcer from the stress of keeping things from my parents and a little confused how they found out about everything.

"Honey how many times do we need to tell you that we lived through raising your brothers. By the time you came along there was never a chance that you were ever going to get away with anything." My mom takes a sip of her hot cocoa like this is a normal catch-up chat between us all then continues. "Your degree came to the house. Those envelopes look distinctive, and we knew what it was immediately without looking at the contents inside. You bought your plane ticket for New York on our credit card. When you canceled your ticket, we were notified of the reimbursement on our card."

The causal way that my mom is talking is blowing my mind a little. "How did you know I bought the dance school?"

My dad starts to chuckle at my question "That was less detective work and more dumb luck and sprinkle of small-town gossip."

"I overheard Frank Jenkins talking to Mrs. Hannigan about the contract for the sale of the school to an unnamed buyer. When you told us you had an internship, we put it together that you were the unnamed buyer."

"We are very proud of you sweetie." My dad says it like I wasn't hiding all this from him.

"I am sorry I kept everything from you. I got it in my head after I broke up with Lawerence this summer that I had something to prove to everyone. I ended up making a big mess of my life and hurting so many people in the process."

"That is part of growing up, learning the tough lessons. I think you are being harder on yourself than you deserve. The things you were keeping to yourself were not bad things, in fact they are quite impressive for a person you age to have accomplished." The way my mom is looking at it makes me feel guilt for not sharing with them sooner. She is right, I should be proud of what I accomplished.

"Okay in full disclosure there might be another secret but with your track record you probably already know what it is."

"Why don't you humor us and share this other secret you are keeping" my dad gently coaxes me into spilling the beans.

"Fine, I am in love with Harrison. We have been secretly dating for months. I have treated him awful, and he has been nothing but amazing to me. Lawrence showed up tonight and caused a scene, and Harrison tried to defend me, but I ran away from him anyway. Oh, I also ruined Harrison and Noah's friendship. Noah is so mad he won't speak to either one of us." I take a breath, this confession feels more painful. "Did I mention I am in love with him."

"Yes! YES YES!!" My mom is fist pumping in the air at what I just said. "You lost fair in square, William. You owe me foot message."

"What is happening here?"

"I just lost a bet to your mother. I don't care about giving her a foot message, but you know I hate to lose." My dad says as he starts to pout.

"I am so confused what is happening."

"The Harrison thing is also not a secret. That boy has been a regular fixture in our home for longer than I can remember. He was always kind to you growing up. As you got older, we noticed that you two started looking at each other different. The last year it has been glaringly obvious that you both had feelings for each other, but the timing has been off. You were with the dufus, and Harrison was too scared to make a move."

"I am creeped out by how much you guys really know. But I am still confused about the bet."

"I bet your, mother, that he would not make a move until the new year. Mom thought it would be this fall."

I sit there in shock thinking I was so mysterious, but the truth was I have been an open book the entire time. "Well did you make a bet on how long it would last? I screwed up royally tonight. He looked so hurt when I turned away from him and walked away. He will never forgive me."

"Nope, sorry, no bet on breaking up because we both know you will go to the distance. You just need a little time to figure it out." My mom smiles down at me. "You know what this calls for? I hide the good cookies in the back of the cabinets just in times like these."

The front door opens and closes. Before I have time to question who would be coming over so late Emma appears in the entryway to the kitchen. She takes in the scene in the kitchen and makes a beeline straight toward me and throws her arms around me. She squeezes my tight and whispers in my ear "So proud of all that you have accomplished, kid." She pulls back and her eyes look a little misty.

"What are you doing here?" I ask as I look over her shoulder fearing Noah will come in any moment.

"Your parents were nice enough to volunteer to watch Lola tonight so we could attend the Ball. It goes without saying that was the best Fireman's Ball I have ever attended."

My dad starts to get up. "Let me help you pack Lola's stuff up, and I can carry her out to the car for you."

"God bless you William, I will not turn down any help carrying her out to the car." Emma absently rubs her belly. "And Ginger we need a girl's night now that you have more free time with the ball being over." Emma and my dad leave the kitchen together.

My mom grabs the cookies and sits down beside me. "Do you know what tonight reminds me of?" She says as she offers me a cookie. I grab one and reluctantly ask, "What?"

"Your senior prom. You came home crying that night too. You were also wearing a beautiful gown."

"I had forgotten all about that." I sit there and think back to that night. My date was a jerk, and I never wanted to go with him in the first place. I secretly wanted to go with Harrison but that was never going to happen. I was 18-year-old senior in high school, and he was 27 at the time. My date ended up being a jerk, and I left early. I came home crying. Noah and everyone had come to hang out that night. Emma and Stella tried to comfort me, but I just wanted to be left alone. I ended up sneaking outside and rocking on the porch swing my dad had built for my mom a few years prior. Harrison wandered out with a blanket in hand and sat with me as I snuggled up under the blanket. At first, we just enjoyed the quiet of the night.

He would point out stars in the sky. I was certain he was making up the names and stories that went with the stars he pointed out. He found things to say that would make me laugh. After a while I had forgotten about the disastrous prom.

My mom pulls me from my memories. "You remember being out on the swing that night with Harrison, don't you?"

"Mom, you are really starting to freak me out with the mind-reading Voodoo you are pulling out of nowhere tonight."

My mom starts to laugh. "I am telling you, darling daughter of mine, Harrison and you have always had a connection. Timing has not always been on your side." She turns to me and looks serious, which is out of character for my mom. "Just promise me that you won't let fear stand in your way. You love that boy, and I am willing to bet he loves you. Let yourself be happy; it is worth the risk."

A tear falls down my cheek at her honest words. "I don't know how Mom. I made a real mess of everything tonight. What if he never forgives me?"

"What if you never try and you never find out if he can forgive you." She stands and makes her way to the sink with her empty cup.

Why don't you plan on sleeping in your old room so you don't have to go back out tonight in the cold? Before she leaves the kitchen, she comes to give me a hug. As she is hugging me, she says, "I am so proud of the woman you have become. Now go get your man and choose happiness."

And just like that, she heads to bed. I am left sitting there reeling from the emotional roller coaster that is my life. I clean up the few dishes left out before heading to bed.

I am not sure how I am going to do it, but I am going to convince Harrison to give me a second chance.

Chapter 34
Harrison

I was the last one to leave the community center. Noah stayed to help me lock up. I am relieved that Noah and I are back to normal and we were able to work out our issues. I just wish that I could say the same for Ginger and me.

I drove by the dance studio and all the windows were darkened, even the ones that I know go to her apartment. I was hoping that she would be in bed sleeping. She had to be exhausted from all the work on the ball. I become a level one stalker when I check the parking lot and don't find her car. She went somewhere else tonight. Not knowing is driving me crazy. After racking my brain of all the places, she could go I settle on her parents' home, that is the only logical option. I finally got home a little before two in the morning.

I feel like I barely closed my eyes to go to sleep before my alarm went off to get ready for work. Seeing I had all the previous week off from work to help Ginger get ready for the Fireman's Ball I can't complain that it is my turn to report for duty.

I drag myself into the station in full on zombie mode. I am not a big coffee drinker but after dropping my gear on my bunk I stumble into the kitchen in search of any caffeine. This is where the chief finds me.

"Son, you look a little rough this morning. Are you dying?" His tone suggests he is serious but the amused look on his face says otherwise.

"It was just a late night with clean up and making sure the building was locked up and secure. I am sure I will hit a second wind any minute now."

"I know I said this last night, but the ball has exceeded everyone's expectations. You have a very special girl there."

I want to argue that she is not my girl, but I think better of it and just nod my head. I take a sip of the coffee and regret that instantly. I suspect this is what battery acid would taste like. I dump the rest of the cup down the drain, resigned to the fact it is going to be a long day.

The day only gets worse when I am careless and drop my phone into a sink of soapy water. Even though I grabbed it, as soon as it hit the water, the damage was done. It is currently sitting on the counter in a bag of rice. I had been incessantly checking my phone, hoping

Ginger would reach out before my phone took a quick swim, it had been radio silence from her.

I welcomed sleep that night. I was grateful for the break in my thoughts that constantly led back to Ginger. I had been going out of my mind worrying about her, wondering how she was feeling. Hoping that she did walk away from me for good.

It was official that by the end of my shift on the second day, I was grumpy and was biting everyone's head off at the drop of a hat. Needless to say, no one loved my company. With my phone still not working, I felt even more isolated from everyone. I didn't even have the guy's text thread to harass me and offer me a laugh at my expense. The only place in town to get a new phone closes an hour before I get off shift. The earliest I could replace my phone would be tomorrow. I decide that I will drop in on one of the guys and hope they will take pity on me tonight.

The end of the shift finally arrives. I head straight to my truck. I load my gear and jump in. The weather has taken a nasty turn the last few days. I sit in the parking lot for a few minutes while my truck comes back to life after sitting for two days. I am lost in thought when the chief comes running out the side door. There is panic covering his face. I roll my window down. "What happened, chief? Has something happened?"

"It is the dance studio. We got a call of a fire inside. I am rolling the boys out now, but I thought you would want to know. The caller is not sure if anyone is inside, son."

That is all I need to hear. I slam my truck into drive and hit the gas. The boys should be right behind me, but I can't wait. I need to get inside and make sure Ginger is safe. I pull in front of the studio. I jerk on the front door a little too hard, and it flies open. The building is all dark and shows no life except for a glowing light coming from the back studio.

I take off in a run, desperate to find Ginger and make sure she is safe. "Ginger! Where are you?" I am hollering as I run. I stop short when I discover what is causing the glowing light that I saw from the lobby. The giant Christmas tree that Ginger and I had decorated together has somehow been transported to the studio. Ginger is standing beside the tree in her red ball gown from the other night.

"What is this? What is happening? Where is the fire?" I am slightly out of breath as the adrenalin rush leaves my body.

"Don't be mad, Harry. I needed to talk to you, and you were not responding."

"So, you report a fake fire. The guys will be here any minute. I have no idea how to explain this to them. I was scared to death that I had lost you forever."

"Technically, I called your chief and asked for a favor. I never called 911 or anything. No one else is coming."

"Oh." I have been dying to talk to this woman since the moment she walked away from me, and that is all I can say.

Chapter 35
Ginger

This is not going well at all. I am mentally kicking myself for listening to my ridiculous friends and the helpful suggestion to win Harrison back. The plan they all came up with seemed plausible at the time but is more laughable at my expense now.

I have to say something, to stop him from just staring at me. "I tried to call and text you, but you never responded, and I know I probably deserve the silent treatment after I walked away the other night."

"I dropped my phone in water at the firehouse, and it's totally fried. I planned on getting a new one tomorrow."

"Oh."

This is not going well at all. How did I let them talk me into putting this dress back on?

"What is all this Ginger?"

Is it a bad sign that he is using my name and not calling me Sunshine? Defeat is starting to set in. I hear my mom's words replay in my head to choose happiness. I need to give this my all. He might still want to walk away, and that will be okay but at least I know I chose Harry and tried to go for happiness with him.

"I know I don't deserve to ask this of you after how I acted the other night at the ball. I need a few minutes of your time, and then you are free to walk back out that door, and I won't bother you anymore."

He is just standing there staring at me. I push the feeling of wanting to throw up down. That would probably be a mood killer if I threw up on him.

"Do you remember that day you came over to my house when I was in high school? I was crying over a bad audition. You spent the day with me. We watched movies and ate junk food. One of the movies we watched had the girl at the end making a big gesture trying to win the guy over. It has been my favorite movie ever since that day for a couple of reasons, but mainly because it was something we shared together."

Harrison continues to stand there and not say a word. I get it. I hurt him so many times. Maybe I ran out of chances.

"I guess this was me trying to make the big gesture. I owed you a dance that we never got at the ball." I have started to lose hope that anything I say will help.

"Ginger…" he starts to say something, but I hate that he is using my name again.

"Wait, Harry, please let me say my peace, then you can walk away." I am freaking leaking again. I can't worry about the stream flowing down my cheeks at this point I need to get this out. "Harry, it has always been you. It was you who sat with me on a swing one night, telling me made-up stories about stars to make me laugh. It was you this summer that brought me back to life after a bad breakup. It was you who held me when I needed to be held. It was you who kept my secrets. It is you that brings laughter into my life. It is you who supports my dreams and goals. It has always been you." I wipe at my tears, hating that I can't get them to stop leaking. "And Harry, PS…I love you, too. I have loved you for so long. I know it is not fair to say those words when I have made so many mistakes and hurt you, but it is how I feel."

I stand in the middle of the room, feeling exposed and vulnerable. Harrison takes a step toward me, then another. It only takes a few steps before he is close enough to reach out and cup my face in his hands. "Ginger, is it okay if I speak now?"

I nod my head even though he is holding onto me. "I have never told another woman in my life that I loved her. I messed up the other night when I told your ex how I felt about you before telling you. Let me clarify it for you. I am head over heels in love with you."

"I have never told a man that I loved him before you either. It has always been you. I am sorry I was scared before, and the mistakes that I made hurt you." He takes his thumb and wipes my tears away.

"Timing was off before, and I had to wait so I could claim you as mine. And you are mine, Sunshine, never doubt that."

That was enough words for both of us. Harrison leans in and starts to kiss me. I am not sure how long we stand there kissing as we hold each other. This kiss seems different from the previous ones we shared. It feels like there is a promise of a future together, of love and all the good things I have always wanted with this man. This kiss is happiness.

We are interrupted by a man clearing his throat toward the entrance of the room. We break apart to see Noah standing there holding Lola on his hip, and she is all giggles and smiles. "Clearly, the big gesture worked. We are all hungry, so can we get this party started? Plus, I am making the rule no more kissing. Lola is too young to see such things.”

Everyone flows in. Harrison sticks to me like glue, refusing to let go of me. The guys take charge and set tables up the girls bring in all the food that was brought. All our friends are here as well as my parents. The chief and his wife even make an appearance. We all settle in and are devouring the takeout with Christmas music planning in the background.

Max stands up in the middle of the room, looking like he is going to make an announcement.

“Ginger and Harrison, I am super stoked you guys finally figured it out. I don’t know if you truly appreciate all the work that went into making this happen.” He waves his hand between Harrison and me.

“Your one plan for the photo shoot was not really the crucial foundation that our relationship is built on. Nice try Max,” Harrison says, looking amused by his friend’s antics.

“Oh, my dear misguided friend. You have no idea. Who do you think looped the chief in so he would pair you guys together as co-chairs of the ball?”

Harrison turns to his mentor. “Chief, please tell me that you did not help him?”

“Of course, I helped him. I even had to come up with a fake illness for Estelle to get you to believe me. We all saw the writing on the wall when it came to you two young people. You both needed a push in the right direction, so I pushed.” He smiled, looking quite pleased with himself. “My favorite part was the fire call that Ginger asked me to say had been called in. I am certain it was an Oscar-worthy performance. I think I captured the drama perfectly.”

“Unbelievable, can’t trust anyone these days,” Harrison says, not really all that mad; after all, everyone’s meddling brought us together.

As the party continues there is dancing and more laughing.

Harrison leads me over to the tree for the dance that we have waited long enough for. He gathers me in his arms and starts to sway to the music.

“Sunshine…”

I lift my head from his shoulder and look up at him. “Yeah, Harry.”

“Ps…I love you.”

THE END

I hope you enjoyed Ginger and Harrison's story as they found their way to each other in their search for love and happiness. Stay tuned for Ralph's story coming soon in I Love You….Like Crazy.